THROUGH SKY AND STARS

Visit us at www.boldstrokesbooks.com

Through Sky and Stars

by
Tessa Croft

2025

THROUGH SKY AND STARS
© 2025 BY TESSA CROFT. ALL RIGHTS RESERVED.

ISBN 13: 978-1-63679-862-2

THIS TRADE PAPERBACK ORIGINAL IS PUBLISHED BY
BOLD STROKES BOOKS, INC.
P.O. BOX 249
VALLEY FALLS, NY 12185

FIRST EDITION: AUGUST 2025

THIS IS A WORK OF FICTION. NAMES, CHARACTERS, PLACES, AND
INCIDENTS ARE THE PRODUCT OF THE AUTHOR'S IMAGINATION OR
ARE USED FICTITIOUSLY. ANY RESEMBLANCE TO ACTUAL PERSONS,
LIVING OR DEAD, BUSINESS ESTABLISHMENTS, EVENTS, OR LOCALES
IS ENTIRELY COINCIDENTAL.

THIS BOOK, OR PARTS THEREOF, MAY NOT BE REPRODUCED IN ANY
FORM WITHOUT PERMISSION.

CREDITS
EDITORS: RADCLYFFE AND CINDY CRESAP
PRODUCTION DESIGN: SUSAN RAMUNDO
COVER DESIGN BY TAMMY SEIDICK

Acknowledgments

Val and Nicole would never have leapt off my laptop and into the world if it weren't for a few crucial folks. Many thanks go to the team at Bold Strokes for bringing this novel to fruition—particularly to Radclyffe for fantastic mentorship that honed the manuscript, and to Cindy for eagle-eyed editing that polished it. Thank you to Heather and Bethany, the novel's first fans, whose enthusiasm brought the work to life. And finally, many thanks go to my parents, who always encouraged me to reach for the sky and stars: Mom, my first editor, who helped avoid many plot holes on the way; and Dad, who taught me that airplanes are really stinkin' cool.

Dedication

To the badass women of the North.

PROLOGUE

Year 587 Post Diaspora [2753 AD, Terran Calendar]
Piscium System, Sh'keth Controlled Territory

Lieutenant Valentina Koroleva raced across no man's land, her ragged breath echoing in her ears. Ahead, a Slug hive loomed from the volcanic grit of Piscium-b. Behind, her platoon of marines followed in an all-out sprint. Thick, putrid rain fell endlessly, coating the planet in warm, wet ash that lent the air itself the taste of death. The muck clung to her clothes, her skin, and her boots. She grimaced as the platoon stomped through the thick mud, their footfalls sounding like a chorus of Slugs snacking on human guts. The noise carried across the open ground, clawing at her nerves, but Val forced the frisson of dread aside. Despite the godawful sound, nothing stirred amid the debris ahead. The sodden, gray world around them lay quiet.

Val threw her back against the remains of the Slug structure. Catching her breath, she signaled sharply for the team to halt, and the slurp of boots gave way to the soft tinkling of gear as they settled into position around her. To each side, her newly-minted riflemen— every single one of them fresh out of Basic—stared back at her with wide eyes gleaming in pale faces masked by black paint. They were so thoroughly coated in pallid muck that only their eyes and weapons distinguished them from the muted world around them. Like her, they hadn't been truly dry in days. Yet all of them were eager, burning with the desire to destroy the enemy who'd haunted them since childhood. The enemy they'd been raised to fight.

This Slug hive, though, was abandoned—bombed within an inch of its feeble, stinking life by an orbital firestorm. Clearing it was the perfect task for a platoon of green marines and their green commanding officer. Still, the nauseating cocktail of fear and adrenaline that accompanied every mission in Slug territory swirled through her veins. This time it wasn't just her ass on the line. She had lives to protect. To lead.

Opaque puddles pooled at the base of the wall. She caught a glimpse of her reflection—young but no longer innocent—before her booted foot obliterated the image. Beside her footprints, thousands of small, rounded depressions dotted the pathway. The traces of insectoid limbs crisscrossing the landscape, remnants of the countless ebb and flow of enemy forces preceding her, were their first sign of the enemy made real. No more bedtime stories: the war was here, before their eyes, and the sheer number of prints made her blood run cold. These weren't just Slugs—the larval form of the alien Sh'keth they hunted—but Protectors. Three meters of armored, insectoid killing machine that tended to drop from the sky, gut human marines like fish, and drag the remains back to feed the larvae they guarded. Val shuddered.

"Deserted, remember," she murmured into her radio, reminding herself as well as her troops. "The Slugs are gone. Let's get to it."

Val gripped her rifle, raised her hand to signal, and choked on a sudden rush of horror as a Protector reared up in her vision. Her world collapsed to cruel, black eyes framed by ebony armor. The giant mouth, flanked by flashing mandibles centimeters from her face, opened with the screech of a deafening war cry. With a whir of blades and diaphanous wings, it attacked.

"Trap!"

She fired blindly, inciting a hailstorm of magshot echoing her own, but her shot went wide. The world ripped from beneath her feet. Blinding pain exploded through her body. The world dissolved into flickering images, a chaos of carnage as she tumbled in a flailing arc above the blood-soaked ground. Bodies and gore catapulted through her field of view. Her scream of pain mingled with the sudden thunder of bullets and war cries. She slammed into a structure, brutal force driving the air from her lungs, and crumpled to the muddy ground.

Her vision went white. She floated on a tortured sea of screams and magshot.

She came to in utter silence. No voices, no alien chittering, no smack of boots or forelegs in the mud. Her ears rang in the stillness. She lay on her side, right arm afire beneath her, head throbbing. A Protector lay at the edge of her field of view. Resinous, amber fluid seeped from multiple holes in the enormous head, the cruel orbs of its giant eyes dull in death. Yet its foreleg blades, thirty centimeters of blue steel, gleamed crimson with a slick of human blood. Beneath its multi-segmented body protruded two unmoving, booted human feet, the attached legs jutting at an impossible angle. Val swallowed the quick rise of bile.

Her crushed arm lay tortured beneath her. When she struggled to sit up, a ferocious, lancing wave of fire raced up her left thigh, overshadowing the agony in her arm. She moaned, gasping for breath, pain mingling with horror as she took in the nightmare the Sh'keth had made of her flesh. Her thigh was rent to the bone, uniform and flesh tangled in a gruesome rift from knee to hip, her blood surging ominously from the cataclysmic gash into the pool in which she lay. The dirty water already swirled a deep crimson. Chest heaving, she breathed through clenched teeth and fumbled for her med kit. Her fingers, slick with red, slipped uselessly on the field tourniquet. Her blood made a mockery of her attempt to stop the flow. Too weak. Too deep. She watched the slow pulse of her life leaking into the muck.

So this was where she would die. Hardly started, hardly worth it, amounting to nothing at all. She needed to do so much more. The unfairness of it, the *failure*, burned as brightly as the pain in her ruined body. The recruits she'd led into this horror lay ambushed and murdered around her. Their sightless eyes, fierce gleam forever gone, burned into her, judging the pitiful mewling tumbling from her lips as she watched her blood pump out onto the ground. They'd wished for so much, wanted to make a difference in the war, and they'd made it five meters. They'd amounted to nothing. The goddamn Slugs had robbed them of it all.

Rage roared through the dimming edges of her consciousness.

The grip of her mag rifle bit into her good hand as the anger poured strength into her dying body. She gripped the weapon hard and stared into the dead eyes of the Protector.

"Fuck you," she ground through clenched teeth.

She pulled the trigger savagely. Yellow fluid burst forth, spattering her as she shot it again. She repeated the mantra over and over, punctuating each word with a shot, but each pull of the trigger left her more drained, made the effort seem all the more useless. Hot tears dripped from her chin as fury subsided into grief and terror. Still she fired, the Sh'keth's disintegrating body rocking with each hit, the gunfire shattering the uncanny silence of the battlefield. She sobbed with rage and fear until the rifle whined, empty. Her arm trembled. Her vision grayed at the edges. The water around her was hardly distinguishable from blood itself.

She closed her eyes on the carnage and let death come.

PART I: *FLIGHT PLAN*

CHAPTER ONE

Year 599 Post Diaspora [2765 AD, Terran Calendar]
UHM Cruiser Alexei Leonov, *Border Systems*

Val grinned, sensing weakness in her friend's attack, and lunged for the exposed wrist as Kass's knife hand arced past her. The slight widening of Kass's jade eyes told Val she'd caught her off guard. She whipped her other hand forward, flowing into the joint lock.

"Ha!"

Her triumphant crow cut short when a leg wrapped behind hers. The bubble burst. *Oh, fuck.*

Val tumbled into a breakfall over Kass's shoulder, world spinning, cartwheeling ineffectually as Kass executed a perfect reversal and sent her catapulting to her back on the mat. She grunted gracelessly, Kass's weight dropping onto her chest to complete the faultless pin. Kass smirked down at her, a familiar, triumphant gleam in her eyes. Dark hair shaded her pale face as she loomed above Val. A surge of frustrated affection blossomed in Val's chest. Yet again, Kass had her at a disadvantage in the dojo.

"What was that, slime sucker?"

Kass punctuated the question by driving her wrists deeper into the rough fabric of the mat. Val scowled. The harder she strained to pull them free, the greater the pressure grew, until further resistance would land her in the med wing with a broken wrist. Which Kass, as chief of the medical wing, would fix—undoubtedly while adding a heavy dose of insult to injury. It would be infuriating if Kass's medical skills hadn't saved Val's ass multiples times since she dragged Val off the sodden battlefield on Piscium-b. That didn't make another loss any more palatable, nor would she give up just because Kass won nine times out of ten. She squirmed, searching for weak points in Kass's stance, while Kass's arrogant smile lingered indulgently.

Val snarled. "Cocky sonofabitch."

We'll see how much she likes it when I kick her out of bed.

The thought cut through her rising frustration. Now *that* wasn't a bad idea... Val paused her struggling, savoring the mischievous idea, and smiled when Kass raised a skeptical eyebrow.

She arched her hips, pressing into Kass with a languid roll, and was rewarded when Kass twitched with a soft grunt. Aha! A slight shift of the mountain. She broke the pin, slipping free as Kass's weight shifted, and seized the minute reprieve to roll Kass onto her back. She took over the pin with a laugh.

When she looked down, ready to assert her uncommon victory, Kass smiled back with a feral gleam in her eye.

Foreboding reared up, quashing Val's triumph.

"You little shit," Kass murmured.

Her heels tucked into Val's armpits. A half second later, Val flew headlong off the mat.

The textured metal flooring ripped Val's *gi* as she rolled, skidding between racks of free weights. Activity in the gym stuttered to a halt. Heads turned when their bout overflowed the sparring area, the crew's quiet evening workouts eclipsed by the prospect of a spectacle.

Val cringed at the gathering audience. Kass was a surgeon. The only thing she loved as much as saving lives was being the center of attention. Val had just given her a grudge to settle with a stage to do it on. "Fuck," she muttered.

She shifted, ready to come up swinging, but the trick had also cost her Kass's mercy. Her breath exploded in a gasp as Kass landed on her back, knees driving relentlessly under her arms and splaying her against the ground. Kass's weight ground her shoulders into the hard metal decking. An elbow snaked under her chin.

The chokehold tightened. Val gulped in a last, desperate breath before her windpipe constricted.

Kass's breath ghosted against her ear with a low, rough laugh. "The benefits go away if you abuse them, Koroleva."

"Say that again toni—*agck!*" Val gagged as Kass's elbow clamped tighter.

Another pin. She had to stay calm if she was going to find her way out of this one, but her animal brain immediately screeched in panic at the lack of oxygen. She fought it, yet again searching desperately for weaknesses. But if the first pin had been a prison, this one was a fortress. With a mountain dropped on top for good measure. The deck beneath her hummed in time with the ship's engines, the frantic energy fanning the flames of fear licking at her logical mind. All around her, marines tossed out wagers on her remaining time. Forty seconds? Thirty?

Vision graying, Val thrashed, grimacing at the audience. Sweat stung her eyes. Her chest burned in concert with her implanted Heads-up Display, which flickered a crimson medical warning across her field of view: LOW OXYGEN. She would've rolled her eyes at it if they weren't already trying to roll back into her skull.

Kass chuckled maliciously. "You gonna tap out yet, shithead?"

Never. Val tried to grind out the word and simply choked on her own frustration. Fog closed in. Her HUD's urgent warnings activated her audio implant and screamed in her ears, which began to ring. The world faded from view. Her limbs grew heavy. She had to focus. This wasn't over, she had a few seconds left. If she could just—

REPORT TO COMMANDANT GENERAL IMMEDIATELY

The message flared across her HUD, overriding the medical warnings at the same moment Kass's grip vanished with a suddenness that left her head spinning. Air roared back into her lungs with an almighty heave.

"*Fuck*," she groaned on the exhale.

Kass's weight disappeared from her back. "Saved by the bell, slime sucker," she quipped, though one hand patted Val's back affectionately.

Ears finally clearing, Val croaked, "You got it, too?"

Kass knelt beside Val and offered a hand as they got slowly to their feet. Her brows screwed together, eyes troubled, and her thin lips drooped into a speculative frown. "Both of us? Shit. What did we do?"

❖

"At ease, both of you."

Val tried, but the swirling current of curiosity and unease in her gut fought the attempt. Kass shifted restlessly at her side. Astrey's office, large by shipboard standards, was still uncomfortably small for four people, and they both eyed the young man with lieutenant's bars standing next to the commandant's desk. Slightly unkempt, his uniform wrinkled, the man stared back at them through a pair of lenses that shimmered slightly with a data stream visible only to the wearer.

"Lieutenant Haskell." Astrey indicated the junior officer.

The lack of explanation for Haskell's presence left uncomfortable silence in its wake. Val's gaze flicked to Kass, who crossed her arms and raised a questioning brow. Haskell, though, practically ignored Kass. When Val's gaze returned to him, the lieutenant still stared directly at her. Like a scientist appraising a key specimen. Val frowned back, ready to get to the point and dispel the cloying tension.

Astrey sank into the chair behind his desk, the metal creaking beneath his muscular form, and tapped one of the many tablets cluttering the gray, industrial surface.

The screen sprang to life, and Val caught a glimpse of her duty record. Her sense of dread thickened.

"Piscium-b."

Val flinched.

Kass's hands dropped to her sides, fingers flexing ominously. Her voice, when she finally responded, could cut steel. "What about it, sir?"

Astrey held up one large, placating hand to Kass, his gaze fixed on Val. "You never really recovered from that, did you, Major?"

Val rocked on her heels, biting back her first response. Adrenaline and guilt poured through her. What did he think? She'd lost her entire platoon. She'd failed in every measure as a commander of troops. So no, *of course* she hadn't. But she wasn't about to admit that to the commandant general of the Unified Human Marines. She'd admitted it only to the woman who'd saved her life that godawful day, who now stood by her side. She took a long, stabilizing breath. "Sir?"

He sighed, tapping the screen again, and scrolled through her record. "Two months after Captain Volkova pulled you out of that battlefield, you applied for Special Ops. In the ten years since, you've served very admirably: forty-eight combat operations, twenty-six confirmed kills, top marks in flight ops and unarmed combat, All-Forces fitness cadre eight years running." He paused, fingers hovering over the tablet, and looked pointedly at her. "Yet you have never, once, accepted command of another soldier."

Kass cut in icily. "Sir, does this line of interrogation have a point?"

Her posture radiated protective rage, muscles flexing in her jaw, and a slight flush mottled her pale cheeks. "Respectfully," she added. "Sir."

Astrey's gaze cut to Kass as she flung the verbal jab. His jaw tightened.

"I assure you, Captain, it does."

Despite Kass's protective fire, Val swallowed a pang of guilt and loss triggered by Astrey's questions. Was her fitness for duty in doubt? But if so, why would Astrey waste his time delivering the news? Was Haskell a shrink, here to pull her away to a padded cell until they deposited her on some remote world to live out her days in a penance of isolation? She braced herself for Astrey's next words.

He said, "While your superior officers, myself included, have never faulted you for that mission's outcome, I don't think you've ever forgiven yourself."

The truth hit her squarely in the gut. Val held back a gasp, squeezing her eyes shut against the sudden, burning threat of tears. She sucked in a breath while Astrey waited. When she met his eyes again, his face held a brutal compassion, somehow worse than the judgment she held against herself.

"I have an opportunity for you, Major," he went on, "to redeem yourself in your own eyes."

He pushed a second tablet toward her. Val stepped forward in a fog and brushed a finger over the surface, waiting while the encrypted lock communicated with the nanotechnology in her blood. The screen sprang to life and she leaned in, frowning as she scanned the data. Kass moved closer, peering over her shoulder.

"The information on these tablets is top secret." Astrey's tone was grave, though Val suspected that a man of his rank saw top secret information on a daily basis. "I don't need to remind you what that means. Do not breathe a single word of this conversation beyond the confines of this office."

"Of course, sir."

"Haskell and his team have unlocked time travel."

Val and Kass reared back simultaneously, nearly knocking heads in their incredulity. "Sir?"

"You heard me. Time travel. Don't ask me how it works—he's tried to explain it to me until my head felt ready to explode, and I don't recommend you trying any more than I did. But what I do know is that we're using it. We will nip this war in the bud before it even starts. Avert the war, avert the Diaspora, avert the slow extinction of humanity."

A sinking, inevitable dread settled into Val's gut. He would only tell them this if—

Kass asked, "Why us?"

Astrey nodded approvingly. "Lieutenant?"

Haskell suddenly seemed to vibrate with barely-contained excitement.

"Algorithms," he said simply. "Monte-Carlo simulations."

The words bounced off Val's brain like debris skittering across a battlefield, but Haskell shrugged at the blank look she gave him like he was used to confounding lesser mortals. "Probabilities. First, we identified a window in which the Sh'keth were susceptible to a single event upset."

"A what?"

"A single change." Haskell leaned forward, tapping an image on the tablet in front of Val. A timeline appeared, events highlighted with red and yellow flags. "We identified the timeframe in which a single change—in our models, a single person—could alter the course of history. Once we identified that window, we modeled the individual upsets. Our quantum computers ran millions of simulations of potential outcomes, each simulating the arrival of one person at this point." He indicated the image: 1996 AD, more than a hundred years before the war began, before brutal war poisoned the Earth and forced the human Diaspora to the stars. "*One* upset averted the war in almost every, single associated model."

He looked up, gaze intent over the rim of his glasses. "You, Major."

Val scowled, skepticism rocketing through her. "Me."

Astrey interjected, "Captain Volkova, here, is a distant second. She'll be your alternate, in the event you can't jump." He shrugged. "People with a hell of a lot more brain cells than us, Major, have identified the course of action with the greatest probability of success. I trust them. I write the orders. You, Major Valentina Koroleva, will go to the First Hive, on Earth, before it hatches. Destroy it. Stop the war before it starts." A sudden, fanatical spark flared in his eyes. "Save us all, Major."

Haskell cleared his throat and pointed to a red gap in the timeline. "But only if you do it before this. You will have five days, once you arrive, to destroy the hive. If you don't, something happens here—we don't know what—and prevents *anyone* from stopping the war for six months. It's a zone of exclusion. After that, the models diverge drastically within days. You might win. You might not. Humanity may survive; we may not."

Val's stomach clenched. She looked askance at Kass, who'd grown uncharacteristically silent, and voiced the awful theory churning her insides. She'd read science fiction. "If I do this, I don't...erase you? If I change everything, does any of this ever exist?"

Haskell crossed his arms and scowled for the first time, annoyance clouding his features. "The models are unclear." He paused, considering. "Time is a mess, Major. Outcomes blend and diverge. Key events spark limitless expansion. Others pull millions of outcomes into a single, catastrophic or formative moment. We don't know, for sure, what kind of upset you will be. We're not even sure whether there are multiple timelines or just this one. But we do know that the timing we've identified is perfect. Regardless of what happens to us, here, if you succeed, you will stop the war in every human existence." He wrinkled his nose. "I don't like the uncertainties, but the models are more favorable to our survival, specifically, in the window before the zone of exclusion."

"What we do know, Major," Astrey stood, his bulk looming over them all as they stared down at the tablet together, "is that losing this universe is worth it if humanity ultimately survives. Your preparation for the mission begins tomorrow." He paused, dark gaze flicking between Val and Kass, and shrugged apologetically "I know it's a lot. Take the tablets—they contain your orders and the fundamentals of the mission. Study them. Process it. We'll meet tomorrow to review the details."

A moment of stunned silence hung in the office.

"Dismissed."

Chapter Two

Year 599 Post Diaspora [2765 AD, Terran Calendar]
UHM Cruiser Alexei Leonov, *Border Systems*

"You know you're going to miss me."

Kass cast a self-satisfied smile over her shoulder and sat up, sheets slipping from her fair shoulders to pool around her waist. Val snatched them back with forced playfulness. She'd seen the brittle edge to her friend's smile, but for the seven thousandth time since Astrey ambushed them with a game of cosmic roulette, she fled the recognition of Kass's pain. She scoffed to hide the answering lump in her throat.

"I'm pretty sure they knew how to have sex back then. I'll probably manage."

Kass pushed her back into the bunk with a snort. "You're so fucking full of yourself. I'd have thrown you out an airlock years ago if you weren't so *vakking* good in the field."

"And in bed."

A long-suffering sigh. "Suck vack, spacer."

Silence fell, slowly drawing tighter as unspoken words gathered between them. Val struggled for the right phrase to dispel the lingering unease.

"Although." A new spark lit Kass's eyes, and Val's breath eased. "It was an absolute, fucking joy when you ripped those plebes a new one in the mess today."

Val laughed, picturing the recruits launching to ramrod attention when she casually interrupted the gossip bubbling in her enhanced hearing. Meals, cutlery, and overturned beverages had clattered to the floor in their haste to pay respect to the subject of their commentary. Had she been similarly roasted as a plebe? Of course. Did she feel even remotely bad for them? Absolutely not. "Poor babies. One strike for forgetting an officer's biomed enhancements, and the second for thinking it was news to anyone on this ship that we sleep together."

Ships were a tinderbox for gossip, and Val and Kass had lived on this one for years. They'd discovered long ago that whenever the strain of constant war wound past the breaking point, when words or tears or a good round of throws in the dojo failed to ease the tension, they could fall into bed together and lose themselves in desperate, physical release. They weren't lovers. The physicality existed solely to preserve their sanity, and sex wasn't against protocol. Their longtime shipmates were well aware of their therapeutic rounds in the sack. The ignorant recruits, however, had been unwise enough to hypothesize within range.

Kass chuckled. "They should be grateful. I can't imagine how dead they'd be if *they* were the outlet of your stress." She sighed dramatically. "But please do come back. Getting myself off just isn't the same."

A litany of retorts rose and fell on Val's tongue, each skirting too close to the underlying truth of Kass's half-hearted joke. She again forced her attention away from the obvious. They didn't need to directly acknowledge the depth of their friendship—their bond simply was, like gravity or time. Yet tension coiled in the shadows, lurking between them, lingering in the space between words unsaid.

Kass's wristcom beeped an unfriendly reminder. She groaned. "Can we not have two slug-fucking minutes of peace?"

In the two weeks since their assignment they'd done little but study. When Val closed her eyes she saw maps, schematics, and battle plans. Her ears rang with equations and theory breathlessly extolled by Haskell as he distilled a lifetime's worth of quantum physics into what he apparently thought were understandable terms. A secretive team had installed impenetrable, black boxes into Val's dropship, *Soyka*. Thankfully, Kass had been forced into flight refresher training at the expense of her sleep, which punctuated the drudgery with flurries of colorful, expletive-laced comic relief. The melee left little time for contemplating their uncertain fate, yet the uncomfortable possibilities quickly reared their heads in quiet moments like this.

"You know what's really bothering me about this whole thing?" Kass asked.

Val's gut tightened at the question. "Hm?"

"Why the *fuck* is a surgeon the backup for a special ops goddess?" Kass threw up her hands. "You could take out that queen with nothing but your toothbrush and your biceps. It makes sense to send someone like you. But...me? How in *vakking* hell am I equal to you in this?"

"Fuck if I know," Val answered honestly, grateful to dodge more difficult questions. "As far as I'm concerned, this whole plan is black magic. But Astrey says 'go,' so I go."

Kass huffed out an incredulous laugh, shaking her head. "You're such a marine."

"And you're usually such a surgeon that I don't worry about you." She laughed softly. "Don't worry. Right before you go, Haskell will have an intern set your instruments up in the operating room. You'll be so fucking pissed, you'll murder the Slugs just by looking at them. It won't matter that I'm dead."

Shit—wrong thing to say. Val's stomach knotted again. Kass stilled. She turned her head slightly, enough to meet Val's eyes but staring down at the rumpled sheets instead. Her hand clenched in the folds. She drew in a breath.

"Sorry," Val cut her off. "Bad joke. I didn't—"

"Shut up, Koroleva."

Val snapped her mouth closed. She inhaled sharply, fighting the words, but the renewed surge of sorrow at last overrode the dam of her control.

"Kass, I will miss you." Her voice cracked ominously. "If..."

She couldn't force the words out. Tears threatened, her eyes burning traitorously. The unimaginable, awful potential of erasing her best friend from existence drew itself into a noose around her throat, murdering the words before they could escape. She swallowed hard around the lump of grief. She'd dodged this conversation like magshot on the battlefield, but now it was here, unrelenting, and she didn't have a battle plan. She froze, throat working, and gripped Kass's wrist.

Kass smacked her upside the head.

Val blinked, pulled back from the chasm of loss.

"Don't get soft on me, Koroleva. Focus on the mission. When you get back—which you will—we'll talk about how much you love me."

Despite the flippant words, Kass's hand lay over Val's where it gripped her wrist. She squeezed gently, releasing Val's hold, and reached behind her neck to undo the delicate chain fastened there. She cupped the necklace briefly, considering it in the palm of her hand, then dropped it into Val's palm with a soft *clink*.

Val gasped. She ran her thumb over the links, affection and guilt warring in her heart. The chain held three simple, metal rings, each worked in a different finish and wound, in turn, through the others. "Kass. You never take this off."

Kass shrugged. "You need it more, right now."

She cupped Val's hand, curling their fingers together over the intertwined rings.

"Beginning, middle, end," she said softly. "Tied together in all things."

She withdrew her fingers and gave Val's fist a sharp shake. "But it's the last thing my mother gave me, so bring this shit back to me, slime brains."

Kass's wristcom beeped again, more urgently. She stood abruptly, picking up the scattered bits of her uniform, and Val pointedly ignored the quiet sniffle that punctuated her footfalls.

"Fucking flying lessons," Kass grumbled "I don't care what Haskell's math says. If you don't go, we're screwed."

Val fastened the necklace around her throat, grateful for Kass's unspoken request to dispel the moment. "They did say the odds were worse if—"

General quarters blared through the cabin.

"The fuck?"

Kass scowled and hastily fastened the rest of her buttons.

Val rolled out of bed, adrenaline spiking despite her irritation at the insistent warble, and threw on her flight suit and boots. "What vack-faced *idiot* thought it would be fun to call a drill at this—"

THIS IS NOT A DRILL

The words flashed across her HUD and blared over the speakers.

"Fuck," she and Kass chorused.

Kass's narrow features dipped into a contemplative scowl. "Here?"

Val was just as surprised. Their ship had been surveying an uncontested backwater system since Astrey's mission announcement, so far from any front that it felt like leave for all but the small, secret team nucleated around her and Kass. Their classified mission had prompted the bland assignment to keep them safe until departure. The chances of the Slugs showing up here and now were preposterously small.

The warbling alarms crashing through the ship defied those odds.

Realization hurtled into Val's mind and seized her heart in a vise grip.

The Slugs *knew*.

Grief welled up, choking her anew, and her feet froze. She swallowed around the sudden, awful lump, hand hovering above the hatch release. "Kass."

Kass gripped her arm and held her gaze. "I know."

This could be the end. Probably *was* the end. The end of their friendship, end of the *Al*, end of the war. *Everything's* end, if Val succeeded, and the cost was more than she could bear. The thought crushed her as mercilessly as Kass's pin. "Kass, I'm not rea—"

"Yes, you fucking are." Kass's fierce embrace slammed the door on Val's protests, smothering the upwelling of grief. Their shoulders rose and fell together. One simultaneous breath, tying past and present around the moment of finality.

"Do your job, Koroleva."

Kass pushed them apart. One dark, slender brow arched above eyes that glinted diamond-hard in the fair lines of her face. The fingers of her right hand dug into Val's shoulder, just hard enough to sharpen Val's gaze, and her lips quirked when Val met her eyes. "I told you not to get soft on me."

Somehow, Val managed a small laugh that eased the agony clawing at her throat. "Shut up."

Kass chuckled and shook Val's shoulder one last time. "Go save the *vakking* universe, you idiot."

Kass stepped back, held Val's gaze for a last, interminable heartbeat, and hit the hatch release. Val sucked in another breath as Kass disappeared into the crowd of sailors and marines racing to action stations. She closed her eyes, searing the image of her friend into her memory. Grief filled her chest, curled around her heart, and drew tight. She didn't want to breathe, to twitch, to open her eyes and see the end of her universe closing in, but she had to.

She had to go. *Now.* She clenched her jaw, pushed down the grief. She jammed it deep, pressing on the opening wound in her soul. No time for wallowing. She slammed the hatches down as best she could, trusting duty to hold the wound closed until she completed her mission. She'd let it bleed her dry after the Slugs were reduced to memories buried under a mountain.

She had no choice. The Slugs were here to kill her, their presence a sword strike cleaving her life in two, and the clock was ticking on her mission.

Val took a last, deep breath and ran for the shuttle bay. *Focus.* Time to fight.

Her dropship, *Soyka*, waited calmly at the center of a maelstrom. Linemen scurried around it, connecting the hoses and cables that writhed across the deck. Barked orders rebounded from the polished deck. The ship's control surfaces wriggled, motors whirring over the din of voices and clanging tools. The entire bay seethed with activity, the *Soyka* one small eddy in an ocean of ships preparing for launch. She wouldn't be alone when she raced to evade her enemy.

She hoped the small force would be enough protection. If the Slugs were here in force, she was in trouble. The squadron just had to keep her alive long enough to jump.

Haskell appeared, shirt untucked and glasses askew, and a tool—probably priceless—slipped from his overcrowded pockets to clatter against the decking as he fell into step next to her.

"I had the primary coils out for calibrating," Haskell said, broad features drooping with irritation, his hands working the air anxiously. Sweat beaded on his dark forehead and dampened the underarms of his hastily donned uniform. "I reinstalled them, but you know the field strength is directly proportional to the winding coefficient, so if the Helmholtz ratio is—"

"Will it work?"

Haskell wiped his sweaty brow on a wrinkled sleeve. Stared at the *Soyka* as techs scrambled around it. Chewed his lower lip.

Val tried not to think about the fact that *literally everything* hinged on this man's ability to solve this one challenge—a problem incomprehensible to the rest of humanity. "Haskell?"

He made a heinously aggrieved face, apparently offended that the universe had marred the precision of his beautiful calculations with cruel reality. "Yeah."

She slapped his shoulder and he jumped, another tool leaping from his pockets to lose itself in the chaos of the docking bay.

"Good man," she said with a smile, then rode a feral rush of adrenaline into her spacecraft.

Haskell's black boxes had to work. Whatever he thought he could or couldn't do, they were out of time. No more tuning, no more planning. This was their chance to take this razor-thin technological advantage and rip it into a yawning chasm to end this war for good. She had to trust Haskell, trust the engineering and the laws of physics—and ignore the fact that in physics, something was only a law because it hadn't been proven wrong *yet*. She shrugged the familiar worry off her back, checking the arsenal of survival gear tied down in the *Soyka*'s tiny cabin. She'd run the odds countless times. Second-guessing was over. Haskell was the best temporal engineer in the galaxy and his calculations had been checked, scrutinized, and mercilessly picked apart by hordes of scientists and engineers desperate to prove him wrong. He wasn't.

He couldn't be.

Val really, *really* hoped he wasn't.

The hatch behind her slammed shut with a bang and hiss, cutting off the din of voices and equipment. Heavy silence draped across the tiny cabin. She settled into the cockpit, the *Soyka*'s systems filling the quiet with small hums and clicks, the symphony of a spacecraft coming alive around her punctuated by the bright snap of her flight harness. Gentle vibrations rose through the control stick as she flexed her fingers around it. The life support system blew a soft breeze that tickled the fine hairs at the back of her neck. Green light from the status board cast an expectant glow across her hands as they hovered above the controls, while the shadows filled with the crimson, tactical lighting of the cabin. Outside, a marshal signaled sharply for Val to engage her engines. A thrill raced through her neurons as the call to action shot through her soul and she grinned, jamming the throttle forward. This, she knew. *Time to fly.*

The cloud of friendly fighters zipped into formation around her as the squadron burst from the cruiser. Other pilots' voices flowed through her audio implant, the cool call and response of professionals preparing for battle. The fighters had one mission— keep Val alive—and she allowed herself a fraction of a second to wonder what they'd been told. Keep her alive *until what*? Until she deployed some kamikaze superweapon destined to shatter the marauding Slug cruisers into billions of slime-tainted shards? Until she escaped, spiriting secrets into the dark of space? The truth lay somewhere between the two. Would they feel it, if they ceased to exist? Would she?

What a completely fucking useless th—the *Soyka*'s cabin splintered with the screech of alarms. Her HUD blossomed into a firestorm.

She dove, whirling through the flock of fighters that broke and surged around her. Tracers exploded across her field of view. Amber-and-crimson icons peppered her displays. Vakking hell, there were hundreds of them.

"Haskell. We won't last long out here."

Static.

"Haskell. Do you copy?"

Enemy fire streaked across the space ahead and Val jerked the stick forward, twirling beneath the stream of death. Voices and alarms rang in her head, earning Haskell a reprieve as the fighter pilots' chatter clamored against the proximity alerts keening for her attention. Her objective collapsed to *stay alive*, Haskell's mute struggle aside, and the cacophony in her ears ratcheted higher. Val scowled. Space was supposed to be quiet, yet humanity had managed to fill it with so many alarms she could hardly concentrate. She slammed a palm against the audio panel, silencing the endless warnings. More fire. Someone screamed across the radio, terror wrenched from a throat and mercilessly cut short. More tracers, this time closer, and Val threw her ship aside again. *Damn it. They should have armored this vakking thing.*

She wasn't *scared*, per se. Riding the knife edge between life and death was nothing new to a soldier twenty years into a lifetime of war. She'd been chased through space by pissed off Slugs plenty of times before, although this was the first time they'd shown up explicitly to kill *her*. Murderous intent was practically a cliché for the flesh-eating bastards. They'd even succeeded in killing her, once, and only Kass's stupid bravery had dragged her back to safety in time to be revived. Since then, death was simply a patient companion. But *failure* curdled her insides.

The most important mission of her life hinged on this moment. She was the blade poised at the pulsing jugular of endless war. Hundreds of years of human history hung in the balance. Millions of lives. Countless futures. The grand game of probability waited to explode or contract the moment she embarked, and she could do *nothing* until Lieutenant P.J. Haskell fixed whatever the fuck was going on aboard the cruiser she'd just launched from. Preferably before she died. Again.

So maybe she wasn't scared, but she *was* a little stressed.

"*Haskell.*" Another mute volley of enemy fire arced past her ship. "Is your plan to send a cloud of debris on this mission? Because in a few seconds that's what you get."

A staticky, mumbled reply finally eked onto the radio
"*I'mtryingI'msorrypleasedon'tdie.*"

At least the radio was working.

Val touched the control stick again and the *Soyka* rolled, evading another burst of tracers. The ship hummed faithfully around her, thrusters whirring as she whipped the craft into an evasive spin, the systems rising to her command as they always had, crisp and obedient. But it was only a matter of time. Her escape, like the war

• 33 •

itself, was an ever-tightening noose. That tended to happen when fighting the very race from whom you'd stolen interstellar travel in the first place. Somehow they always had the technological edge with which to whittle away at humanity.

Her HUD screeched in her ear a millisecond too late. *"Fuck!"*

The comfortable hum of her spacecraft shattered as magshot rippled across the hull with a bang and the sudden hiss of escaping air. Her ears popped. Something gave with a screech of metal. The universe beyond her windows whipped into streaks as the *Soyka* spun wildly. *"Haskell!* You need to get me out of here *right. Fucking. Now* or so help me I will—"

Val's tirade stuttered to a halt, curled in on itself, and reemerged as an undignified heave as the bottom dropped out of her stomach.

The *Soyka* fell from an alien sky.

CHAPTER THREE

August 1, 1996 AD, 5:00 p.m.
In the skies over Seldovia, Alaska, Earth

"Baker, you read?"

Jack Reeve's boisterous voice crackled over the company frequency, just loud enough to overcome the thrum of a massive radial engine and the spatter of raindrops on the canopy. Nicole Baker smiled at the unexpected interruption. The flight home from Kodiak had become a turbulent slog against headwinds that added nearly an hour to her journey, complete with endless gray skies and petulant bursts of rain that suppressed her usually buoyant mood. Alone at the controls of her airplane, she'd been selfishly indulging in seductive fantasies of a good meal and a warm bed before Jack's voice cut through her reverie. She loved flying—she really did—but flights like this were enough to test any bush pilot's patience. With Alaska's boundless beauty shrouded in clouds, rough air taking her and the Beav on an invisible roller coaster, and nothing to do but hold them both on as straight a line as possible, finding joy in the experience was like trying to catch a salmon with her bare hands. Possible—theoretically. Jack offered a welcome distraction, and the tension and fatigue of the marathon flight lifted from her shoulders just enough to put a smile into her voice. "Loud and clear, Jack. What are you doing on this frequency?"

"Oh, stirring up trouble." She could hear his answering grin. "Where you at?"

TESSA CROFT

Nicole looked down through the driving rain, barely able to make out the coast a mile below. Wispy clouds and a haze of rain threatened her clear path home. The ocean beat against a rocky, black coastline. A few structures peeked out between the trees, and a familiar cluster of large islands signaled her nearness to home. "Just at the southern tip of the Peninsula. Why?"

"Dispatch got a call 'bout a kid needing help." Nicole's heart constricted. "Needs a ride to a hospital ASAP, and you're right on top of 'em. It's a cabin on MacDonald Spit. Think you could put 'er down on the beach and take a couple passengers to Homer?"

She eyed the precariously thin strip of tidewater below. She'd flown over MacDonald countless times in her voyages across the Cook Inlet. The houses dotting the narrow spine of land were beyond the reach of any road. Without an airplane, the residents clinging to its flanks faced a trek—by foot, four-wheeler, or boat—just to reach the road into town, at which point they still had to find a car and get to the tiny airstrip miles away. At that point, who knew how long they'd wait for another aircraft to pick them up? It would be hours before they made it to a doctor. She could get them to a hospital in twenty minutes.

Considering, Nicole glanced at her fuel gauges. She'd been charging into the wind for hours and barely had enough gas to make it home. That same wind still howled outside the aircraft, and the ocean below roiled with whitecaps, seething against its sandy bounds. The trees clinging to the mountains leaned ominously away from the coast, rocking in the gathering storm. A narrow beach offered precious little room for error. The thought of saying no, though, churned her insides worse than the turbulent air knocking her airplane about. She'd been rushed to a hospital in this very plane as a child, her grandfather's steady piloting and her grandmother's soothing voice ferrying her to an unexpected appendectomy in Anchorage. She'd lain in the back seat, curled around herself, and let the drone of the engine soothe her fear. She wouldn't leave a child to suffer.

She pulled the throttle and began her descent.

"Wind straight in off the ocean," she murmured, watching the waves crest and burst against the beach.

Jack grunted agreement. "Pretty sure everyone else around Homer's happy as a clam to sit this crap out. Kid's lucky you're the one flyin' over. Nobody else's actually gonna go out and get 'im in this."

"Which either makes me insane or an idiot," she said softly, frowning at the swaying trees below. Either way, the choice was obvious.

She glided lower, visibility improving as she eased below the thickening rainclouds, skirting the foothills of the Kenai Range rearing up from the tumultuous sea. She strained to see through the spackled windshield, leaning against her window and peering down at the beach zipping beneath her low pass along the coast. Dark, scraggly spruce and writhing, silver birch waved up at her as she swept past, leaves and needles buffeted in the blustering winds off the sea. Mist spewed from the crashing waves, blowing across the black sand in harried, white bursts whipped from the water. The wind tugged her off course, eating away at her improvised runway and urging her airplane toward the rocks and driftwood cluttering the line of high tide. The nose fought her, eager to weathervane into the gale, and she pressed hard on the rudder to keep herself in line with the narrow expanse of gravel. Her feet and hands moved in an unconscious dance, twenty years of pilotage guiding her motions without thought as the beach inched closer to her tires.

Then figures, their arms waving. A family living a life like hers, remote and pristine, wonderfully independent but for these moments when life in the bush clashed with the harsh reality of a frail, human body. These moments when machines—on dry land, over snow, across the sea or through the air—became lifelines. "Tallyho, Jack. I'll check in with you from Homer."

She fought the wind with throttle and yoke. The engine pulled her through the recalcitrant air. A wing dipped precipitously. One massive tundra tire bit into the sand, then the other, and a tumultuous clatter arose as grit leapt into the air to spatter the aircraft's tail. Her feet went into overdrive, steering the airplane's momentum to a controlled stop upwind of the family scurrying toward her along the beach. When the De Havilland Beaver finally rolled to a standstill, wings rocking in the unforgiving gale, her legs burned with the effort of holding a straight line in the sand. The family, unaware of the difficulty, rushed toward her as the propeller at last twitched to a halt. A little boy wailed in his father's arms. Tears streaked his mottled cheeks. Nicole leapt from the cockpit and flung the passenger door wide, beckoning for them to climb aboard. The relief in their eyes instantly defused the lingering tension of the challenging landing.

"Thank you," the woman gasped as her partner climbed into the rear seat.

Nicole nodded, one hand on the door, the other clamped over her ballcap as the wind snatched at it. Even at low tide the waves were deafening, booming breakers muting any thought of a reply. Strands of hair pulled free of her braid and plastered themselves across her face. She eyed the continually building rain clouds. *Just another beautiful day in Alaska.* On cue, the drizzle became a downpour. The Beav's wings deflected the onslaught, shielding the harried family as they loaded the whimpering child into his father's arms, but Nicole's flannel instantly glued itself to her skin in a frigid layer when she stood aside to let them in. Raindrops leapt from the brim of her cap and disappeared into the wind. They ran in rivulets down the back of her neck, trickling under her collar. She shivered as she got the family buckled in, glancing between seat belts and the lowering mist beyond the windows. The mountaintops had vanished into the clouds. Streaks of rain fluttered across what remained of the horizon. The ocean beckoned, churning. She hid a spike of worry from her passengers. The cloud ceiling was dropping fast, the brutally rapid deterioration common of Alaska's seething weather. She eyed the diminishing margin between sand and sky one more time, made her decision, and turned the key. The thunder of the engine beat back the tempest. In moments, they were airborne again.

The drone of the engine dipped and wobbled as they bounced and shook in the gusts. The little boy mewled and cried above the roar. Nicole set her sights on the other side of Kachemak Bay and pressed the throttle forward. Flying on fumes into a gale, scud running across the bay as a storm closed in…she smiled despite it all.

THROUGH SKY AND STARS

At last, the Beav's massive tires touched down on wide, unblemished asphalt. The flash of an ambulance whirled on the ramp nearby. Paramedics rushed toward the airplane, stretcher between them. The wind howled in protest along with the child. As they lifted the stretcher into the ambulance, tiny payload tucked aboard, the mother turned back. Her eyes darted between her child, the airplane, and the paramedics waiting to close the doors and speed away. After a brief hesitation she ran back, wrapped her arms around Nicole, and squeezed hard enough to knock Nicole's ballcap off her forehead.

"Thank you," she said again.

Then she was gone, the hug vanished as unexpectedly as it had appeared, and Nicole watched the ambulance rush away with a bloom of hope in her chest. She smiled despite the chill working through her sodden clothes.

Her stomach growled as the flashing lights disappeared up the road.

"Okay, okay." She chuckled, turning back to the plane. Fantasies of a good meal and a warm bed reawakened. Though the propeller tilted upward, ready and willing to pull her back into the sky, the horrific weather had closed in. Plus, they both needed fuel.

"Sorry, girl," she said to the plane, patting the dripping fuselage. "Even an insane idiot would stay home in this."

She threw down the chocks, tied down the wings, and went to find a taxi. Home would wait until tomorrow.

• 39 •

CHAPTER FOUR

August 2, 1996 AD [Terran Calendar], 0300 hrs.
In the skies over the Kenai Mountains, Alaska, Earth

TERRAIN. PULL UP.

Vakking what? Val yanked back on the stick, adrenaline bursting through her veins. The *Soyka* ignored her, whipped into a violent dive, and screamed downward like a demon headed for hell. Was it down? It felt like it, but her equilibrium abandoned her faster than oxygen from an airlock. The ship tumbled from her control. Her inner ear went dumb under the onslaught from her screaming HUD. Every agonizing jolt of the sudden turbulence went straight to pit of her stomach, nestling in beside dread and the sudden urge to lose her lunch.

She gritted her teeth. Growled at the fog of confusion. Her ship was designed to *counter* accelerations, preventing her from smearing into a slimy mess while maneuvering at incredible speeds in the vacuum of space. Feeling anything at all was a bad sign, but *this*...this was fatal. Her control systems were completely and utterly screwed. The ship tumbled and bucked, rising and falling in the grip of an invisible demon trying to shake the life out of her. The stick jerked again, ripping itself from her grip and slamming into her knee. She pressed her palms to the instrument panel as her arms tried to wriggle free of her shoulders.

And the *noise*. Seconds ago, she'd been racing through empty space, deceptively quiet despite waves of enemy fire drawing a

TESSA CROFT

slowly tightening noose about her neck. Now the very darkness screamed at her like a thousand angry banshees out for blood. *Air.* Alarms screeched through her HUD and filled the tiny cabin of the *Soyka.* Her dropship struggled in vain against mortal wounds, a parting gift of the squadron of Slug fighters. Val's equilibrium slewed farther with each jolt of turbulence. Gravity toyed with her. A gust lifted, then harshly dropped, her guts. The *Soyka* was losing the battle against a sudden, alien atmosphere, but she couldn't focus on the instruments long enough to figure out why. She couldn't even see the *vakking* altimeter. Squiggles of amber and red danced in her vision as she fought to bring the control panels into focus. She reached blindly for the switch for her backup controls...nothing. Her HUD screamed again, this time overpowering mewling alarms and howling wind alike.

SINK RATE. PULL UP.

Her mind raced down channels of cause and effect. Backup computer? No response. Auxiliary power? Nothing. Secondary control surfaces? The spin bucked harder and Val cursed, her fist cramping on the stick. A whisper of desperation slithered up her spine. If Haskell had done his job—likely, given Haskell was a damn genius—jagged mountains and icy water hid in the furious darkness beyond her windows. Their invisible maw closed in on her as surely as Slug cannons a moment before, just as eager to consume her. Crimson warnings crept like lava across her displays.

SINK RATE. PULL UP.

She had one option left, and she didn't like it. It was a long shot—and a stupid one, at that—but she had no choice. She was out of time, out of altitude, out of luck. She ripped the safety cover off the *Soyka's* primary power switches.

Her ship powered down. Completely.

The computers let go. The control surfaces reverted to simple, aerodynamic equilibrium and the ship assumed a straight—if no less fatal—descent. The world stilled for a glorious heartbeat. Val took one breath, giving her ship every precious second she could afford, before she slammed her palm into the switches and prayed to every god she'd never believed in.

The panel flickered to life. The altimeter—

"Fuck!" She jerked back on the stick and slammed the throttle forward. The engines sputtered, then screamed. Spray erupted beyond her windows. Val flinched.

The *Soyka* went dark, blackness crashing down in a screech of rending metal and the terrifying, gurgling rush of water forcing itself into her wounded ship. Time skidded. Seconds slipped past in a daze. Minutes? She wasn't sure, but when she came to, her feet were numbing in a pool of icy liquid. Warmth dripped from her chin. She couldn't see but she could hear the water pouring in behind her, bubbling gleefully as her ship sank.

Val dragged herself out of her seat, stumbling in the dark, and staggered when the ship rolled with her steps. Inky death sloshed at her calves. She felt her way along the bulkhead blindly, searching. The chill reached her knees. *There.* Rough fabric slid under her fingertips, her pack still strapped into the stowage compartment. Part of her whispered to leave it, abandon it in favor of escape while the ship still bobbed near the surface, and she hesitated with one hand on the clasps. She'd survive without it, but she'd be useless against the Slugs without the weaponry within. Val shook off the urge to flee. The *Soyka* tumbled, rolling like a fat slug in the pitch darkness, and the invisible waves swallowed her pack. "Damn it!"

She had to focus. She could do this. This ship was her home—hundreds of hours, innumerable missions. She could free that goddamn pack blindfolded, hands tied behind her back, while enemy fire crisscrossed the air above her head. This would be easier than getting out of Kass's pins. The cold encroached like a thousand needles, a steady onslaught of numbness creeping up her thighs. She wouldn't last long, but she didn't need much. Val dove into the frigid dark.

The searing cold sharpened her senses, channeling her mind's eye into her fingertips as she worked the invisible clasps. Her pack surged upward with an explosion of bubbles that fizzed against her cheeks. She surfaced with them, triumphant, but her crow of happiness came out in a fierce yell as a fucking icy sea sluiced from her clothes. "*Fuck, that's cold!*"

She worked her way to the hatch, teeth chattering as the soul-numbing water reached her armpits, dragging her pack along the surface behind her. With the ship sideways, the hatch release sat somewhere near toes she could no longer feel. She heaved in a breath and dove again. Her fingers scraped over metal, spreading out from the hatch release, searching, until—*yes!* A metal door sprung outward. Val snatched at the mask inside, smashed it against her face, and breathed a literal sigh of relief as oxygen blasted the water from the emergency mask. She would make it out of this shitshow of a landing, after all.

The hatch release groaned and scraped, the *Soyka* resisting abandonment to the last, but the door finally slid free as Val lost feeling in her legs. A burst of bubbles swirled about her as they fluttered into the invisible, infinite depths. Floating in a wasteland of fatal darkness, Val's heart skipped. She could've been swimming up, down, sideways, *backwards* for all she could see, but the pack saved her. It rose like a buoy, rocketing for the surface, and Val clung to the lifeline with lifeless fingers.

She broke the surface with a yell. Cool air rippled over her exposed skin like the draft from a blast furnace. Relief bubbled through her. She ripped the mask from her face and gulped in the unlimited, precious air.

A white whale bumped into her shoulder. Val jerked, nearly falling from her precarious perch, and scowled at the offending iceberg. What the fuck? Haskell said she'd arrive in late summer. She knew from brutal exposure that this was fresh water. She was in a lake. Why were there icebergs? Ghostly, white blobs drifted around her, bobbing in the wake of her graceless thrashing. They were everywhere, blotting out the shore, and ahead of her, a wall of the stuff reared up into the night. Val gaped. She'd almost flown her spacecraft straight into a goddamn *glacier*.

At least now she understood why it was so goddamn cold.

With a sigh of relief, she dragged her pack from the water, slipping on algae-draped stones. She scanned the shore, alert for enemies or predators, but it was jarringly peaceful. Brush crept down to the water's edge, leaves swaying in a gentle breeze sloughing from the mass of glacial ice dumping into the lake, and beneath them lay only shadows, downed logs and rocks glistening with reflected moonlight. Her HUD kept mercifully quiet. The system's only flicker of color highlighted the scurrying of a rodent escaping the tumult of her graceless arrival. Alone. *Perfect.*

She stripped off her sodden flight suit and immediately warmed without the frigid fabric clinging to her skin. Still, she shivered as she worked her pack open and laid her supplies aside, neatly, until she found what she needed: Dry clothes, the tight plastic around them the saving grace that had kept them dry while also making them—and her—float. She'd never been so grateful for the irritatingly tight, difficult packing strategy, even as her tingling fingers fumbled with the tight bindings.

Her shivering subsided. The warm, clean fabric smelled of her quarters on the *Al.* She tried not to dwell on the fleeting nature of the scent as it brushed past her. Her past, and that future, were gone. The stars she'd plummeted from were now as inaccessible as the twenty-eighth century. A final shudder rippled through her, the magnitude of what she'd done rocking her core like an earthquake twisting the foundations of the Earth, immense and inconceivable. Val shook her head as it passed. The enormity of it would crush her if she let it, and she couldn't afford that. The price she'd paid—that they'd all paid—demanded she keep going.

Warm at last, Val finally spared a moment for her injuries. She'd lost time after the crash, and the gash across her forehead still burned. The nanotech in her blood had clotted the gash in her forehead and stopped the bleeding, but a quick dash of salve from her pack, cleverly disguised as a tube of *Neosporin* (whatever the fuck that was), boosted their response. Val grimaced at the hot tingle of skin knitting itself back together at inhuman speed. Still, she was grateful for the small bit of the twenty-eighth century tech she'd been allowed to carry with her.

The horizon began to pink, a tantalizing glow kissing the mountaintops, and Val raised her eyes skyward. The stars she'd left behind still laid out before her, spinning across the sky in a glimmering river holding fast against the encroaching day, but the swirling universe she'd known was bounded by great mountains bisecting Earth from sky in ominous, jagged lines glowing faintly in the imminent dawn. The great flanks swept upward, shrouded in brush, then scraggly pine, and finally vast fields of grass and

TESSA CROFT

wildflowers that shifted and sighed in the gentle wind off the glacier. Vegetation gave way to rock as she scanned higher, the habitable slopes giving way to unforgiving rock inhabited only by the hardiest creatures. The crescent moon—exactly as she knew it, unchanged despite the cataclysmic leap in Val's own existence—squatted serenely above the ridgeline. The mountains were at once vast and encroaching, untamed but limning her new world in insurmountable walls.

At her feet, the quicksilver surface of the lake spread between the nearest peaks, shimmering with ripples that flitted between rafts of pure white ice. The glacier held court over the scene, flowing from unseen heights to crouch at the water's edge. Greens of every shade emerged from the brush around her as sunlight seeped into the morning. The breeze caressed her cheek. Val closed her eyes and pulled it deep into her lungs. *Unlimited oxygen.* The smell of salt. The hint of soil and living things. The faint stirring of water and soft shush of wind through the trees forming a quiet, uninterrupted duet. Beautiful and haunting; in Val's time this was gone, sunk beneath chemical fire and horribly polluted oceans, as lost as the *Soyka.* Countless worlds dotted her memory, from volcanic, tide-riven hellholes to lush rainforests filled with eerie foliage never seen by human eyes, but nothing compared to Earth. Cradle of humanity, home of biodiversity vaster than anything in the known galaxy, an oasis among worlds. This was what she came to save.

Val knew precisely where she was, though no human had laid eyes on this scene in hundreds of years. She recognized the valley, though the reality was more beautiful than she'd imagined while poring over maps in her quarters. The combined miracles of physics, mathematics, and Lieutenant P.J. Haskell had placed her, the *Soyka*, and the Earth in the exact right places at the exact right time. Still, she tested the theory by sweeping her hand across the inside of her forearm. A faintly-glowing map appeared, the lines a ghostly tattoo, and she smiled with predatory glee as the perfection of Haskell's navigation illuminated in glowing ink. *Right. Vakking. On.* She hadn't really *expected* Haskell and his geek gang to get it wrong, but she hadn't been able to ignore the niggling possibility that her life and mission would be wasted by blinking into existence deep

THROUGH SKY AND STARS

inside the planet's mantle—a certain outcome if Haskell's numbers had been off by even a millionth. A surge of pride stole through her as she thought of his aggrieved scowl, the worry in his voice as he'd strained to complete his work and Val struggled to stay alive. *You did it.* Val stood on the southern coast of the North American State of Alaska at the end of the summer of 1996 AD.

Eight hundred years of human history, erased in the blink of an eye.

Her stomach clenched.

She blew out the ache in a huff. Every second spent second-guessing was a second wasted. She snapped her hand to her elbow and the map vanished. Kass's voice rose in her mind. *Do your job, Koroleva.*

She afforded herself one last, wistful look at the lake and considered her ship lying at the bottom. She couldn't help regretting its loss, though the odds of her returning to it had been slim to start with. Even *if* she lived and *if* she returned to this place, the ship simply wasn't capable of a return journey—Slug-induced perforations aside. When she'd asked, Haskell had simply smiled apologetically and suggested she spend the rest of her life imagining that they roamed the galaxy without her. Of course, the luxury of doing so required that she survive what was essentially a suicide mission *without* the added complexities of quantum phys—

She froze, listening. A deep whir had crept into the background of her new world, rising so subtly that she'd nearly missed it. She turned slowly, trying to locate the direction of the sound, and was facing the lake when a small aircraft burst over the horizon at its far end. *Vack!* There was just enough gray, predawn light illuminating the shoreline that an attentive pilot would already have spotted her. The plane arced out over the lake. Too late.

Wingtips dipped and flared red in the first hints of morning sunlight as the craft circled back toward her. A tiny, white fuselage gleamed in the first rays of light, just large enough for a handful of humans or a small load of cargo. Broad, spindly wings and a single, round engine kept the craft aloft. Two bulky wheels dangled below the cockpit. A third, smaller wheel sat beneath a tail sporting the craft's identification code. *Cute.* Or it would be, if she weren't so

TESSA CROFT

suspicious of its presence. *Ancient.* She squinted, trying to make out the pilot as the plane drew nearer.

"Please just be a boring Terran," she muttered.

With her enhanced vision, she made out a cap, sunglasses, and the bulk of a communications headset. Definitely human, and definitely looking at her. The wings rocked. She tentatively lifted one hand in return. Then, deciding that confidence was probably best in the face of a local circling overhead, she waved vigorously in her best impression of, "Hi, neighbor!"

"Nothing to see here," she muttered through clenched teeth, watching the small plane begin a slow circle overhead.

She wasn't worried about being seen—the odds of a random Terran pilot being a Slug operative were extraordinarily slim—but the sight of a woman alone in this vast wilderness was bound to worry any local flying over such remote terrain. The last thing she needed was a search and rescue squadron deployed to find her. So she put on her best impression of an unconcerned hiker gawking at an airplane—which wasn't hard. A cocoon of sound enveloped her as the aircraft banked above the lake. It swept across the water, reflection frolicking across the waves, as sunlight fell upon the mountain peak beyond and painted the backdrop in slate, pine, and snow running with golden light. The sound filled her, bolstering her determination with a bubble of joy. She smiled at the sight of the tiny craft drawing dawn across the sky like a tiny, mechanical Apollo. Primitive but beautiful.

Satisfied, the plane wagged its wings in farewell and leveled off, the sound releasing its grip on her chest only once the craft finally disappeared over the mountain. Val was almost sad to see it go. Almost. She was 99.9 percent certain that the stranger peering down from the aircraft had been no more than a concerned Terran, given Haskell's team had reported that the Slugs were weak in this time period. Most reports suggested they hadn't emerged from the hive for at least another hundred years. But 99.9 wasn't good enough when the stakes were this high. Humanity didn't get a second chance. She tightened her pack, checked her wristmap one last time, and started to run.

PART II: *PREFLIGHT*

THROUGH SKY AND STARS

CHAPTER FIVE

August 2, 1996 AD [Terran Calendar], 1700 hrs.
Kenai Mountains, Alaska, Earth

Val put several kilometers between herself and the lake before full daylight. Her wristmap's seamless hacking of the planet's primitive positioning satellites provided ample guidance, but she hardly needed it as she drank in the stunning beauty of her new world. She was caught between elements, clinging to the flanks of the impossibly huge, geological beasts as they reared up from an icy gray ocean below. Waves crashed against the mountainsides along the coast, rumbling and worrying at the steep cliffs below her as she jogged. Precarious hillsides rose above, populated by seabirds that whirled and complained at Val's intrusion. She passed through a series of valleys, each with a glacier at its head and an icy lake in its base, an unfathomable quantity of ice pouring from the peaks around her. In daylight, the lakes were stunning, bright turquoise, though icebergs bobbed mockingly in all of them. Gurgling streams, running away from the relentless melting above, cut into loose, gravelly sediment beneath what little grass took root in the valley floors. Above them, the mountainsides were *pink*. Millions of fuchsia flowers, growing on stalks as tall as Val herself, carpeted the wild and wonderful landscape. They swayed in waves as gusts of wind whipped playfully down the valleys.

Unlimited, guaranteed oxygen. Unlimited clean water. A pristine, indescribably beautiful landscape unlike any planet she'd

• 51 •

ever seen. It was luxurious and practically mythical to someone like her who'd grown up in overcrowded cities and still more crowded space stations, where the far-flung remnants of humanity huddled close and the relentless vacuum of space waited beyond the walls to consume the careless or unlucky.

Yet the beauty hid demons.

Familiar loathing surged through her each time she contemplated the lurking threat drawing her onward. She shuddered at the thought of these very mountains desecrated by chemical fire, when human militaries drove the Protectors back into their hive long before she'd been born. They'd brought the First Hive of Earth to the brink of destruction. Yet just when victory seemed near, the fault in the human strategy became abundantly and horrifically clear: humanity had assumed that the First Hive was alone. The Colony vessel returned in the closing phases of that first battle, raining retribution and regretful hindsight upon a world that had killed its kin. Centuries later, Val and her fellow soldiers still bore the consequences.

She forced herself to run faster, until the burning pain in her muscles drowned out the unease in her heart, until she couldn't think about the thousands of people aboard the *Al* whose fates hung in limbo while she sprinted across the mountainside. She might never know whether they'd winked from existence the moment she appeared in the skies over Alaska. Most likely wouldn't. What she could control, now, was whether she completed her mission quickly and decisively. The sooner, the better, to increase their odds of survival. She leaned into the call, the invisible thread pulling her onward, and let the fire in her muscles burn away thoughts of the life she'd left behind.

She ran until the ground flattened into a riverbed guiding her north. Until alpine scrub gave way to leafy brush, dark pine, and silvery trunks rising from cobbled banks dappled in evergreen shade. Until the sun beat down on her shoulders and she chased her shadow upstream.

Until her HUD exploded to life, amber-and-crimson warnings flaring across her vision in a dizzying array of furious cautions.

An *airplane*. Her implants struggled to recognize the unfamiliar technology, metal and plastics and unknown materials flagged and analyzed in a dizzying swirl of icons while her human mind struggled to process the flood of information. She blinked. The messages diminished. And then she saw the *person* kneeling next to the machine.

Vakking idiot! She dove into the brush at river's edge, praying that her inglorious flailing went unnoticed, and landed in the shadows with a soft grunt. A rock dug painfully into her ribs, chastising her in lieu of a disappointed drill sergeant. She knew better than to waltz around a blind corner! She'd gotten complacent in the peaceful hiking, let her sulking dull her senses. Had she given herself away? Blown her mission to smithereens in a blind fit of moping? She gritted her teeth and waited for the sound of approaching footsteps—or worse, the skittering of insectoid limbs over stone. Her HUD dimmed to a faint reminder of the unknown apparatus now beyond her field of view. The river burbled innocently, a soft presence calming her nerves. Nothing stirred but leaves. Still, her fingers itched for a mag rifle that wouldn't exist for seven hundred years. She scowled and pressed a finger to her temple, silencing the agonizing bleat of her HUD before it blinded her, and peered again at the unexpected presence on the riverbank.

Val blinked as a chill of recognition raised the small hairs on the back of her neck. The same aircraft that had circled above her this morning now sat on the riverbank. The same white fuselage still glowed, bathed in the afternoon sun, and the wide wings rocked gently in a soft breeze pouring down the valley. The clear blue sky shimmered on the canopy. Red accents at the wingtips shot through the calm gray and evergreen of the river valley, the rogue streak of color demanding adventure. Yet it stood still, poised on a long gravel bar that snaked toward her along the stream, and the Terran pilot crouched at its base with an open toolbox. Val scowled, suspicion tightening her shoulders. To find it here, now, with its pilot placed perfectly along her route... Had they been lying in wait? Any Sh'keth scout with half a brain could've inferred her path.

She dismissed the suspicion, and her rising unease, with a soft snort. If they'd spotted her—which was, admittedly, plausible—they would also have to deem her a threat before they took action. *That* seemed unlikely, as this planet was currently crawling with humans and a lone woman hiking through the wilderness was hardly outside the realm of plausibility. Most importantly, though, if they *had* deemed her a threat they'd have murdered Val as she ran. No questions asked, no messy fight. The Sh'keth didn't need a human pilot's help to drop out of the sky and gut her. Which meant that nearly running headlong into plane and pilot *probably* hadn't sacrificed her mission in an appalling feat of rookie idiocy, but the question remained. What were they doing out here?

Val held a finger to her temple, blinked twice in rapid succession, and her field of view raced forward as magnification brought the aircraft to her fingertips. To the uninitiated the shift was a sickening flight at dizzying speeds that lurched to a halt just before slamming bodily into the propeller, a sensation that often deposited newly-enhanced plebes on their knees in a pile of vomit. Val rode the rush with practiced indifference and inspected the riverbed scene in crystallized clarity.

The Terran in question was engaged in battle against a tire nearly half his own size. Another lay limply to the side with a cruel shard of driftwood protruding from it, pointing into the sky like a mocking, rude finger, and Val's enhanced hearing caught a wordless grunt of effort as the Terran knelt to wrestle the replacement into position at the base of his aircraft. Tools littered the ground around him. The knees of his beige workpants sank into the coarse, black sand as he hefted the bulk of the tire. His hands, where they gripped the tire, were dark with grease and dirt. Flannel sleeves, rolled up to the elbows, revealed fair skin tanned by the late summer sun. A faded cap shielded his face in shadow. He lifted the tire, back straining, and his chin came up.

Val blinked as a bolt of pleasant surprise shot through her. *She* wobbled slightly under the weight of the tire, found her balance and set her shoulder into it, shifting the massive thing toward the aircraft's landing gear. A blond braid fell into view and the Terran woman huffed at it, blowing renegade strands away from her face. The tire lifted achingly slowly toward the axle. It swayed against the woman's efforts, threatening to topple, but she pushed it relentlessly closer to success. Her smooth jaw set in determination, brow furrowed over a frown of concentration. Her eyes glinted with determination. But just as she neared success, the axle sneaking tantalizingly close, the sand below her feet shifted and the tire dipped, slipping sideways and tumbling from her grasp. It rolled aside petulantly and flopped to the sand with a *whumpf* Val could hear *without* enhanced hearing. The Terran woman muttered at it and shook out her hands.

Val closed her eyes and touched her temple to reset her magnification, considering. Her rational mind told her to sink back into the forest and be on her way; A Terran and her problems were nothing but a distraction from Val's mission. She should circle through the trees, remain out of sight, and continue toward the hive without leaving so much as an inkling of her presence. The idea, though, left her unsettled. She looked again at the airplane. The ancient propeller tipped skyward, challenging, and the mighty wingspan looked ready to pull the Terran back into the sky with sheer strength of will. But the mountains loomed above them both, huge and untamed. She imagined the empty kilometers behind her. Ahead lay many more. Though the woman seemed capable of getting herself out of this mess, what if she didn't? Val was here to *help* humanity. Turning a blind eye to a Terran in distress went against that directive.

Mind made up, Val rose and stepped from the trees.

Not even replacing a flat could dampen Nicole's spirits. She crouched on the riverbank, troublesome tire firmly in her grasp once more, inching the stubborn beast closer to the axle while ignoring the mounting strain in her arms. She was riding high on life and coffee. She'd woken to a phone call, the kid's parents filling her in on the emergency appendectomy that their son, Kelly, had sailed through with flying colors, and he'd even gotten on the line to ask when he could ride in her airplane again. The eagerness of his plea—and the fact that he'd sounded vastly better than the day before—would leave her smiling for days. After a gorgeous flight home in the smooth, clear skies of a picture-perfect autumn morning, Nicole's mood danced right over the flat like the northern lights skimmed over mountaintops. She'd knock this tire out and be back in the skies tomorrow, ready to face the next adventure Alaska had in store.

Until a voice sounded behind her. Here, in her haven in the woods where visitors unfailingly announced themselves with the roar of an aircraft engine, providing ample warning of their approach. Twenty-five miles from her nearest neighbor. The absolute middle of nowhere.

"Can I help with that?"

Nicole screamed.

Her corresponding jerk of surprise loosened the sand under her boots and she slipped, flopping gracelessly onto her rump in the gravel. The fifty-pound tundra tire followed, dropping mercilessly into her lap and eliciting a pained grunt that turned into an undignified *oomph* as it toppled further, landing flat on her chest and knocking the wind from her.

At which point she lay on the ground, gasping for breath, and looked up at the most gorgeous women she'd ever seen. Copper skin split by a dazzling, perfect smile. A lock of ebony hair falling over dark brows. Silver eyes flirting with mirth. Every perfect bit of her completely upside-down from Nicole's perspective.

What the hell?

The woman's expression shifted to abject guilt as she took in the minor catastrophe unfolding in front of her. She reached out and the weight of the tire vanished.

Nicole sat up, wheezing, mortified and confused. "I'm sorry, but who…what…?"

The stranger's gaze lingered on the knife edge of schadenfreude, a sparkle in her eyes despite the apologetic grimace on her face. "I'm very sorry I startled you."

Her rich voice rolled over deep vowels, the accent dancing around recognition.

"You looked like you needed help, but it seems I've made things worse." She held out a hand. "Val."

Nicole took it, allowing herself to be helped to her feet. She brushed sand from her thighs, her heart still going full bore, and took her first deep breath since Val's terrifying arrival. Her thoughts skittered like pebbles on a frozen lake, ricocheting away from the reality of the stranger now standing in front of her. She was forty miles from the nearest road, for God's sake! People didn't just *show up* on Nicole's riverbank. She shook her head with a soft laugh, trying to quell the racing of her heart, and had to push back several strands of hair that escaped her hat in response.

"*Jesus*," she finally got out. "You scared the absolute hell out of me!"

"I really am very sorry," Val repeated.

"What the heck are you doing way out here?"

Val's gaze sharpened with a spark of suspicion. She hesitated, gaze flicking upriver, and Nicole pulled in another deep breath. *Odd*. She shouldn't care—Alaska attracted more than its fair share of folks who simply wanted to keep to themselves or leave something behind—but the splash of icy distrust trickled through her like unease after the first bump of turbulence.

Val's gaze slid back. "Just hiking," she said at last.

"You're a long way from any beaten trail."

"I like to stay off those."

Nicole pushed her sleeves up and tried to set suspicion aside. Val's behavior was odd, but whatever drove her this far into the remote wilderness remained her own story to tell—and though she couldn't put her finger on *why*, exactly, Nicole sensed no danger in the woman's presence. Val wouldn't be the first odd duck to wind up in the small pond of the North. She let it go with a shrug and a reassuring smile. "Apparently."

Nicole considered Val as she studied the pass upriver. At first glance, Val was exactly the hiker she claimed to be, from her laced leather boots to the large pack she carried on her shoulders, but her conformity ended at first appearances. Her golden-brown skin stood out against the cool grays of the riverbank, her square jaw framed by short, jet-black hair that fell in an orderly cascade across her forehead. Her clean, simple attire stretched taut over strong shoulders and thighs, but though she stood relaxed—arms crossed, feet planted confidently at shoulder width—her lean body radiated power, and command presence hung in the air around her like an invisible uniform. Her eyes were filled with calculation as she stared into the distance, and when she turned her gaze back to Nicole, the quiet confidence in them held her fast.

Nicole fought the urge to hold her breath, waiting for Val's next words, waiting for those eyes to finish their assessment. At last, a small smile played across Val's features and the icy suspicion melted beneath the wry flash of mirth. "Trust me, I was as surprised as you to run into another person out here. I wouldn't have bothered you, but," she looked pointedly at the tire now resting in the sand, "do you need help with that?"

Nicole regarded the tire. The damn thing sat smugly in its little crater of gravel, staring up at them with its singular, recalcitrant eye, and she didn't relish the prospect of wrestling it back into submission. She did her best to keep a straight face as she deadpanned, "You did just knock five years off my life. I think I *deserve* a hand."

Val barked a sharp laugh, her smile broadening until it crinkled the edges of her eyes. "Fair enough."

Her grin dissolved the awkwardness of their unlikely introduction. It was a hotshot grin, oozing with bravado and confidence, the sort generally seen on a pilot more interested in his own ego than flying, and which Nicole usually deflected with an eye roll. Wielded by a gorgeous woman radiating genuine, competent authority? It was downright dangerous. Nicole found herself smiling stupidly back. *That grin is a weapon.*

She forced herself to ignore it. They had work to do.

The task, however, became appallingly brief when a jock materialized out of thin air. Even Jack, who was burly enough to complain that most bush planes weren't big enough for "real" men, never turned down help with a tundra tire big enough for her plane. Yet Val gracefully picked it up and floated it onto the strut as if positioning a feather pillow. She struggled to keep her jaw from dropping as Val reduced the effort to breezy seconds.

Then Val stood back, wiping her hands together with a satisfied hum, and cast a playful look in Nicole's direction. "Better?"

"Show-off," Nicole said, fighting in vain against the combined forces of Val's impressive strength and effortless charm. She was *not* going to be affected by either one. Absolutely not.

And dammit if Val's grin didn't widen precisely as if she could read her mind. "I would apologize, but I think you'd still prefer it to being stranded in the wilderness."

Nicole blinked, confused, and looked around her wilderness home. "Stranded?"

Val waved one hand at the riverbed, the valley, the ruined tire lying to the side. "I assume you weren't going anywhere soon."

"Aha." She gestured to the well-worn path leading to her cabin. "I'm not stranded, Val. I live here."

The crevice between the trees would have been easy to miss, especially if Val's attention had been drawn to an apparent damsel in distress, but she chuckled as Val's bravado faltered. Yes, she'd had to change the tire before she could head back to Seward. And yes, it was an onerous task. Even if she'd failed to do it alone, though, Jack would've eventually flown out to check on her and help. That's how life in the bush, the life her grandparents had taught her, went. The people who lived out here, in rugged country where even life "in town" came with its share of grizzly bear sightings, looked after each other. So she was anything but *stranded* here, with her home through the trees and her friends on the lookout. She crossed her arms and skewered Val with an accusatory stare, though she softened it with a smile. "You thought you were *rescuing* me?"

Val had the good grace to look chagrined. She shrugged apologetically. "I suppose so."

She gestured to Nicole's airplane, now standing on its own, and the roguish confidence flared again. "I should have known that a woman who commands such a beautiful machine would be able to take care of herself."

"Complimenting me *and* my airplane in the same breath. Nice recovery, Casanova."

A cloud of uncertainty wobbled Val's grin.

Nicole scoffed gently. "Don't tell me you usually get away with that kind of talk."

The rumble of a chuckle rewarded her as Val's expression turned sly. "Sometimes."

Nicole laughed despite herself and waved again toward the path to her cabin. "Well then, would you like a cup of coffee for your troubles?"

The apologetic smile returned, and with it a surprising, irrationally strong tide of disappointment struck Nicole, belying the gentle chiding she'd just delivered. She'd wanted Val to stay.

"Any other time, I would have liked that," Val said. Her gaze turned upriver, following its path through the valley into the distance. The relaxed twinkle in them hardened to steely resolve. "But I need to make a few more kilometers before the sun goes down. I still have a long way to go."

Nicole shoved futilely at the disappointment. She'd had no reason to expect Val would stick around. She'd materialized from thin air, clearly following a plan of her own, on a trip that just happened to pass through Nicole's life. Still, she couldn't help the feeling that Val was someone she wanted to know. Unwelcome restlessness gripped her at the thought of Val simply walking away. She grasped at ideas. Should she give Val the number of Jack's shop in Seward? But then what? Unless Val lived in Seward, it'd be nearly impossible to catch her there. And then she'd have Jack in the middle of it…but what was *it*? Maybe her gaydar was off. Maybe she'd been alone out here too long, if she was so quick to assume a woman's charm was anything more than friendly. But no, Val had clearly been flirting. Hadn't she? Nicole's thoughts derailed, catapulting into one another, until Val held out a hand.

"I should keep going, now that I know you're safe and sound. It was good to meet you…"

The jumble of Nicole's spiraling thoughts screeched to a halt. She blinked. She hadn't introduced herself!

"Nicole," she blurted, blushing, and laughed to cover her embarrassment at the failure. "Baker. Nicole Baker." Val's hand was warm and dry, her grip assured and her palm rough. *Heck with it.* "Look me up if you're ever in Seward. I fly for Aurora."

Val's grin returned, slowly dimpling one cheek. She gave Nicole's hand a squeeze and let go, the absence of her grip leaving Nicole inexplicably bereft. Then she flicked a mock salute, said, "I will," and resumed her trek upstream.

She took off with a purposeful stride at odds with the casual confidence of her flirtatious assistance, the charm of her presence dissolving into the pace of a woman on a mission. Nicole watched her go with growing bewilderment. The momentary gleam of purpose sharpening Val's gaze flickered into her memory. A casual backpacker, looking on her upcoming miles like an inmate on death row? Something more than a peaceful hike drew Val onward. Yet even as Val's lithe form shrank into the distance, Nicole fought the sense that she ought to have done or said something to keep Val around, or to at least get her number...she shook her head. *What am I, fifteen?* She'd made it clear that she wanted to keep in touch—with a directness that was unusual for her—and Val had offered nothing in return. Her disappointment swirled again at the thought. Nicole had never been so instantly, compellingly attracted to a woman she'd just met. It seemed wrong to feel such a strong connection and accept that she'd never see Val again.

Yet she was gone, and Nicole couldn't stand on the riverbank forever.

She gathered her tools with a sigh. Her gut was usually right, and today it whispered that Val was important. Her fingertips tingled with the urge to seize the opportunity disappearing upriver. But what could she do? Follow Val into the wilderness like a madwoman? She scoffed at the absurdity of her own suggestion. *Let it go, Baker.* She'd asked Val to stay and told her how to find her. The ball, if there was one, sat squarely in Val's court.

She let out a long sigh and scanned the pass again, one last time. No silhouette approached through the gathering dusk. Val had melded back into the wilderness from which she'd come, but her absence felt like a puzzle piece Nicole couldn't place. She could force it into the space it *ought* to go—a chance encounter and a good story—but doing so warped the experience in a way she couldn't put her finger on.

She stood on the bank for a long while, watching shadows creep down the valley while she waited for her restlessness to settle. The gurgle of the river seeped into her body. A cool wind picked up, shifting the alders along the bank, and chickadees flit between the branches in oblivious glee. But peace eluded Nicole.

TESSA CROFT

At last the shadows fell over her airplane, casting the white paint in a chromium glow, and she shivered as the sun's warmth retreated. Her ennui shattered.

Distraction. That's what she needed. Something to draw her focus away from the encounter that had her fumbling for balance. Inspiration struck as she shoved her tools into place in the small shed behind her cabin. A row of old coffee cans, riddled with small holes, peered at her from the gloom inside. *Target practice.*

❖

Val's steps were a hundred times lighter when she broke into a run again. The happiness lingered long after Nicole's riverbank disappeared from view. She thought back to Nicole's shocked yelp of surprise, the tire falling into her lap, and chuckled even as sweat broke out anew on her brow. Her breath echoed in her ears as her footfalls quickened. Gravel crunched beneath her boots. Somehow, her encounter with Nicole had cleared her mind and soothed her churning thoughts. The Terran and her peaceful existence, here in this remote corner of a land teeming with beauty and potential, reminded Val that she was here to save more than just a planet—she was here to preserve the innocence, the *hope,* inherent in humanity before centuries of war against the Sh'keth ground her race down to bitter dust. *Humanity* was no longer a faceless mask divorced from the mere thousands she'd left behind in the twenty-eighth century. Nicole was a living, breathing, caring example of the kindness and resourcefulness of humankind before the war. And—she smiled, climbing over a boulder—it didn't hurt that Nicole was as beautiful as the land she lived on. Val was a *little* guilty for scaring her, but Nicole's recovery—and the subsequent, flawless skewering of Val's misguided chivalry—would lighten her step until the Sh'keth hive crumbled around her. The twinkling mirth of Nicole's smile would be a gift if it graced her final thoughts. Not a bad way to go.

Shadows poured into the valley as the sun sank below the ridgeline. She leapt over boulders and downed logs, the path growing steeper as she gained speed, and the mountains closed in. The hillsides drew close as cupped hands, squeezing the river

THROUGH SKY AND STARS

into a narrow stream cascading over boulders stuck in the cleft of tectonic upheaval. Her trail narrowed as the valley walls closed in. Leaves and branches reached from the gathering gloom, snagging and catching as she skirted the boundary between rock and forest. Her run became a scramble, legs and arms straining as she lifted herself over granite tumbled from the mountainside above. The effort energized her, the rush of blood in her veins pushing her up the mountain. In the wake of Nicole's smile she was more relaxed than she'd been in weeks. She was ready to complete her mission.

Until a gunshot split the murky dusk.

Val skidded to a halt, shoulders heaving, sweat skittering down her back with a chill. The *crack* of a chemical round was unmistakable to her enhanced ears. *Oh, no.*

Nicole.

Had she led the fucking *Sh'keth* right to her doorstep? The mistake crashed down around her, shredding her peace like a shell falling on the battlefield. Ruthless certainty flooded her chest. She should've stayed out of it. Left the Terran to her work and her life, left her innocent of the war that had followed Val across centuries, steered clear of even the *thought* that she could help another human without exposing her to danger. But that was the problem—clearly, she *hadn't* thought. She'd waltzed right up to a beautiful woman as if there wouldn't be consequences. Just like she'd waltzed around a corner and practically walked face-first into the same woman's airplane. And now Nicole was in danger and Val was an hour's run from her home. It was too far, but Nicole was in danger because of her. She had to go back.

Another shot split the darkness. Nicole was resilient. Maybe she'd found cover, a place from which to make a stand and fight back. *Give them hell, Terran.*

Val careened back down the valley.

❖

Nicole sighed contentedly and leaned against the cabin as the last rays of sunlight faded from the mountaintop above her home. Warmth seeped from the sun-soaked logs as the air cooled into

TESSA CROFT

night. The river bubbled happily beyond the trees, a gentle breeze whispered through the alders, and the softly stirring leaves called a soothing lullaby that urged her to go inside, settle in by the fire, and sink into a good book. She closed her eyes and let the peace of simple sounds lull her earlier anxieties into memory. She'd finally managed to put her unease aside and accept that Val—whoever she was—would be no more than a curious anecdote in her life story. Target practice was good for that.

Sleep tugged at her. Maybe she could chalk the restlessness up to fatigue, after all. The satisfaction of getting a child the care he needed was enough to push her through the grunt work of a flat tire and the surprising encounter with Val, but she should have realized she was running on fumes. Now, savoring the dusk, a deep contentment held her in place despite the darkening sky.

Dusk came slowly this time of year, the day lingering long into the last, diffuse light left by the sun as it regretfully dipped below the horizon. The mountaintops clung to the meager gray light of evening, gleaming softly in the twilight, and drew her eyes skyward. Orion rose regally above the jagged line of rock and ice. She smiled at her grandfather's "three lucky stars" angling up into the night sky. Her grandmother had constantly ragged him for calling them that— *it's everyone's damn constellation, dear*—yet he'd persisted. She felt his presence strongly today. Everything that had enabled her to help that child, she owed to her grandparents. She missed them, but she couldn't help smiling as she gazed into the starlit sky. They'd be proud of her. Yes, it was a good night to savor.

The crunch of gravel froze her with a bolt of fear, shattering the brief contentment. *Bear?* She raised her gun, cautious, and the fear exploded into a rush of adrenaline as something huge and black burst around the side of her house. The surging mass of shadows careened around the corner with a growl, drawing a frigid spike of fear through her chest and freezing her breath in her body. Pebbles skittered and clattered in its wake, pattering against the side of the house. She stumbled back as the thing reared up in her vision, looming closer, the midnight sky vanishing behind the hulking shape. She chambered a round.

"Wait!"

Too late. The crack of the weapon split the air a millisecond before Nicole's brain recognized the *human voice telling her to—Oh, no—*

A muffled curse and the shape toppled. A thud.

Nicole scrambled to find her flashlight. *Oh shit oh shit oh God—*

The beam focused on a crumpled body, bronze features slack, limbs akimbo, blood oozing from her temple.

Val.

She came back! Somehow, ridiculously, *inappropriately*, her heart beat faster.

I killed her! Perhaps her elation was premature.

The Ruger fell to the ground. Nicole dropped to her knees in the grass, heart thudding in her chest, breath trembling over her lips as terror receded and horror poured in. Oh God, she'd *shot* her. She stared at Val, slumped on the ground before her, guilt and confusion swirling through a new fear as the adrenaline seeped slowly from her shaking hands. Val was so *still*. It didn't matter if she was back if Nicole had…

She gulped, unable to finish the awful thought. "*Shit,*" she breathed aloud, urging her swirling thoughts to still long enough for rationality to kick in.

Well. Only one way to find out whether she was going to prison, accidental or not. She reached out, hesitated a moment in awful foreboding, then pressed two, trembling fingers to Val's throat. A strong, steady pulse beat beneath her touch. "Oh, thank *God.*"

She swayed in the tide of relief as it rushed in on her shaking breath. Alive. Val was alive and Nicole was safe—as much as her animal brain refused to believe it. She pulled in a deep breath. Blew it out slowly, lifting the free strands of hair that had fallen across her forehead as she flailed in the wake of Val's second terrifying arrival. She sat back on her heels, pushed her sleeves up to her elbows. The frantic seconds replayed in her mind's eye: the twitch of her finger, the recoil as she staggered back, Val's grunt of pain and the solid *thud* as she toppled.

Ah. She looked at the cabin wall, standing stoically beside them. The dots connected between the solid wall and the lump swelling

TESSA CROFT

on Val's temple. An unfortunate knockout…and a sliver of selfish hope wormed its way into Nicole's mind. Maybe Val simply tripped, dodging Nicole's bullet, and hit the wall on her way down. Maybe she'd missed. Maybe… Her guilt latched onto the hope and gripped it like a lifeline, but that rope was anchored to a sapling. She sighed. She needed to take stock, approach this objectively, use the first responder skills she learned as a guide to assess her unlikely patient before she jumped to any conclusions. She leaned forward, careful, and gently patted her way along Val's body, searching for further injuries. She skimmed her fingers through fine, dark hair, along the muscles of Val's neck, over broad shoulders and across the trim waist, and Nicole's relief grew as she passed critical organs without finding injury. She was about to give her hope free rein when she passed Val's hip. Blood streaked her fingers as she touched Val's pants. She bit her lip, hope vanishing, and slowed to find the source. *Oh, my God.*

She flushed, her cheeks heating, embarrassment riding over her concern like a 747 on a short runway as she completed her assessment. She hadn't *quite* missed. The grazing wound, relatively minor, had probably been just enough to unbalance Val with a twitch of pain. If she *was* going to accidentally shoot someone, this was the place to hit them…but this would be oh, so awkward to apologize for.

"*Shit,*" Nicole groaned again.

She suddenly desperately wished for Val to wake up to treat her own wound.

It was minor, true, and Nicole was relieved enough to be mortified. Still, she had an unconscious stranger lying in her backyard who'd leapt out of the darkness like something straight from her nightmares. Why the *hell* would Val come rushing back like that? She'd come barreling around the house full-tilt, actually *growling* for God's sake, instead of going to the front door like any sane person would. Who *was* this person? Val's neat attire, command presence, and chiseled body screamed *military* as loudly as her unwillingness to share the details of her journey. She'd lifted that tundra tire like a leaf and could probably break a neck with her bare hands. What would a woman like that do when faced with a near-stranger who'd *shot* her? A chill of anxiety trembled through Nicole. Part of her suddenly wanted desperately to run away, hide in the cabin, and hope that Val simply disappeared back into the wilderness.

But she'd shot another human being. She owed Val care, comfort, assistance. She didn't know her, but the swirl of confusion, fear, guilt, and even—she admitted—happiness at Val's ignominious reappearance paled beside compassion. Responsible or not, she'd never leave another to suffer. She'd do everything in her power to make this right. She reached out to release the clasps on Val's pack.

"I'm sorry," she whispered.

She lifted Val into her arms.

• 68 •

THROUGH SKY AND STARS

CHAPTER SIX

August 3, 1996 AD [Terran Calendar], 0400 hrs.
Kenai Mountains, Alaska, Earth

Val crawled back from oblivion with agonizing slowness. Her mind slogged through a tortured sludge of memories and unease as thought dragged itself from the depths. With awareness came pain, every flavor of it, from nails across steel to the pounding of jackhammers to the bright, hot fire of a star burning behind her eyes. The migraine drove itself into her temples and throbbed between her ears, surging in time with her heart, and her newly conscious mind recoiled from the rude awakening. She groaned. A wave of nausea rolled through her. *Vakking hell, what have I done?*

She pulled in a long, slow breath. The scents of pine and woodsmoke filled her nose. A fire crackled nearby, the warmth alighting on her shoulders as she lay on her stomach, head pillowed on her folded arms. Carpet fibers tickled her fingertips. Warm, dry—she'd almost say *comfortable,* if her brain weren't busy sliming itself against her skull. She tentatively flexed each limb, assessing, looking for injury, until—*Ow.* A hot needle of pain when she moved her right leg. She'd had far, far worse, but the sheer indignity of it drove deeper than the wound itself. Here she'd been trying to save a Terran and—

Nicole. Her eyes flew open.

She was in Nicole's home. It had to be—the cozy space was built of rich wood, beautifully finished and glowing soft amber in the firelight, and a familiar ball cap was tossed carelessly on a worn

• 69 •

sofa just beyond Val's reach. A similarly recognizable blue flannel was balled haphazardly next to it, streaked with drying blood. Concern twisted Val's middle. *Fuck.* Beyond the sofa, the night lay so dark and still through the windows that even her HUD struggled to resolve the gentle twitch of leaves. Inside the cabin was similarly, confusingly, quiet…except for slow, steady breathing behind her. Val raised herself cautiously to her elbows and turned her head, hissing through clenched teeth as the fury of her migraine protested every agonizing degree. The pain coalesced into a hard, cold knot in the pit of her stomach and she struggled not to throw up. She closed her eyes and pushed through. Another breath, eyes closed. Then she blinked, finding Nicole a few feet away, and bit back a harsh laugh despite her pain.

The Terran was *asleep.* Not a single trace of struggle showed on Nicole's body as she dozed in an armchair by the fireplace—and confusion wreaked havoc on Val's tenuous consciousness. Her headache spasmed. What about the blood? The gunfire? She blinked as pain blurred her vision. *What the fuck happened?* She'd heard more gunshots as she raced back down the mountain pass, flying over rock and sand as she retraced her steps to Nicole's home. They'd echoed off the valley walls, each one a stark reminder that she'd left Nicole alone against the goddamn Slugs. When they ceased, she feared the worst, and the utter silence she'd found upon returning to the airplane had turned her blood cold. She'd tried not to imagine what she would find as she followed the short path into the blackening forest. The dark, quiet cabin only confirmed her fears. And then she'd rounded the corner of the small home, her HUD blared a warning, and—*oh.* She'd tried to dodge, twisting away from the rising weapon as her HUD screamed at her, but she hadn't—quite—made it. A surge of admiration overrode her pain as the memory burst past her migraine. Nicole *shot* her.

I need to stop startling this woman.

A flare of respect dimmed the flame of her headache as she looked up at Nicole now. Strands of her unruly blond hair had escaped from her braid, framing her face in a wispy halo of reflected firelight. A book lay open in her lap and her strong hands, nails still dark with traces of grease from her earlier struggle with the tire, rested on the open pages. A clean flannel, soft with age, had been pushed up to her elbows. She'd changed into a new pair of faded, beige workpants that ended above hiking boots fraying slightly at the seams. Her head tilted to one side, the firelight gently illuminating a tanned neck and the vulnerable line of her jaw. Her full lips were parted slightly in sleep. Beautiful, unharmed, perfectly capable of defending herself in the dark, and apparently strong enough to haul Val's unconscious ass inside after knocking her flat. Despite the circumstances and the accompanying twinge of pain, Val smiled. The more she got to know Nicole, the more she liked her.

Behind Nicole, wall-to-wall shelving formed a library crammed with books of every size and color. Actual fucking paper, thousands of pages of it, stacked and sorted and clearly well-loved. The covers crammed the shelves in a riot of colors and textures. Val hadn't seen paper in years—it was a luxury when society existed aboard tin cans hurtling through the void. To see so much, riotously stacked and piled on simple wooden planks.... She itched to reach out and touch the pages.

A ladder rose past the books, leading to a loft above them, and she could just make out a stack of blankets folded atop a battered traveling trunk in a bedroom filling the space at the apex of the small home. To the right of the library was a simple kitchen, divided from a cozy dining area by a narrow peninsula of countertop. Organized chaos reigned there. A bouquet of multihued coffee mugs hung on pegs by the sink, a knife block sported handles of all shapes and sizes, and the small dining table was overrun by stacks of charts and aviation references. The furniture was mismatched but comfortable and well-loved. The space spoke of contentedness and warmth, and every inch of it clashed with the harsh lines and sculpted metal of Val's life before Earth. She liked it. Wistfully, she imagined living here: quiet evenings fending off cold nights, mornings filled with the promise of adventure in a wild land. The exact opposite of waking to curdled, familiar fear and slipping on her mask of indifference. *Bullshit, Koroleva.* She dragged her addled mind away from the irrational, impossible thought and back to the matter at hand. It was time to extricate herself from a random Terran's home without compromising herself further.

Nicole was completely fine. Whatever she'd been firing at, it hadn't been the Sh'keth—from the looks of it, it hadn't been *anything*. Val, stampeding back here in a fit of idiotic heroism, had not only delayed her mission but gotten herself shot. The gunshot was more damage to her pride than her body, and the salve in her pack would take care of it in minutes, but her headache was a vastly different story. Even in the twenty-eighth century the brain was still a mystery, and her nans would do little to repair a concussion. No silver bullet there. Her gray matter would heal at a normal, infuriatingly slow, *human* pace, and she could only hope that her skull finished splitting open before she reached the hive.

Her attention returned to the Terran. Nicole had slipped further into sleep, shoulders slumping, and her grip on the book in her lap had faded as she relaxed. It slid toward her knee. Val thought about rescuing it, but the fear of a cranial supernova held her back. It tumbled free. *Poor, abused paper…* The novel hit the floor with a soft *thwack.* Nicole snapped awake at the sound.

❖

Nicole sat bolt upright, adrenaline sizzling through her chest. *Shit—*

She stopped short as her eyes locked onto Val's, the starlit irises alloyed gold in the shifting light of the fire, and her breath caught on the small smile dimpling one corner of her mouth. She'd expected Val to be upset when she woke—angry, wounded, sprawled on the floor in the home of woman who'd shot her—but Val stared at her with a touch of humor and a new measure of respect in her dark gaze. She looked like she might break into a laugh at any second.

"You shot me," Val said, rich voice dripping with mirth, "in the *ass*."

So much for Nicole's dignity. The heat of a blush rose rapidly up her neck. "God, Val, I'm so sorry! It was dark, and you came flying around the corner and I jumped, and—" she caught herself babbling and cut herself off. "What the hell were you *doing* running around my property in the dark like that?"

THROUGH SKY AND STARS

Val grunted a laugh and her grin faltered, gaze turning inward with a grimace. Nicole's thoughts clattered confusingly between mortification and disbelief as Val levered herself slowly into a seated position. Corded muscle flexed in her arms as she did so, graceful despite her injury, and a pulse of unease slithered through Nicole as the panther of a woman stretched in front of her. Val, however, hissed softly as she shifted her weight, as disinterested in a fight as any wild creature crossing paths with a human.

"Apparently," she said grimly, "nothing useful."

Nicole sat up straighter as concern centered her thoughts.

"Here," she said, willing her blush to fade as she held out a pair of aspirin. "I couldn't give you any painkillers while you were out."

Val eyed the medication for a moment, gaze calculating, before she extended her hand, accepted the pills, and popped them into her mouth. She chewed.

Nicole gaped.

Val stared back, perplexed. "What?"

"Isn't that…disgusting?"

Val shrugged, then flinched. Swallowed. "Getting shot in the ass is worse."

This is insane. She'd shot another human being, that person apparently wasn't that concerned about said incident, and the woman in question now lounged in her home comfortably enough for witty banter. Nicole ran her hands over her face with a sigh to dispel her embarrassment and confusion. At least there wasn't blood on them anymore. The blood—and the scars she'd seen on Val's body as she treated the comparatively minor wound—sat uneasily in her memory. "Val, seriously, what were you doing? You scared the *shit* out of me. Again!"

"I really am sorry about that. For both times."

Nicole exhaled sharply, incredulous. "I *shot* you! Why are you sorry?"

Val cringed at the exclamation, spearing Nicole with regret, but it was Val who gave a small, apologetic shrug. "It was very stupid of me."

Nicole pushed the sleeves of her flannel up with a soft laugh. "That's true."

• 73 •

"I heard the gunshots and I thought…" Val trailed off, a flicker that resembled self-reproach passing across her face. She forged ahead. "I thought you were in danger."

"*What?*"

Val had the grace to look sheepish. "I thought—"

"You thought I was in *danger*? You came racing around the corner, in the dark, when you *knew* I had my gun out, because you thought you were rescuing me…*again?*"

Laughter bubbled up. She couldn't help it—the absolute, heartwarming stupidity of Val's actions, laced with bravery and a dose of utter irony, dismantled her dismay into such a thoroughly confusing jumble of emotions that only laughter made it past the logjam. She stood abruptly, full of a hundred emotions she didn't know how to express, and paced to the small kitchen a few feet away. She couldn't decide whether to be furious or happy that this charming stranger had done something so indescribably, sweetly stupid. She let her thoughts settle as she filled the kettle with water, then returned to the fireplace.

"Haven't you ever heard of target practice?" she asked, setting the kettle over the fire, "This is *Alaska.*"

Val looked away and rubbed the back of her neck.

"Well," she said, wilting a bit as a fresh wave of pain ghosted across her dark features. "It seems I got what I deserved."

Nicole's bubble of exasperation burst, replaced by concern. She knelt next to Val. Softly, she said, "You're lucky it wasn't worse."

Val's eyes darkened and she frowned, raising one ebony brow at the admonition. Her mouth opened slightly, threatening argument, but the thought seemed to die unspoken as she held Nicole's gaze. She blew out a soft breath instead. "As I said, very stupid." Her smile returned, sly. "Clearly I didn't learn my lesson about women who fly beautiful airplanes."

Nicole scoffed and looked away, tucking a loose strand of hair behind her ear, then cast a mock glare at Val. "Do *not* try to weasel your way out of this one so easily, hotshot. You were unconscious for almost an hour."

A ghost of concern fluttered across Val's handsome features almost too fast to see. Though she quickly replaced it with another grin, forcing levity over the truth, she clearly didn't like the news that she'd been out for so long. As if she'd sensed Nicole catching her true reaction, Val made a show of wiggling her eyebrows suggestively. She gestured to the unfamiliar pants she now wore. "Long enough to miss all the fun, apparently."

It worked. Nicole reeled. *Shit.* Of course she couldn't have avoided that particular topic forever, but she'd hoped her dignity might recover a *little* before having to justify taking off an unconscious woman's pants on the floor of her living room. The impulse seemed silly, now—she could simply have cut the fabric away to get to the wound—but an irrational part of her had wanted to avoid adding "destroyed your pants" to "shot you." She pressed on before another blush revealed her awareness of the questionable logic. She would *not* let Val flirt her way out of the seriousness of the situation. "The wound is shallow and clean. Take care of it, and you'll be fine in a week or two. But I'm worried you have a serious concussion."

Val frowned. "I'm fine."

"I should take you to the hospital in town. It's—"

"No!"

The harsh interruption startled them both. Nicole blinked, taken aback, and even Val looked surprised by the force of her own outburst.

"Sorry," she said quickly. "I just...hate hospitals. And there's not much they could do, right?"

Nicole's eyebrows rose. Military physique, disproportionate response to danger, avoiding town...Val was absolutely hiding something. Never mind the accent, which skirted close to that of the Russian immigrants common in this part of Alaska. Nicole had the sneaking suspicion that she was helping a foreign agent, though she couldn't imagine what lay in the uninhabited peaks beyond her home. Although the soldier's innate desire to help had drawn Val out of the shadows, the force pulling her into the mountains remained, but so, too, did Nicole's resolution not to pry. She would let Val keep her secrets. It seemed the least she could do, under the circumstances. Still, she couldn't let Val—who'd helped her and, though it made no sense, cared enough to rush to her defense— wander into the wilderness in her current state.

• 75 •

"Okay," she said slowly. "Then how about you recuperate here for a few days?"

She frowned at the troubled expression on Val's face. The stoic resolve she'd glimpsed on the riverbank was back. Whatever waited in the mountains, it called to Val with inevitability and finality.

"I'll be on my way tomorrow," Val said suddenly, sternly, and Nicole blinked in surprise.

"You have a gunshot wound and were unconscious for an hour. I don't think it's just my guilt telling me that you ought to stay put for a few days."

The steel in Val's eyes was a gate slamming shut before Nicole's protests, her face as chiseled as the immovable mountains in the darkness beyond the windows. "I appreciate your concern, but I cannot stay."

A chill crept down Nicole's spine. "Why?"

She regretted the question as soon as it was out of her mouth. Unease curled in her gut. Val's expression closed further, a thunderstorm in the set of her brow and the line of her lips, and her eyes proclaimed, *None of your fucking business* while her mouth said, "Because I'm fine."

Val surged upright like an iceberg breaking the surface of the sea, bursting upward with an aggressive heave only to bob uncertainly upon arrival. Concern sizzled through Nicole. She held out a hand, ready to catch her before she toppled again.

"Val—"

"I'm fine," Val insisted, despite the sweat breaking out on her brow and the sudden pallor in her cheeks. She batted away Nicole's steadying hand and gripped the back of the armchair hard enough to bleach her knuckles. "Thank you," she gritted out, "for your care."

Nicole watched as the proverbial train wreck rolled on, at once incredulous, infuriated, and everything in between. It was a short journey. Val took one, abortive step toward her pack where it leaned against the wall by the door, swayed, reached out for something that wasn't there, and fell to her knees. A sound of commingled frustration and pain, somewhere between a growl and a groan, tumbled from her lips as she sank to her knees. Her fingers dug into the rug. The muscles in her jaw stood in stark relief, futile stubbornness writ large across her rigid features, and she fought it just long enough that a flicker of grudging respect danced behind Nicole's irritation. Finally, with a soft gasp, Val crumpled and lay still.

Sighing, Nicole bent to retrieve her from the floor. Again.

Oh, Koroleva, you are so fucked. Waking up to the reality of her incompetence was a thousand times worse than waking up to her migraine. This time, Val knew exactly where she was, how she'd gotten there, how utterly stupid she'd been, and how thoroughly she'd sabotaged her own mission. She knew without opening her eyes that she was on the couch, lying on her back with one arm thrown over her eyes. The fire still hissed and the room was still warm. Not much time had passed since her embarrassingly short-lived attempt to muster out under her own power. She was right back where she'd started, but worse: she couldn't ignore that her concussion was the debilitating icing on a true fuckup cake. There was no denying, now, that she had to rest. Had to waste time letting the most important—and the least enhanced—part of her body piece itself back together on its own. The thought of sitting on her ass like a slime-brained invalid turned her stomach. She really had fucked up her mission in a fit of blind incompetence, after all. "Ugh," she ground out the single syllable of disgust as if she could cough up her own failure and spit it out.

Sadly, it remained stubbornly lodged in the center of her brain, pulsing merrily around the throb of her heartbeat. The concussion and its effects cavorted on.

"Val?" Nicole's soft voice tickled at her migraine.

Val raised her arm and peered out gingerly. The pain flared, briefly, then guttered as her eyes adjusted to the flickering firelight. Nicole's expression sat somewhere between concern and the overwhelming urge to smack Val upside the head. Which was fair. Nicole had been completely right, and *Val* wanted to smack *herself* upside the head…except she'd probably black out again if she did. "Sorry," Val murmured. "I was an ass."

A gentle scoff. "Let's chalk it up to your brains being rattled."

Val sighed grumpily. The Terran was still right. Her brains were scrambled worse than something Kass would wolf down in the mess hall. Val only hoped that giving her stubbornness free rein hadn't alienated Nicole, considering she'd become her unwilling houseguest. The chances seemed slim. In less than a day she'd managed to terrify Nicole twice, bleed all over her, and aggressively black out on her floor. Not a great first impression.

"Can we start over?" Val asked, aware of just how ridiculous the request was.

Nicole laughed softly. Her expression turned thoughtful as she paused, staring at the flames dancing in the fireplace, and her tone was careful when she responded.

"Val, I can tell you don't trust me. Under the circumstances, that's completely reasonable." She grimaced and pushed up her sleeves, finally meeting Val's eyes, and she lifted her shoulders in an apologetic half shrug. "I shot you, and even if it was an accident, just raising the gun was totally disproportionate."

It was nothing. The thought hovered on Val's lips, but she could never explain the chasm between the wound Nicole had inflicted and the things Val had survived before this. Instead, she waved it away. "You were right about how completely fucking stupid I was."

Nicole raised an eyebrow at the expletive, a slight, rueful smile curving her lips. "I'm glad you agree, but I feel responsible. I don't want you traipsing off into the woods with a concussion and a gunshot wound." She leaned forward, elbows resting on her knees, and folded her hands together. "You seem very capable, despite your... questionable decisions so far, but you're clearly in no shape to hike solo through the remote wilderness. So." The emerald gleam of her gaze settled like a heavy blanket over Val's attention, gently dissuading protest. "I want you to stay here until your headache is gone."

Val's hackles rose instinctively. Her shoulders bunched, the offending headache screamed, and she fought the sudden, panicked sense of her mission slipping through her fingers like smoke. Even knowing Nicole was right, she couldn't help the tide of unease. Too much was at stake. She only had four days left... Her mouth opened to argue, despite her rational mind, but Nicole raised a placating hand.

"After that, I will fly you wherever you need to go."

A shocked heartbeat froze Val's protests in her throat. "You... anywhere?"

Nicole's smile widened, her eyes sparkling, and Val's disheveled mind zeroed in on the delicate green, rich as the rainforest canopy of Gliese, where she'd spent three months on a survey of—

She blinked. *Focus.*

"The Beav and I can get you within a day's hike of anywhere around here," Nicole continued, oblivious to Val's mental detour. "I'll drop you off wherever you want to go, no questions asked, if you spend at least a day here."

The kettle demanded attention, distracting Nicole while Val considered her offer. *Too easy.* Yet a tendril of hope broke through her suspicion. She could wait out the concussion, recovering in comfort, and arrive at her strike point in perfect fighting condition. When Nicole left, safely disappearing over the horizon, the medical salve in Val's pack would boost her nans and erase every outward trace of her wounds, leaving only a small hole in Val's pants as souvenir. Neat, effective. *Efficient.* She *wanted* to be suspicious. Paranoia was a habit that had kept her alive this long, a companion as familiar as the hovering threat of annihilation, but as she watched Nicole mix cocoa into two steaming mugs, she found herself struggling to embrace it. How the hell could a woman who'd shot her somehow make her feel...safe? Val turned the word over in her mind. Despite everything, she wanted to stay with her. Get to know her. Indulge in the ridiculous fantasy of living in this peaceful haven in the woods with her.

Nicole turned, a rueful smile on her lips, and Val's defenses crumbled further. *It doesn't hurt that she's fucking gorgeous.* Nicole handed over a cup. "I can't say the cocoa will win you over. It's powdered, but nothing else keeps out here."

Val smiled anyway. "Thank you," she said, and her stomach betrayed her. Loudly.

Nicole laughed, the sound bright in the dim light of the fire. Val's hunger had shattered the tension lingering in the air. "So, will you let me help you? As soon as your headache is gone, I promise I'll take you wherever you need to go."

The offer hung in the air between them. Val closed her eyes and took a long breath. Suspicious or not, she didn't have much of a choice. "Very well," she said at last.

It felt right. It felt awful. The guilt climbed up inside her, clamping down on her heart, even as her rational mind told her that the plan was sound. Not defeat. Hardly even delay. Still, her head throbbed and her stomach churned. Was she acquiescing too easily, addled as she was? When she met Nicole's eyes again, not even her own awareness of her ragged emotions could keep them from her face. Nicole, however, was smiling—and the sight of it drove the demons back long enough for a small, answering bubble of happiness to swell in Val's chest.

Nicole's voice was laced with humor, warm as the ceramic in Val's hands, when she continued. "But, Val?"

"Hm?"

"If you try to rescue me again, I'll drop you in the middle of the ice field instead. And I won't give you your pants back before I do."

THROUGH SKY AND STARS

CHAPTER SEVEN

August 3, 1996 [Terran Calendar], 0800 hrs
28 kilometers south of the First Hive, Earth

The sludge and stench of Piscium-b clung to her in a suffocating blanket of filth. The dead Protector lay beside her, huge, empty eyes staring accusingly at Val as she moaned helplessly in the mud and blood. Her rage was spent, the battlefield a mess of crimson and amber, her vision graying at the edges.

This is where it ends, she thought. No more.

The Protector stirred.

It rose on shattered forelegs, a grotesque puppet of her own nightmares.

NO.

"You failed," it screeched, its words echoing with a thousand human voices.

It reared back. Regarded her with cruel, merciless contempt. Two foreleg blades glinted blue-black in the fading light.

"FAILED," it roared, and drove the blades through her chest.

Val awoke with a gasp, fingers closing instinctively over imaginary blades, the image of the dead Protector's lifeless eyes seared into her consciousness. Her shoulders heaved as she gulped in breath. She lifted her shirt. Nothing. *Holy fuck.* The killing blow had felt so *real*, grafted seamlessly into the memory of that awful day in combat. The dream—every bloody moment—had been just as real as that horrific morning on Piscium-b. She shuddered. Goose

• 81 •

TESSA CROFT

bumps prickled her skin as the terror of the nightmare relinquished its hold on her chest. *And I thought that memory couldn't get any worse.*

With a shaky breath, Val willed her consciousness back to the present. The stillness of the Terran home clashed painfully with the echoing trauma. The weight of the silence pressed down on her unsteady thoughts. Nicole's soft breathing, deep with sleep, drifted down from the loft above. A gust of wind stirred the trees outside. A log popped in the fireplace, last gasp of the fire that had dwindled to embers as they slept. Cool air kissed her clammy skin. Calm, quiet, peaceful—everything her life *hadn't* been, and in the vacuum the pull of her mission reached out and twisted its fingers of guilt around her heart. Cruel images of her murdered platoon flickered again. Val ran her hands through her damp hair and sighed. Whether it was the nightmare or the lingering effect of the concussion, her head throbbed. The mission must wait, still, but she had to quell this maelstrom of unease.

She threw the blankets back and cautiously lowered her feet to the thick rug she'd awakened on the night before. The aging, soft pile tickled between her toes. The gunshot wound sparked, irritated, but the pain was a mere grumble relative to the wound she'd just relived. *Silver lining.* She settled into her first stance. Familiar motions flowed from her limbs, slowly at first, then gathering speed as her body loosened and the ritual soothed her addled focus. Decades of practice drove her hands and feet. The knot in her chest reluctantly relinquished its hold, grief and guilt slinking petulantly back to their prisons. Freed, she moved faster. *Cut.* Her hand arced out, an invisible knife severing an invisible foreleg. *Blend.* She sidestepped an imaginary counterstrike and extended her arms, snapping them downward as her knee came up to meet them. *Break.* Her unease faded into the background, swamped by focus.

Until, partway through a kata she'd performed every day for ten years, she *forgot what came next.* Val stood frozen in a stance she'd sailed through thousands of times, her pulse racing while discomfort poured through her anew. *What the fuck?* She scowled. Shook her head—which was a mistake, as the dull ache behind her eyes exploded into bright spots across her vision. Her stomach clenched and a cold ripple of fear coursed down her arms. *It has to be the concussion.* Her frazzled mind steadied at the whisper of explanation. *Focus.*

Val blew out a long, slow breath. A last ripple of gooseflesh trickled down her body. She shuddered. *Focus.*

"Cold?"

Val jerked in surprise. Her eyes shot upward, instinct driving her into a stance even as her brain recognized the absence of threat. Nicole crouched at the top of the ladder, gaze calculating as she paused in the act of climbing onto the ladder, and Val's heart fell. *Vack.* She was trying *not* to alienate her. Yet waking her up with military exercises definitely fell into the *suspicious* category, while responding to her arrival by dropping into fighting stance would put her right at the top of the list. Val forced herself to relax, letting her hands fall to her sides, and grinned up at Nicole. *Be nice.* It hadn't escaped her notice that Nicole was particularly susceptible to a bit of flirtation, and she wasn't above using it to her advantage to get out of the corner she'd painted herself into. "Good morning."

Nicole dropped her gaze, a flush brightening her cheeks, and started down the ladder. Val, despite her worry, couldn't help a bolt of satisfaction sizzling through her at the response. Nicole guiltily caught staring was infinitely preferable to Nicole being afraid of the crazy woman trapped in her home. If she was going to be stuck here, she might as well enjoy it.

"For the record," Nicole said, reaching the bottom of the ladder, "you're welcome to stoke the fire if you're up before me."

She glanced at Val as she knelt next to the fireplace, reaching for fresh logs, and as she leaned forward her hair, free of its braid, fell in a captivating, golden cascade nearly to her elbows. Val stared, lips parted, caught in appreciation of the rare and beautiful sight. Aboard ship that kind of luxury either got caught in machinery or got you hauled around the dojo. *Nobody* kept their hair loose, and *nobody* was blond after the melting pot of humanity's diaspora. She burned with the desire to run her fingers through it. Nicole, however, caught Val looking and simply smiled before catching the tresses up in one hand, holding the blond waves effortlessly over her shoulder.

"It's a pain sometimes." She blew gently across the embers and tiny flames leapt across the kindling. "But it's a bit of a guilty pleasure."

Val ran her fingers through her own short locks instead, her senses rejecting the poor substitute. "I prefer simplicity," she said, disconcertingly incapable of forming a more interesting, coherent statement. "I'm impressed that you keep from lighting it on fire."

Nicole chuckled, tucking a few errant strands behind one ear. "Lots of practice. Matches don't grow on trees, you know." She stood, brushing her hands against her workpants. "Hungry?"

She moved to the kitchen and produced a box of foil packets, colorful writing splashed across their twinkling surfaces, while Val tried to reel her unruly thoughts back from fantasies of sinking her fingers into Nicole's hair. Blissfully unaware, the Terran tore a packet open and handed over a thin, rectangular pastry with an expectant gleam in her eyes. Val, distracted from her distraction, eyed the thing suspiciously despite her growling stomach. It reminded her of a military calorie bomb from a pack of field rations, something to be consumed in the line of duty with a salute and a *sir, yes sir,* but Nicole's expression fairly glowed with delight. She raised an eyebrow at Val's hesitation. "Haven't you ever had a Pop-Tart before?"

"Should I have?"

Nicole laughed. "I guess they don't have them in Russia. Here." She took it back from Val and laid it on a metal grate over the fire. "Give it a minute, then enjoy. There's a reason I save them for special occasions."

She disappeared through the front door to something called an "outhouse"—which Val assumed was the Terran equivalent of a head—while Val stared dubiously at the rectangular, beige cookie sitting over the fire. She eyed the thing until the edges began to brown, then took it gingerly into her hands, the heat tingling her fingertips, and brought it to her nose for a tentative sniff. A surprisingly pleasant scent teased at her memories. Encouraged, she took a cautious bite.

A cascade of flavors exploded across her tongue. *Oh, vakking hell.* Sugar, yes—more than any "breakfast" had a right to contain—but paired with a sharp, spicy note that danced across her tongue. She took another bite. And then another. By the time Nicole returned, she gazed forlornly at her empty hands.

Nicole laughed. "You can have mine."

Val promptly disposed of that one, too.

"What is that taste?" she asked, trying not to sound awestruck at something so obviously commonplace.

"Cinnamon sugar," Nicole answered slowly, as if surprised Val couldn't tell.

Smothering her preposterously strong reaction to what Nicole clearly considered commonplace, Val cleared her throat. "I haven't had real cinnamon in...a long time."

By which she meant *ever*, because cinnamon had died with the Earth. Having tasted the real thing, Val suddenly understood why culinary masters had striven to reproduce it ever since...but she also now recognized that without a shadow of a doubt, even the best reproductions fell heartbreakingly short. The uniquely sweet, spicy combination left her tastebuds sparkling in a flurry of heat and pleasure simply indescribable to a woman raised and sustained by mass-produced ration packs. Just wait until she told—*dammit.* A gut-wrenching wave of loss gripped her chest as her thoughts ran ahead of her reality. She might never share this experience with Kass. She might have already erased her. She could tell herself that she was following orders, averting catastrophe, saving untold millions of lives...but the mere act of sitting here, enjoying this moment, meant that her friend might never exist, would never enjoy this simple pleasure of her ancestral world. The traitorous lump rose again in her throat, prickly with guilt. *Fuck.* She slammed a mental door on the thoughts and turned her face away from Nicole to hide the tears threatening to spring into her eyes.

Nicole patted her on the shoulder and stood. "And you still haven't. That's about as processed as it gets. But you've given me an excellent idea for later."

PART III: *CLIMB*

CHAPTER EIGHT

August 5, 1996, 8:30 a.m.
Kenai Mountains, Alaska

"So, Val, what do you do when you're not materializing from the woods in the middle of nowhere?"

The question drove a bolt of unease through Val's gut. *Vack.* She'd hoped to avoid this conversation, since sticking to her briefed cover was likely to go over about as well as holding her breath in an open airlock. So she did the brave thing and feigned fascination with the scene playing out beyond the cabin's windows. Maybe, if she was lucky, the question would die of neglect.

Fortunately, the scene *was* mildly captivating, and Val's admiration for Earth's biodiversity rose as she watched the minor drama unfold. A diminutive, furry creature made its way slowly, upside down, along a treacherously long, thin wire in a feat that would make her toughest drill sergeants proud. Its goal was clear: a cylinder full of seeds and nuts, clearly failing in its mission to be inaccessible to fluffballs with nefarious intent. The line swayed dangerously as the puffy tail bounded along undeterred. She had to admit that it was cute—honestly, it was fucking *adorable*—and it appeared to be a naturally-evolved ninja, but it was also clearly a huge pain in the ass. A bird swept in as she watched, squawking angrily to dissuade the interloper, and the thing let loose with the most godawful series of high-pitched chittering Val had ever heard. Amplified by her enhanced hearing, the noise threatened to bring her concussion-induced headache roaring back with a vengeance. Her admiration disintegrated to disgust and she pulled her eyes away with a grimace. Her disdain, however, was softened by a brief flash of relief as her headache remained mercifully at bay. Finally, on the third morning of Nicole's attempts to undo her lifetime of fitness via every imaginable cinnamon-laden recipe, Val was cautiously optimistic.

Nicole laughed knowingly. "That's Reggie. And yes, he's both obnoxious and amazing."

"Reggie?"

Nicole shrugged and smiled at the nefarious ninja mouse beyond the window. "Named after a character from a book I like." Her gaze returned to the cutting board in front of her, the sharp knock of the blade punctuating the air of the cabin as she prepared yet another meal to whittle away at Val's fitness for battle. "Anyway. What do you do for work?"

Damn. Val hesitated. If she tried to improvise at this point she'd probably back herself into an airlock, but this was going to be painful either way. "Actually, I'm a pilot."

Nicole's eyes brightened and a smile burst across her face, the expression so delighted that a pang of guilt shot through Val along with her rising unease. "No! Why in the world haven't you mentioned this yet?"

"I was a bit distracted." Val gestured at her own backside, grinning, and waited gleefully for the blush to rise on Nicole's face.

Nicole, however, was getting good at disarming Val's bravado. She pressed on with a mock scowl and only the slightest flush creeping into her cheeks. "What do you fly?"

"Jets."

Nicole smirked knowingly. "So you're in the Red Air Force?"

Val blinked. *Vakking what?* She stuck with the byline she'd briefed. "No, no. I fly for Boeing. I deliver 727s from the factory to the airlines."

Nicole's jaw dropped and her hands stilled. "You're kidding. My grandmother was a WASP!"

Val's mind raced. What—? Nicole's awed expression faded into a slight frown at Val's confusion. "You know, in World War II? The women who ferried fighters and bombers for the Army Air Forces?"

Damn, she's going to be harder to fool than I feared... "Oh! Of course! Sorry, my brains must still be scrambled. I thought you were calling your grandmother a horrifying, stinging insect...which seemed unfair, although I've obviously never met her..." Val let the statement trail off suggestively. Her concussion *had* made it hard for her to focus for a day or two. Despite her growing optimism this morning, she wasn't above using the excuse to get out of a jam.

Nicole snorted softly and resumed making breakfast. "No, she was incredible. Flew everything from P-51s to B-25s, then moved up here after the war. Once the Army didn't want her anymore, this was the only place where she found challenging pilotage. She met Gramps flying charters out of Anchorage, they built this cabin together, and the rest is history." She winked at Val, who was busy trying to stifle relief at the change of subject, and gestured with the knife to a point over Val's shoulder. "That's them."

The image, locked in fading color, hung alone in a simple wooden frame adorning the wall nearest the fireplace. A lanky man stood next to Nicole's airplane. His socks peeked from the abbreviated hems of long, khaki pants and a flannel shirt escaped from the waist of a puffy vest, while the smile on his face was as big as his frame. It emerged like daylight from a short, sandy beard. His eyes were trained adoringly on the woman around whose shoulders his arm was slung. The woman looked back at him, a wry grin on her face as if patiently accommodating a familiar joke, but she had one arm looped around the man's middle with fond familiarity. She wore denim, tucked into sturdy work boots, and in her free hand held a radio headset as if she'd just climbed down from the airplane. Soft curls of a familiar, golden hue were tucked over her ear but, like Nicole's, a few strands flew loose in an invisible breeze. Val recognized the riverbank that curved into the distance behind the aircraft. A shadow reached out from the base of the photo, the ghost of an unknown third person capturing the image of two happy Terrans who were clearly deeply content and disgustingly in love.

"Who captured this?"

Val looked back over her shoulder and caught a brief, quizzical expression on Nicole's face before she answered, "My mom."

"She was raised here?"

TESSA CROFT

"Yes." Nicole crossed in front of her and set the cast iron over the fire. "And she hated every second of it, so she moved to Anchorage before I was born. Of course, in what she always felt was a cruel twist of fate, I constantly dragged her back. I've always loved this place."

Nicole paused, standing at Val's shoulder, and her expression softened. Her gaze settled unseeing on the world outside the windows. "I still see her every once in a while, but we don't talk much."

"Hard to send an email when you don't have a computer."

Nicole laughed, her gaze returning to Val as disbelief quirked her eyebrow. "Email! You must have some pretty fancy technology at the airlines. I'd have to fly nonstop for a year just to afford a computer. But no, Mom and I just have…philosophical differences." She paused, an unspoken question hanging in her eyes. "You know?"

Uncertain, Val shrugged. "Mothers," she said vaguely.

Val grasped for a response, inexplicably distressed by the disappointment clouding Nicole's sharp gaze. "Mothers," Nicole agreed, and went back to cooking.

❖

This day promised a thousand things to look forward to—the breakfast whose delicious aroma had just begun to permeate the cabin, the gorgeous sky taking shape outside the cabin, or the flight up to the icefield that such weather would allow, to name a few—but instead Nicole's focus remained stubbornly riveted on the woman standing a few feet away.

This morning she'd lain in bed, savoring the decadence of a loft warmed by fire stoked long before she woke, and marveled at how utterly comfortable it was to have Val here. It seemed absolutely ridiculous, considering the circumstances under which they'd met, that Val fit seamlessly into her days. Val had an easy smile and a wholehearted, infectious laugh, and Nicole found her fascination with Alaska endearing. She'd been nothing but relaxed, friendly, and helpful in the three days they'd spent together. Nicole liked her.

THROUGH SKY AND STARS

In the quiet of that first morning, though, when she'd caught the barest sound of soft footfalls in the living room below and, curious, crept to the edge of the loft, she'd seen a side of Val that she was clearly trying to keep hidden. Below her, Val had worked through flowing kata, her body fluid and surprisingly graceful despite her injury, while her hands, firm and steady, snapped through motions almost too quick for Nicole to see. The look in her eyes had been sharp enough to cut through rock. The deadly power burning in Val's angry eyes had kindled a heavy respect in Nicole's gut. It was the sort of respect she held for a grizzly—not fear, but an innate awareness of…potential.

Still, Val had gone out of her way to avoid even the pretense of threat since that first night, and the chilling focus had dissolved into her disarming grin the moment she caught Nicole watching her. That glimpse of lethality had reminded Nicole that the woman in her home remained a mystery, though, and this first, unsatisfying attempt to prod at Val's background had left her more certain than ever that Val was hiding something. Which just made it more unsettling when Val's grin elicited hers despite her misgivings, or when the mischievous sparkle in Val's gray eyes stirred up…ideas. Though she'd been convincingly oblivious to Nicole's gentle prodding at lifestyle choices, Val *had* parried her flirtatious jousting that first night. Not to mention the simple and straightforward clothes, the lack of jewelry, and the short hair. *I'm trapped at home with a gorgeous woman who's setting off my gaydar left and right. Woe is me.*

If only her story added up. Val certainly had the cocksure attitude of a hotshot pilot. The shit-eating grin and effortless confidence fit perfectly into every *Top Gun* stereotype. She held herself as if she were used to being in charge, her shoulders back and confident, her mannerisms relaxed but certain. She hummed with true power and competence—not empty bravado, but the surety of someone who'd led others through mortal danger and come out the other side intact. Nicole saw the same in rescue pilots or climbers who routinely faced the harrowing edge between life and death in the Alaskan wilderness. She doubted, though, that Val's leadership experience came from transporting airliners. The fact that she'd never heard of the WASPs or offered up any of her own flying stories was a red flag

• 93 •

that screamed *cover story* louder than Reggie on the birdfeeder. Hell, the fact that she'd waited three days to mention it was all the proof Nicole needed. No pilot could resist bringing up flying, particularly to an obviously avid aviator like Nicole, or avoid spinning a good yarn when given half a chance. Unless she wasn't allowed to talk about it because she actually flew MiGs.

In which case, Nicole decided once again, she didn't need, or even want, to know. She liked Val. In the weirdest turn of events that Nicole never would have imagined, shooting Val seemed to have led to friendship. *Maybe she's been shot before, so it's no big deal to her...* she shook her head to dispel further thoughts along that line. She respected Val. If the she couldn't, or wouldn't, talk about her past, then Nicole wouldn't pry. Especially not after the heart-wrenching grief she'd glimpsed in Val, and *definitely* not within days of shooting her. She could respect the sanctity of Val's reasons for trekking alone into the wilderness. The unspoken truce they'd brokered that first night still held. Nicole didn't ask questions, Val didn't offer up details, and they got along just fine.

"Well then, what do you think about going flying? Since the weather's good, I'm due for a charter out of Seward in..." She checked her watch. "...about two hours."

Val's smile burst across her features, knocking her previously uncertain expression into yesterday. "Oh, hell yes."

Well, that's consistent.

They hurried through breakfast, Nicole forcing herself to remain methodical despite her eagerness to take to the air. After days cooped up in the cabin, she itched to feel the roar of the engine through the yoke and watch the treetops fall away below her. A good flight would fill her mind with something besides Val and her mysterious backstory. Nothing, however, killed a pilot faster than rushing into the air. Her grandparents would kill her if she showed up at the pearly gates because of a bad preflight.

Regardless, excitement buoyed her steps as she at last grabbed her flying bag and swung the door wide. It bloomed into anticipation as she looked up, spying the utterly cloudless blue expanse above the trees. *Finally.* She took another step—and held up sharply when Val's arm snaked around her waist from behind.

"Hold," Val said quietly, next to her ear.

The distraction of flying crashed back into the thoughts she'd been trying to avoid as Val's strong embrace held her in place. She couldn't help the thrill that ran through her, nor the disconcerting catch of her breath. Warmth pooled in the pit of her stomach. *"Val—"*

"Shhh." Val's breath tickled her throat. She reached out and pointed.

Not thirty feet away, a sow and cub ambled out of the trees.

"Oh, shit," Nicole breathed, her jumbled nerves sharpening. At once beautiful and terrifying, the bears embodied the untamed force of the wild in hulking bodies covered in thick, coarse brown fur rippling in golden waves against chocolate undercoats as they lumbered closer in long, powerful strides. Their massive paws left swathes of flattened brush in their wake. A few more steps and Nicole would have discovered firsthand how deadly those paws could be. The sow lifted her head in their direction as if sensing Nicole's thoughts. She sniffed, then huffed a warning. Nicole pushed gently but insistently back against Val, urging her into the cabin, eyes trained on the bears as she desperately tried not to think about the muscular body she pressed herself against. *Get it together!* Her inner monologue railed as her subconscious relished the moment. *What the hell?*

The door closed between them and the bears. Nicole paused, one hand on the doorknob. A span of heartbeats passed as her adrenaline receded.

"Whoa," she whispered.

Val released her and stepped to the window. "Whoa, indeed. I see even Reggie is hiding from these two."

Nicole forced her mind away from the lingering details of Val's embrace. "I'm glad you saw them. I'd have been breakfast for sure."

"I'm sure you'd have noticed them in time," Val said, but her attention remained outdoors. "I suspect you get used to them passing by from time to time."

Nicole shook herself. "Well…yes. A couple of times a year, I guess. Usually I'm better about keeping an eye out. I guess I got excited to introduce you to bush flying on a day like today."

Val spared her a mischievous glance. "Hurrying to fly usually kills in other ways."

With a shrug, Nicole joined her at the window. "You know, you're right about that. Probably a good thing to have to take a deep breath."

Of course, she'd never admit that she needed those few deep breaths because her imagination refused to let go of the moment just after the door had closed. If she had just turned, they'd have been so close... She blinked. She'd literally almost walked into a mauling and all she could think about was making out. She shook her head ruefully and gave Val a gentle punch to the shoulder. Her very firm, very muscular shoulder.

Get a grip. Get a grip. Get a grip...

Val looked at her quizzically.

Nicole laughed awkwardly, uncertain where the gesture had come from. "Sorry, that's probably the second time I've almost died today." Val's raised a skeptical eyebrow. "Thanks for saving my butt."

A disarming smile spread slowly to Val's eyes, and Nicole's cheeks flamed as she realized the opening she'd left for a woman who'd already demonstrated willingness to turn a flirtatious riposte. Mercifully, Val turned back to the bears and let the obvious lie. "Don't worry about it," she said. But the smile never left her eyes, and Nicole's stomach did a small flip.

The coast cleared as Nicole's embarrassment finally started to fade. They ambled down the path to the riverbed at last, Nicole with her flying bag slung over her shoulder and one eye on the sky. Beside her, Val grumbled, wincing each time she took a step with her right leg. "I still can't believe you shot me in the ass!"

Nicole cringed. "I really am sorry. You just scared the shit out of me."

Val waved her apology away. "I deserved worse. I'm just..." she grimaced again, "not used to feeling helpless."

"I very much doubt that you're actually helpless." Thoughts of rippling muscles leapt involuntarily into her mind.

Seriously, brain, we just got off that track. "But I understand."

"Humans are just such delicate *meat sacks* sometimes."

That was a unique turn of phrase...Nicole arched an eyebrow at her. "You say that like you're not one."

Val chuckled. "Oh no. I very much am."

Again, a tone implying there was more to the story that Nicole couldn't understand. But they'd reached the Beav and questions of Val's background took a back seat to getting ready for flight.

It was a gorgeous day. The fog that often settled in her little valley was burning off in the bright sunshine, revealing a cloudless sky that beckoned enticingly. Nicole hopped up onto the strut, opening the door and pulling out her checklist.

"First step in coming home alive," she said, waving the laminated paper in front of Val.

"Vakking right," Val said.

"What?"

"Fucking right," Val repeated.

Nicole shook her head and moved on. *I must need more coffee.* "How much do you know about bush flying?" she asked.

"Assume I know nothing, because I want to know it all." Val stopped to appreciate the aircraft, shielding her eyes against sunlight pouring into the valley.

"Careful what you wish for." She smiled, taken by Val's earnestness. "I'm liable to talk your ear off. I may be biased, but a DeHavilland Beaver is about the finest example of bush flying you'll ever know. She's a dream, capable of short takeoffs and landings while ferrying up to two thousand pounds of passengers or cargo. This one was built in 1962 and still flies as good as the day she rolled off the factory floor."

Val's brows drew down as she did the math. "1962?"

"Don't worry," she said reassuringly, though Val's surprise at flying an elderly aircraft was yet another sign that she lacked true familiarity with general aviation. "My grandfather took exceptional care of her after he bought her from the Army. She's practically a member of the family. Been with us through everything from search and rescue missions to ferrying dogs for the Iditarod."

They walked around the aircraft as she spoke, Nicole inspecting and testing as she went. Val followed, gaze sharp, and knelt with Nicole as she checked the tailwheel. "Do you primarily fly cargo?"

"Mainly passengers. I'm on contract with Aurora Ventures, out of Seward, so I mostly fly tourists on scenic flights like the one we're headed to today. Resurrection Bay, Kenai Fjords, and the Harding Icefield are pretty much an endless draw for flightseeing tours." She stood, satisfied with the tailwheel's condition, and chuckled. "Of course, I've had my fair share of weird cargo. I learned not to ask questions when I got paid to deliver a hundred McDonald's cheeseburgers and two hundred condoms to a lodge on the shore of Kenai Lake in the dead of winter."

Val sputtered, aghast. "*Two hundred?*"

"Like I said, I learned not to ask questions."

Val shook her head.

"It's weird, but I love it," she continued. "I never get tired of flying over this land, whatever the reason. It's beautiful, and every flight gives me the opportunity to appreciate the incredible place I get to live in. It's…a sort of communion with a place that's supported me, body and soul, for my whole life."

When she paused, Val was eyeing her with a small smile, head cocked. A flush crept up her cheeks. "Sorry," she said, hunching her shoulders. "I guess I waxed a bit poetic on you."

The small smile grew a bit, crinkling the corners of Val's eyes. "Don't apologize. Flying is your soul."

Despite the words, Nicole blushed further. "I suppose." She raised her eyes to the wings, focusing on inspecting the flaps to quell her embarrassment. "I guess you could say that this airplane is my connection to the land and to my own history. It's a phenomenal aircraft, but I also just truly love it."

Val followed her gaze. "These flaps go all the way to forty?" she asked, indicating the mechanism Nicole had deployed at the start of their inspection.

"Full flaps is fifty, but I wouldn't use that unless I was working into a very tight field."

Val squinted up at the wing. "And the ailerons are tied to the flaps."

"Good observation," she answered, happy that Val's vague cover story at least translated to real knowledge of airplanes. She at least *looked* like she was locking each detail away for reference.

Maybe she wasn't very familiar with general aviation, but she'd caught the subtle shift of the ailerons with the flaps down. She paid attention. "I think you'll do alright in the right seat."

Nicole climbed into the airplane first, then offered her hand as Val managed the same feat with a couple of one-legged hops. *Holy shit.* She caught the words before they tumbled out of her mouth, smothering an astonished gape as she considered the sheer strength required. The Beav was a big plane, and the initial leap alone was a few feet over the tundra tires and retracted skis...which Val had just managed with one leg. Val took her hand in a firm grip as she hauled herself the last foot with her arms only, deftly maneuvering herself through the narrow doorway and settling gently into the right seat.

Nicole cleared her throat and handed over her spare headset. "I suggest you fasten your seat belt before you close the door."

Val complied as Nicole plugged in her headset. Her eyes followed Nicole's hands as she completed the preflight checklist. *Prime...starter, mags...* the radial engine roared to life, splitting the quiet morning with mechanical thunder that resonated in the pit of her stomach. Joy rushed through her each time she turned that key, felt her grandfather's presence, and recalled his hands on the same switch. A thousand adventures and happy memories rolled into a single sound as the powerful rumble shook her body. God, she loved this airplane.

One eye continually on the instruments, Nicole gave Val her standard briefing as the huge engine warmed. The radial engine purred while she dialed in settings as familiar as the back of her hand. Finally, the plane perfect, ready to race into the sky, she closed her eyes and took a deep breath, hunting for the calm at the center of her swirling emotions. The comforting perfume of old upholstery, oil, and metal filled her nostrils. For the next thirty minutes, nothing mattered but the controls in her hands. She pushed the throttle forward and the huge tires surged across the runway of her personal airport.

Val let loose a *whoop!* of unadulterated joy as the aircraft leapt into the air, her grin sparkling in the bright sunlight as they ascended from the valley into a brilliant blue sky.

Nicole amended her list of Val's joys as the trees fell away below: cinnamon and airplanes.

They followed the valley south, the mountains sweeping past in shades of slate, fuchsia, and spruce, until finally bursting free of it and arcing out over the ocean.

"Resurrection Bay in all its glory," Nicole narrated, waving one hand at the scenery as she maneuvered them onto a course for Seward.

She banked over the coast, dipping a wing briefly toward the rocky shoreline. The day was unquestionably gorgeous, bright sunlight sparkling on a thousand ripples in the broad expanse of ocean, the silvery surface abutted by sheer, dark cliffs and the foaming white of crashing breakers. Seabirds whirled and darted below them. The sky arced above them in a cerulean dome stretching between stark gray ridgelines that cut the horizon into massive teeth. Every color seemed brighter, the contrasts more acute, the world more alive beneath the warm sun.

"*Fuck* it's beautiful," Val blurted, gaping out the window.

Nicole couldn't disagree. "These are the days I fly for. Smooth. Sunny. Perfect!" She elbowed Val playfully across the small space between them. "You must be good luck. Even the sea is calm!"

She smiled down at the coast zipping by below, so different from the angry beach she'd landed on just a few days before, and a cluster of brown shapes caught her attention. "Apparently, the locals agree. We caught them out sunbathing!" She pointed at the cluster of Steller sea lions, their huge, auburn bulk visible even from altitude.

Val's jaw dropped as she gazed down at the massive animals lolling on their stone bench at the edge of the sea. She turned to look at Nicole, eyes ablaze with delight, and Nicole beamed. "I'm glad I didn't run into any of them on my hike!" Val exclaimed over the purr of the engine.

"And there's town." Nicole gestured toward the buildings coming into view at the head of the bay.

The tiny community of Seward, Alaska, clung to the strip of land between mountain and sea. Homes draped the lush, green flanks of the mountain, clustered together along the few streets that angled sharply down toward the waterfront where businesses crowded the few level roads. The busy harbor bristled with bobbing masts. Fishing boats, sightseeing tours, even a few sails—ships' wakes crossed back and forth beneath them as they approached, tens of vessels peppering the blue-gray water on a beautiful, sunny day. Behind it all, the mountains reared majestically into the sky, forming the flanks of fjords carved by glaciers thousands of years ago. Nicole let her gaze slide over the familiar landscape, endlessly scanning for other aircraft. Traffic was always heavy on a lovely day like today, and Seward's airport lacked a control tower to keep everyone in line—making her undivided attention critical. They set down to the south, the sun glinting off waves breaking just past the end of the runway ahead of them, and taxied toward her favorite hangar.

"You're right," Val said, grinning like a kid with a candy bar as they climbed out of the cabin, "that is a hell of an airplane."

Nicole patted the fuselage lovingly. Jack approached with a wave, wiping his hands on an oily rag as he sauntered from the open hangar doors. The one person on Earth who knew the engine of the Beav better than she did, he was a bear of a man, tall and broad-shouldered, who constantly complained that airplanes weren't made large enough for real Alaskans. She could see his smile from fifty yards as it shone through his bushy, brown beard. "Hey, Rescue Ranger!"

Nicole laughed, waved away the words, and shrugged as Val arched one eyebrow. "I flew a kid to a hospital a few days back," she explained.

"Landed in a hell of a gale, too. Kid was lucky Baker, here, was flyin' by." He held out a beefy hand to Val. "Jack Reeves. Chief mechanic for Aurora. You are…?"

Val took his hand and held it for a beat, no shake. "Val Koroleva." Jack cocked his head, processing Val's accent. "Temporary mechanic's assistant."

"Do tell." He enfolded Nicole in a tight hug before leaning back, hands on her shoulders. "What'd you do to our girl?"

"Left main. Flat's in the back. Think you can give her a quick once-over and sign it off?"

Jack scoffed. "Consider it done, pal."

She turned to Val. "See if you can't impress Jack with a feat of strength, too, while I check in with the office?"

• 101 •

TESSA CROFT

Val crossed her arms, regarding Nicole's friend with a confident smile, and looked so goddamn dashing next to the airplane that Nicole nearly couldn't look away. "I think I can do that," she said breezily.

Jack guffawed, his booming laugh echoing across the tarmac.

As she walked away, Nicole caught herself focused on the sound of Val's rich vowels as they faded from her hearing. She couldn't help it. Next to Jack's boisterous laughter, Val's deep tones and rolling accent were undeniably sexy. She cast a guilty glance over her shoulder as she reached the door to the charter office. Val leaned into the open cargo door, snagged the flat tire like it was a leaf, and presented it as an offering to Jack, whose delighted laugh practically rattled the office windows a hundred yards away. Val noticed Nicole's attention and lifted her chin in acknowledgement, smile visible across the tarmac. Nicole only hoped her blush was invisible as she waved back and stepped hurriedly into the charter office.

The brightly-lit lobby was clean and neat, lined in stunning photographs of the nearby Kenai Fjords National Park, and on a sunny day like this it was crowded with late-season tourists hoping to catch a sightseeing flight over one of the many natural wonders nearby. The park itself boasted opportunities to glimpse an incredible array of wildlife, while the coast promised views of several large glaciers that calved dramatically into the sea and left trails of icebergs drifting ominously out into the bay. Meanwhile, the Harding Ice Field from which they flowed offered hardier adventurers the opportunity to land and step out on its surface. It was one of Nicole's favorite trips to guide. The beauty of the icy landscape aside, she loved the humility that the ice sheet demanded. Standing on the pristine white surface she imagined the glacier flowing beneath her feet, relentless and patient, a mere hint of the ponderous motion of the Earth, and recognized her own insignificance next to the power of the planet. The perspective granted on the ice never failed to clear her mind of petty frustrations.

Ray Sweeney, owner of Aurora Ventures, looked up as the bell over the door signaled her entry. Like Jack, Ray had known Nicole most of her life. He'd grown up in Seward, his parents part of the tight community around the small airport, and had been a recurring character in nearly all of her childhood visits. Though they were roughly the same age, at thirty-two, Ray's black hair had already taken on a rugged salt-and-pepper that lined an expressive, handsome face lit by baby-blue eyes that crinkled at the corners as he recognized her coming through the door. "Mornin'!" he said, beaming at her.

Nicole returned his smile, leaning against the counter as he handed her a clipboard with her preflight packet clipped to it. "Seems like this is one of those magical days when everyone's in a great mood," she said, her anticipation for the upcoming flight building with each smile she saw in the lobby.

"Every day you wake up with Bonnie is a great day," Ray said with a chuckle. The chocolate lab in question perked up at the sound of her name, happily plodding over to press her head against her owner's palm. He scratched behind her ear and she leaned merrily against his knee, tongue lolling, the two of them the picture of rustic contentedness. "Couldn't ask for a better day to be flying, either." He indicated the clipboard with his free hand. "Got a group for your usual run up to Harding. I made it up there in the Cub this morning. The strip's in good shape."

"Great," Nicole murmured as the indicated paperwork absorbed her attention. The forecast was flawless, with clear skies until long after they'd return from the icefield, and the small group of tourists were well within the Beav's carrying capacity. "This weather *is* fantastic. These folks are in for a treat."

Ray nodded and waved over the small gaggle of tourists clustered in the outfitters' waiting area. Bonnie plodded excitedly from behind the counter to meet them, tail wagging furiously, and proved a wonderful icebreaker as introductions were made all around. The small party buzzed with excitement, wide-eyed as they chatted amongst each other, but she noticed one of them—an older woman, her posture rigid and her eyes darting from Nicole, to the airplane outside, to her friends—hanging back, reticence in her eyes. *Uh-oh.* She recognized that look, and as she led the group into the briefing area, where an aeronautical chart and enormous photos of the area were tacked side-by-side on the wall, she watched the

TESSA CROFT

woman peel off for Ray. Her friends called out to her, but she shook her head, brushing off their protests as she made a stiff beeline for the counter. Tense murmuring reached Nicole's ears as the woman reached her target. Ray met Nicole's eyes apologetically.

She was pulling out because Nicole was the pilot.

Weight and balance about to get easier. Nicole stifled a sigh. This happened occasionally, enough that by now she simply regretted that this woman would miss out on the trip of a lifetime on one of the most gorgeous days of the summer. It always stung, but over time the bite had evolved from that of rejection to a deep disappointment in passengers who, for whatever reason—and Nicole tried not to guess, because most of the options that sprang to mind were uncharitable—felt that the gentler sex were incapable of safely flying an airplane.

She turned back to the remainder of the group and her frustration faded as she took in their eager faces. The photographs of the ice field reminded her of the phenomenal experience ahead. She would be introducing the grandeur of the icefield to Val as well as this small group of friends. A flutter of anticipation rose in her chest, gently dispersing the thin fog of disappointment. "I'm sure I don't have to tell you this," she said with a smile, "but today you're going to visit one of the most stunning, alien landscapes on Earth: the surface of a glacier at an altitude of four thousand feet, where there will be nothing but ice and rock for miles around you. Some of you may have even seen this ice up close already, if you visited Exit Glacier on the way into town. The Harding Icefield, more than seven hundred square miles of ice, feeds almost all of the glaciers you'll see as we fly up there."

She traced a finger along the chart, following a meandering blue line up the valley north of town, then arcing into the vast expanse of white. "We'll fly up here, along Resurrection Valley, before heading up over the ice. We'll land near here." She indicated a wide, flat expanse near the broad summit of the ice. "We'll be very far from the dynamic edges of the ice, where crevasses form, so you will be quite safe up there and we won't need to rope up. However, once we're on the ice, I'll ask you not to stray too far from our landing strip—just to be safe."

THROUGH SKY AND STARS

The tourists' brightly colored windbreakers swished as they nodded excitedly, cameras swaying on their necks, and she spied more than one fanny pack stuffed with spare film canisters. Every single one of them would likely be used on such an unusually gorgeous day.

"A woman pilot!" An enthusiastic, willowy woman decked out in well-worn hiking gear latched herself to Nicole's elbow as they left the office, headed for the plane. "I'm surprised," she continued. "I expected our pilot to be a grizzled old man. You're what, half my age?"

Nicole laughed and slid her sunglasses down in the bright glare of the ramp. These were the women she loved to meet, the ones who relished the experience of flying with a woman at the controls. The ones who considered it part of the adventure to be embraced, not feared, and who would share their joy and excitement with others. One impression at a time, these were the people who helped make women pilots less of a novelty. "You're thinking of my grandfather," Nicole said. "And to be fair, he taught me to fly and I inherited his plane." She waved toward the Beav. "But the people who fly out here are as varied as their reasons for coming to Alaska. Don't worry, though. If it's an experienced pilot you want, I've got over six thousand hours as pilot in command."

"Oh, I have no doubt about you, young lady!" the woman exclaimed, the crow's feet around her eyes peeping around her own sunglasses as she laughed. "It's a pleasant surprise. But I'll be sure to tell Frank." She paused, then leaned in conspiratorially. "His son's a pilot for the airlines."

Jack, who probably saw the *Rescue Me* expression on Nicole's face at this inevitable turn of conversation, sidled up to Nicole and shoved a clipboard toward her as if he had pressing business. "All signed off and ready to go."

The well-meaning tourist fell back to chatter with her friend as the two of them separated from the crowd. As they approached the Beav, the tourists trailing like a row of ducklings, Val dozed in the rear seat. Feet crossed over the doorframe, a borrowed cap tipped over her eyes, Val cut a striking picture. "She's a hell of a gal," Jack said, out of the customers' earshot. "Cracks me up, but I get the impression she'd kick my ass to Sunday and back if I got on her bad side. Where'd you find 'er?"

Nicole eyed the muscular figure stretched lithely in her plane. "It's a long story, but the gist of it is that she was backpacking through my valley." She paused, reflecting on Val's grace and focus moving through her kata. "And yes, I think she'd intimidate a grizzly."

"But not you, huh?" He guffawed, slapping her on the shoulder. "I saw she was limping. You kick her ass first?"

"Something like that."

He gave her a loaded, sidelong glance, held it just long enough to be obvious, and then burst into a deep laugh that doubled him over as he walked. "*Jack*," she muttered under her breath.

She slapped the clipboard good-naturedly across his chest, acutely aware of the customers clustered just behind her, and wondered whether Jack *had* saved her from an awkward conversation after all. "Did you fill 'er up?" she asked, trying to change the subject.

Jack doubled over again.

Nicole scoffed, furiously willing her blush to fade before she had to face the customers again. She never regretted being honest with her friend, but sometimes... She gave him a friendly glare over her sunglasses before beginning to settle her passengers into the rear seats. Still, she could practically hear him cackling until he disappeared into the shadows of the hangar. She climbed into the cockpit and Val swung into the front seat beside her with a cocksure grin that sent an unexpected, tingling wave through Nicole's gut. Focus, she told herself, taking a deep breath and trying to ignore the pleasant suspicion that Jack was right to pick up on something there.

"Alright, ladies and gentlemen..." She launched into her passenger briefing and started the engine for the second time that day.

CHAPTER NINE

August 5, 1996 AD [Terran Calendar], 1130 hrs
In the skies above Resurrection Valley, Seward, Alaska

The sky stretched in a glorious, unbroken blue bowl as they banked over the valley once again. Below them, a stream of glacial meltwater glittered as it flowed across a broad, gravelly plain between the mountainsides, beckoning them toward the ice that flowed toward them in a fractured, blue-marbled river streaked with dark moraines. The Beav's shadow rippled and danced across amber moss and stark, gray outcrops. A few small mountain drafts gently rattled the plane, but the tourists were so busy pointing their cameras out the windows that they hardly noticed. They'd never know how absurdly lucky they were to enjoy the adventure of a lifetime on a day like this.

Val stared down at the jaw-dropping landscape below and let Nicole's confident, comfortable narration wash over her. Even over the radio, with the thrum of the engine cutting in between her sentences, Nicole's voice was relaxed and assured as she brought the landscape alive for her passengers. From the front seat, Val could see the way her eyes scanned the world outside the windows, occasionally pinging the instruments in front of her before returning to monitor the air around them, and the casual manner in which her hands rested on the yoke. There was no question that Nicole commanded this aircraft and knew it, but she managed the massive machine as effortlessly as she'd handled her own hair. Even after hundreds of hours in the *Soyka*'s cockpit Val had never escaped the subtle, subconscious line that lay inevitably between herself

TESSA CROFT

and her spacecraft. As much as she loved her ship, the *Soyka* was a machine—a vehicle slaved to her will. Nicole flew as though her plane were simply an extension of her own body.

And it was vakking *impressive*.

Her HUD flashed in her vision, snapping her attention to a dark spot on the landscape below, and she reluctantly let her focus shift from Nicole. She touched her temple casually, as if leaning against the window frame, and allowed her vision to race ahead. Her spine straightened as the scene snapped into focus. She reached out instinctively to draw Nicole's attention with a touch. "Hey."

"What is it?" Nicole asked, her posture stiffening at the tone of Val's voice.

"There are people down there who need help."

"What?" Nicole craned her neck to scan the ice on Val's side of the aircraft. "Are you sure?"

Shit. It was impossible for Nicole to see anything more than dark blurs against the bright white of the snow. It was impossible for *any* Terran to see more than that. Backing up her instinctive comment required revealing her enhancement to a person who could never know or comprehend the technology hidden within Val's body. Her training told her to let the moment pass, to protect her secrets and pass her comment off as a mistake, but her conscience rebelled. She couldn't leave them to die on the ice. "There are people waving their arms at us, and it looks like someone lying on the ground," she said tersely, filtering out greater detail that lay plainly in her sight. "They are clearly in distress."

Guilt seeped through her as Nicole banked the airplane without further question. She wouldn't be in this situation, clumsily trying to cover up her seemingly inhuman abilities, if she'd extricated herself from Nicole's care as soon as she awoke in the cabin the morning after getting herself shot. With hindsight as crisp and clear as her view of the distressed Terrans below, Val realized that she'd let her mission slide to the periphery of her focus. Worse yet, she'd hardly resisted the dulling of her intent. She'd welcomed the comforts of Nicole's care, the soothing pace of life in her cabin, of life with her. And if it weren't for her HUD she'd probably still be sitting here mooning over a gorgeous pilot. *Damnit, Koroleva, you let yourself*

• 108 •

lose track of the mission because you're crushing. Shame crowded in with her guilt as the revelation sang through her. She scowled. *Well, that's just vakking perfect.*

Unfortunately, she'd just committed them to a rescue operation and her focus would have to remain distracted a little longer. Nicole eyed the peaks around them, telling her passengers that they were going to make a low pass to give them a better view. They skimmed down the valley just above the ice, pristine white at high altitude giving way to spackled, cerulean ice littered with rocks and gravel, streaks of blue and gray whipping by as they returned to lower altitude on the glacier. Val gritted her teeth and watched the terrain race by. She had to focus on this mission, now. "There." She pointed as they buzzed the crevasses opening up along the edge of the ice sheet.

Val watched a curse form on Nicole's lips and be absorbed by the roar of the engine, too quiet for the radio to pick up. At this altitude Nicole, too, could see the person lying on the ground, clutching a pickaxe they'd driven into the ice and snow. A rope around their waist stretched to the lip of the nearest crevasse and disappeared into it. Two others waved frantically at the plane speeding past over their heads.

Nicole scanned the ice around them. "Official rescue takes a National Guard chopper, likely out of Anchorage, which will take an hour to get here. Can you tell if they're stable down there?"

Details swept through Val's vision. The prone hiker's red face was rigid with terror, their boots slipping impotently on the ice as they fought for purchase, and their arms were stretched out fully toward the anchoring axe. All far more detail than she should be able to see, but, "I don't think so," she reported.

"If I land I can at least get a stable anchor in for them." Nicole handed Val a folded paper chart. "I'm going to find a good spot. Can you call Anchorage Center and inform them of the emergency?"

Val stared at the piece of paper in sudden panic. Lines and symbols spattered it like some kind of demonic spell. *Call Anchorage Center...* Thankfully, Nicole waved at the radio before Val's brain shredded in the confusing morass of unfamiliar symbols. "The frequency's already on standby. Just swap it."

She clamped her lips around a sigh of relief and jammed the intuitive button that brought up the right channel. Using the terminology she'd heard Nicole use on the way in to Seward, she stumbled her way through the initial call. Fortunately, Nicole took over the conversation once she'd chosen a landing location—even if she did cast a confused, sideways glance at Val as she stepped in. Val cursed herself; she clearly didn't know what she was doing. Her cover seemed about as secure as that hiker down there, clinging to a last-ditch spike on a wet, icy slope.

The hiker was having better luck, though, because an unbroken, smooth stretch extended away from the heavily-crevassed edge where they lay. Nicole's body language shifted, the casual tour guide rigidizing into determination as she spied the landing strip. It looked impossibly short to Val.

"Ladies and gentlemen, as you may have noticed, we appear to be first on the scene to a potentially injured climber." She looked into a mirror above her head, catching their gazes. "Val and I are going to assist. While we are gone, you absolutely must remain with the aircraft. You may get out, but do not under any circumstance move away from the aircraft. There are crevasses in this area and you may fall if you wander too far. Is that clear?"

There were a few gulps as they took in the solemnity of the situation, but all four nodded. "Very good. Fasten your seat belts. This could be a bumpy landing."

The ice loomed like a wall in front of them as they slanted into the valley once more. Walls of rock raced by on either side, bands of dark, open ice gaping below the skis as Nicole cut the margin to zero and skimmed low over the crevasses. Instinctive protests welled up in Val at the suicidally small gap between the aircraft and catastrophe. She clamped her lips on them, forcing herself to trust the pilot she'd marveled at just moments ago. As the skis kissed the snow and their smooth flight transitioned to a bumping, rattling landing, Nicole erupted in a flurry of motion, her hands dancing across the controls and pulling back on the yoke in a precise choreography, her gentle features hardened with concentration. One hand returned to the throttle, ready to slam it back to full power if the snow showed any hint of collapse beneath them. One of the tourists let out a yelp of

THROUGH SKY AND STARS

fright as the uneven ice bounced them all a few inches off their seats, the roar of the engine replaced by rumbling and shaking as they skidded to a stop. Nicole held the nose steady on their improvised runway. Despite the shuddering resistance of the unmarred snow and the bone-jarring, controlled chaos of the landing, her quiet, calm focus permeated the tiny cabin. Slowly, mercifully, the aircraft came to a halt on a stable, firm expanse of white.

A moment of tense silence ticked by in the cabin as Val watched Nicole, who sat stock-still as if feeling the stability of her plane with her body. Soft clicks from the cooling engine counted down a timer only Nicole could see or feel. Finally, her shoulders relaxed, and a breath of relief flowed out of her. Only then did Val release her vise grip on the edge of her seat. Her palm stung as the leather seam peeled away from it.

A blast of frigid air burst through the warm interior of the plane as Nicole leapt out onto the glacier. It jolted Val into action, and she too leapt from the aircraft, ignoring the lance of protest from her wound as she dropped to her feet on the snow. The wet snow crunched like gravel under her feet, water between the icy pebbles squeezing into the seams of her hiking boots as they sank into the layer of surface melting. Icy wind immediately cut through her jacket and carried away the comfortable warmth of the airplane, clearing her thoughts and crystallizing her focus. "What can I do?" she asked as Nicole threw open the plane's cargo door and began pulling out equipment.

"Put this on." Nicole tossed her a climbing harness. "I wish I could leave you with these guys for safekeeping, but with crevasses everywhere I need to rope up. You're coming with me."

The panicked hikers' cries reached them long before Val and Nicole arrived at the scene. A man rushed toward them as they neared, a battered yellow helmet with *Wild North Adventures* scribbled across it swaying on his head as he ran across the snowpack.

"Stop!" Nicole cried, so forcefully that Val nearly tripped on a stuttering step.

Nicole held out her hands. "Stop! Stay there!"

He skidded to a halt, breathing hard, his eyes wide and panicked. He pointed back toward the other two hikers. "Chris! Chris fell!"

• 111 •

Both of the others now lay on the ground. One of them, a woman, was the one Val had seen from the air; she gripped a pickaxe with arms that trembled under the strain, her expression fiercely reminiscent of a plebe about to slide off the obstacle course and take half her buddies with her. A deep trench ran away from her across the ice, scored by ragged, futile gouges from her axe before it had finally gained purchase. Her face stood out red against the snow, streaked with tears, and her labored breath hitched in and out of her through clenched teeth. The second man had simply thrown himself down on top of her to lend his mass in the fight against gravity. The taut rope attached to the woman's harness cut deep into the ice where it disappeared over the lip of the crevasse. Only her grip on the ice axe prevented her and her unseen companion from slipping into the icy chasm forever.

"Hurry!" the woman gasped. "I...I'm slipping!"

Nicole knelt next to them. Again, her hands flew into action, whipping a metal stake from her pack. When she spoke her voice was remarkably calm. "I'm Nicole. I'm certified in crevasse rescue, and I'm going to help you."

The exhausted woman's eyes latched onto Nicole's face, her expression overflowing with relief and hope as Nicole's quiet certainty settled over her.

"What happened?" Nicole asked.

"Chris—our guide—he's the one down there," the man wrapped around the woman said, his face white with terror. "Julie managed to get her axe in, but we didn't know what to do, and every time we moved she started to slip, and—shit!"

Both hikers jerked sharply toward the crevasse as their current patch of snow and ice gave an ominous lurch. The woman let out a tremulous, terrified wail but held her grip.

The clang of metal on metal rang across the glacier as Nicole hammered the anchor into the ice with her own axe. Val waited, ready to help, but Nicole was firmly in control of this situation. She deftly tied one knot, then another, almost faster than Val could follow, until at last she slipped a knot around the other woman's harness. "Okay," she said, "You can—"

A strangled cry drowned out her words as the woman's fingers slipped free of the axe. The pair slid toward the crevasse with the

THROUGH SKY AND STARS

sickening, crunching grind of wet snow over ice, limbs flailing for purchase as their bodies tumbled toward an icy death—until they stopped abruptly, Nicole's anchor line snapping taut. Their shrill, terrified cries cut short in a pair of matching grunts as ropes took the weight of the fallen guide. Beneath the rumble of human noises, too quiet for the Terrans to hear, the ice creaked ominously as the anchor twisted under the sudden load. Val tensed. A moment of shocked silence echoed across the ice.

Then the woman started laughing. "Oh my God!" she yelled, craning her neck to look back toward Nicole. "You did it!" Her wide eyes turned back to the taut ropes, wide and amazed. "You did it!"

"We're not done yet," Nicole cautioned them. Still, she looked up at Val and a small, triumphant grin pulled at her lips.

The insistent, ominous creaking of the ice quelled Val's tight, answering smile. "Better get them out of there."

Nicole's momentary jubilation withered visibly under her tone. Val winced internally. She *wanted* to celebrate with her, but this wasn't over until everyone was firmly back on solid ground. She couldn't relax while the ice groaned like a dying beast. Nicole worked swiftly, transferring the weighted line from the buddy to the anchor, and the woman gratefully backed away from the ropes and leapt into the arms of the man who'd been curled protectively around her on the ice. Val's stomach clenched as the motion set off a symphony of protest in the ice. She kept one eye on Nicole as the Terran began to rig up a pulley system. She should probably warn her—

A sudden cascade of noise erupted in Val's enhanced hearing and she lunged toward the rope a fraction of a second before the anchor gave way with a crack like a gunshot, the metal stake flying toward the crevasse as a spray of icy shrapnel exploded into the air around them. With blind instinct, she closed her fists around the rope and she threw herself back against it. The strain screamed through her arms and shoulders. Her feet slipped out from under her and she fell onto her back. *Vakking ice—*

She fought for purchase with her boots, but the rubber soles glanced off the cold, wet surface as if greased. *Not* a good plan. Frigid water and sharp, icy shards drove themselves under her shirt

• 113 •

and cut into her back as she ground across the ice. The edge of the crevasse skittered toward her like a Sh'keth Protector moving in for the kill. Her injured leg shrieked in pain as she drove her heels in again, futilely. She was going to have to drop the rope. Her palms burned and her fingers went numb. After all this, she was about to let a Terran die.

"Val!" Nicole's voice cut through her concentration at the exact moment her harness caught, slamming her breath from her body in a pained grunt as the hiker's inertia tried to rip her shoulders out of their sockets.

"I've got you!" Nicole cried. "Hold on!"

The rope sang with tension. Val strained to hear the ice again over the ragged static of her own breathing, willing it to hold, knowing that any slide toward the crevasse meant releasing the hiker's lifeline from her hands. An eternity ticked by. Her fingers had gone white, her palms bright red with strain and blood where the rope chafed across her palms. She wouldn't be able to hold it for much longer. "Nicole!"

Nicole skidded to a stop beside her in the snow. "I've got you," she repeated, dropping to her knees yet again. "Please just hold on."

The fear in her voice snagged Val's attention and pulled her gaze up from the ice. Nicole's cool exterior had cracked, revealing the well of concern that had already gotten Val into trouble once. As much as she appreciated it, the hiker's survival relied on Nicole keeping her wits about her. She had to keep her focused. "I'm fine," she lied gruffly, and watched Nicole's gaze sharpen at her harsh tone. "Just get this fucker on an anchor."

She pointedly returned her icy glare to the rope in her hands. Nicole grabbed the first anchor and drove it back into the ice. By the time Nicole transferred the weight from her, Val almost couldn't let go of the rope—her numb fingers cramped and spasmed as she relaxed them, flopping onto her back on the ice and ignoring the freezing water soaking into her jacket, every muscle in her body threatening mutiny as they relinquished the strain of holding the hiker above the abyss. She would pay for this later.

She lay there for a brief eternity, eyes closed, panting, the ice mercifully quiet.

"You alright?" Nicole asked quietly.

Val nodded and opened her eyes to the baby-blue sky stretching endlessly above her. She sat up slowly, every muscle in her body chastising her for losing sight of her mission. She was supposed to be figuring out how to recover *faster*, not wrecking her body saving the life of a random Terran idiot who'd fallen in a big, icy hole. She looked over at Nicole, who sat on her knees, face turned toward the crevasse, her eyes filled with calculation as she scanned the rope stretched to its edge. Her braid fell over her shoulder, several strands fallen loose and tucked behind on ear, held at bay by her cap. She either didn't realize or didn't care that her workpants were soaked through or that crystals of wet ice clung to her knees and elbows. As she looked at Nicole, Val realized that she *wanted* to be near her, that she was drawn to Nicole as if in the gravity well of an oasis world. Something in Val wanted desperately to stay close to her. No wonder she'd let her mission slide.

Nicole glanced back, her gaze softening slightly as their eyes met. She smiled tentatively. Val's answering smile settled into place like the blanket of regret falling over her shoulders. Nicole stood and held out a hand. Val took it and rose, ice and snow falling away from her, and for a half second, they stood on the ice hand in hand. In that moment Val thought she felt Nicole's thumb trace the back of her own hand, a half-imagined caress, just tenuous enough that she wondered whether her imagination was running away with her newly acknowledged infatuation. Nicole let go. "Let's get this guy out of there."

No matter how much she wanted to linger with Nicole, wanted to let her heart find purchase in this new world, the stinging pain in her hands and back reminded her sharply that her own desires were irrelevant. Her mission called. Her window of opportunity was dwindling rapidly, and with it her friends' chances of survival. As beautiful as Nicole was, body and soul, she couldn't. Wouldn't. There was too much at stake.

But damn if Nicole didn't fly that plane like a *vakking* goddess.

Val let loose a resigned sigh. Maybe in another lifetime.

Tomorrow she would leave for the hive.

THROUGH SKY AND STARS

CHAPTER TEN

August 5, 1996, 2:15 p.m.
Harding Icefield, near Seward, Alaska

At last, as the shuddering sound of the National Guard helicopter faded away with the guide and his group safely onboard, Nicole and Val stumbled back to the Beav. The moment they arrived, two things happened simultaneously: bone-deep weariness struck Nicole so powerfully that she wanted to curl up in the front seat and sleep for days, and the group of waiting tourists burst into excited chatter. She looked at her watch. *Hardly past two...* They'd been on the ice for just under two hours. Two hours that felt like a lifetime. She waved off the tourists' jubilant and appreciative chatter, ushering them back into the plane. Thank God they were excited about witnessing the rescue, rather than upset at having been left waiting all morning—tired as she was, her patience probably wouldn't have made it any further than shoving an annoying tourist down the nearest crevasse and negating the whole misadventure in one fell swoop—but now they wanted to know every detail. When had she learned crevasse rescue? Had she done one before? Would the injured man be alright? How could she tell this was a safe place to land? She painted a smile on and forced answers out past her exhaustion because she had to and someone had to fly them all back, but at the moment she wanted only a massive dinner and a soft bed.

Her back and shoulders began to ache as she climbed out of the cabin in Seward. It seemed an eternity of smiling and posing for

• 117 •

pictures before the customers finally dispersed, gleefully promising to send pictures of the rescue along with rave reviews to the office. Their heads bobbed like silver buoys in a multicolored sea of windbreakers as they trundled toward the office. Nicole smiled, watching them go, but she sagged against the Beav the moment they disappeared.

"Are you alright?" Val asked, her dark brows drawn together in concern.

"Yeah," Nicole said, although she let her head rest against her seat as she stood on the strut. She closed her eyes and welcomed the warm sunshine seeping into her aching muscles. The coarse fabric pressed into her cheek and the familiar, comforting scent of the aging upholstery filled her nostrils. She could almost fall asleep there in the warm cabin. Val's fingertips rested on the back of her hand, Val's concern diffusing through the touch. Exhausted, she simply leaned there, kept her eyes closed, and savored it. *Just for a moment.*

"Are you certain?" Val asked.

God, yes. The response rang through her with surprising clarity. She opened her eyes and gave Val a small smile, pulling her hand back. "Really, I'm okay. I just..." She rolled her shoulders speculatively. "God, that did a number on my back."

She glanced at Val, recalling her sigh of utter relief after she'd relinquished the guide's rope. "Aren't you at least a little sore, too?"

Val shrugged, eyes unreadable behind the mirrored surface of her borrowed sunglasses. "I'm sure I'll pay for it tomorrow."

Nicole eyed her skeptically. "Well, *I'm* wrecked, even if you're Wonder Woman, and I'm starving. Let's go."

She waved Val after her and made for the office. In a few, short minutes they'd borrowed Ray's truck and were pulling into one of Nicole's favorite places in the world. The Bear Hug was one of the busiest restaurants in town, frequented by fishermen as often as tourists, all drawn by the promise of pancakes for dinner or a massive, mouth-watering burger at any hour of the night. The interior was bright and cozy, the classic diner counter and booths peppered throughout by eclectic Alaskan kitsch: photographs of bears everywhere you looked, of course, along with fishing poles and dip nets, taxidermized salmon, a few old snowshoes and skis, a

THROUGH SKY AND STARS

can of bear spray labeled "Seasoning"...the list went on the longer you looked, a lifetime's slow and steady accumulation of garish paraphernalia that the locals tolerated like a salamander tolerates ever-warming water. The bar abutted the kitchen, terminating by the cash register at a glassed-in counter filled with T-shirts and hats. An old gumball machine sat just inside the door, filled with candy that Nicole could swear hadn't moved in a decade. The welcome aroma of sizzling burgers overwhelmed her senses in a glorious bouquet as they passed the multicolored sentinel. She'd hardly drawn a single, appreciative breath before Jackie Reeves, the second half of her best friends in the world and the establishment's proprietor, practically leapt the counter to wrap Nicole in a bone-crushing, eponymous hug. For a moment, her world became a whirlwind of fleece and pine and wild, curly hair. "How you doin', kiddo?"

Nicole chuckled into Jackie's shoulder, accepting the hug gratefully along with the familiar, loud greeting. A hug from Jackie Reeves was *exactly* what she needed after their adventurous, exhausting morning. Strong as a black cup of coffee and just as uplifting. "Good, J. Starving, but happy to see you."

Jackie stepped back, holding Nicole at arm's length, and inspected her with a concerned eye, tut-tutting at her still-damp Carhartts.

Nicole sighed and raised her hands apologetically. Apparently, she looked like she was about to keel over—which, admittedly, she'd been thinking about doing back in the plane, so Jackie wasn't far off the mark. Plus, Jackie was a quintessential Alaskan, always on the lookout for a friend in need. She'd known Nicole for over twenty years and could clearly see when she was running on E. Nicole gave her a small, guilty smile for running herself into the ground, but Jackie simply squeezed Nicole's hands in a second, miniature hug.

"Your fingers are freezing." She scolded her, then pushed a warm mug of black coffee into them. The heat of the mug instantly permeated her palms, sending a frisson of pleasure through her chilled body. "Ray called ahead. I've got your usual on, times two." Her eyes flicked to Val, curiously, and she raised an eyebrow. "You need something warm too, stranger?"

TESSA CROFT

Val pulled off her sunglasses and settled her hip against the counter with a nonchalant air, but Nicole recognized the tightness in Val's jaw as her weight shifted. She'd seen the same tension in Val's posture each time her migraine reared its head. A bolt of concern arced through her. How much pain was she in? Val, however, cast a dazzling smile at Jackie, propped one elbow on the counter, and leaned in conspiratorially. "Cocoa?"

Jackie let out a merry, rumbling laugh. "Cute," she said, and caught Nicole's eye with a wink as she turned to fix up a mug.

Tamping down a traitorous blush, Nicole turned to Val.

"Are you okay?" she asked quietly, indicating Val's injured leg.

Val shrugged. "I've had worse."

"I'm sure. But the way you caught that rope…" Nicole trailed off, looking pointedly at Val's hands. Val *had* to be hurting. Catching that rope in the first place should have been impossible, let alone holding onto it for a bone-jarring arrest when Nicole's hasty anchor caught her and the fallen guide. She'd suffered rope burns from much less.

Val shook her head dismissively. Nicole stared her down. With a sigh, she raised one hand. "It looks worse than it is."

Nicole blanched. The palm was raw and red, chafed near to bleeding where the guide's rope had cut into it. *Jesus.* "Are you sure we shouldn't go to—"

"Here you go." Jackie turned back to them, derailing Nicole's concern by sliding a mug across the counter toward Val. It was piled so high with whipped cream, the only sign of cocoa beneath the small mountain was a drip running down the side of the overfilled cup. Val's eyes lit with such childish excitement that Nicole momentarily forgot her worry, giggling at the sight.

Val eyed her sidelong and affected an aggrieved air. "Excuse me. I *earned* this," she said regally as she lifted the ridiculous mug of cream and sugar to her lips. Still, Nicole noticed the careful way she held her palms away from the hot surface.

"That you did," Jackie said, leaning close across the counter. "I hear you two are a couple of heroes who just pulled a man out of a crevasse."

• 120 •

Warmth flooded Nicole's cheeks as heads at several nearby tables turned to look. She shrugged and busied herself with pushing up her sleeves. "We just happened to be in the right place at the right time, J."

And I'd have flown right by if Val hadn't been there.

Val's eyes were closed as she savored the outlandish beverage in her hands, looking for all the world like a simple, hungry tourist. Yet she'd seen those people when Nicole had barely seen smudges on the ice, and she'd snatched that rope out of thin air while avoiding impalement by the metal spike streaking toward the crevasse with it. For the hundredth time, Nicole wondered who—and what—had fallen into her life.

In the silence, Jackie glanced between the two of them with a knowing, if skeptical, frown. She set her hands on her broad hips. "Well then. Sit your butt down and tell me about it."

Nicole sat as Jackie slid a plate in front of her, a burger smothered in pepperjack and green chiles dwarfed by a mountain of fries still hot to the touch. Val, spying a second plate, cast a smoldering come-hither stare as it crossed the small space from the kitchen. Nicole hummed appreciatively. The glorious, mouth-watering scent made her stomach growl. "Oh, Jackie, have I mentioned that I love you?"

She took a bite, giving herself a moment to let the perfection of flavor caress her senses, before she said, "Val ought to start. She's the one who saw them." She paused her assault on the burger long enough to cast a questioning look at Val. "Honestly, how *did* you see them? I could barely make them out until we descended!"

"I saw a flash," Val said around a mouthful, eyes trained on the food as if it might flee.

"A signal mirror?"

Val nodded and kept eating. Nicole frowned, confused by Val's terse response and disappointed in herself for failing to see the distress signal. "I guess I missed it."

She hadn't seen any mirrors on the hikers once they'd landed, but after her first, low pass had confirmed Val's observation of hikers in distress, she'd stopped worrying about whether Val had seen them and focused instead on how the two of them would rescue the guide. Still, someone with as much flying experience as she had, and as much knowledge of the landscape over which she'd been flying, should have noticed the unusual flash of a signal mirror. "Maybe I ought to get my eyes checked next time I'm in town."

Val looked askance at her and paused with a fry halfway to her mouth. "The customers were distracting you. I seem to recall one of them being quite…"

"Chatty?" Nicole chuckled. The older woman had continued to bend Nicole's ear throughout the flight on the fine qualities of the young, male pilot she knew, until her friends had cautioned her that if she didn't shut up and let Nicole guide, they were going to throw her out the cargo door. "True."

"And to be honest, the fact that I saw them was not nearly as impressive as that landing." Val's attention shifted to Jackie, and she waved the forgotten fry eloquently while the crooked grin crept up toward her eyes. "That landing. I was either about to die, or already had and was in heaven."

Jackie chortled as Nicole scoffed, but she busied herself with another fry to distract herself from the bubble of pleasure she took in Val's approval. It *had* been a challenging landing. Unproven ice always came with the threat of hidden crevasses or ponds of glacial meltwater that would wreck her landing gear in half a second. But she'd also made enough landings on the ice that it hadn't been *that* exciting. Had it?

Val leaned into the drama as she described the unexpected descent. Jackie, who'd experienced many trips up to the ice and therefore knew *exactly* what landing on skis felt like, offered sympathetic, shocked murmurs as Val related the experience. Nicole's suspicions returned as Val related the rescue in dramatic detail. Sure, she wasn't a bush pilot, but was an unexpected off-airport landing *that* thrilling? The apparent novelty was unusual for a pilot who supposedly had enough experience to break into the male-dominated realm of the big jets.

"I probably owe her new upholstery, given my death grip on the seat when we hit the ice."

She scoffed good-naturedly and nudged Val playfully with her knee. Val nudged her back. They locked gazes. Something in her eyes echoed the unguarded expression Nicole had captured on the ice, in that moment after they'd reestablished the anchor and halted the guide's descent into the crevasse once and for all. She'd caught Val looking at her with...what? Respect, a bit of admiration, and a touch of—*oh, God.* Val wasn't shocked by the landing. She was *flirting.* Nicole realized that her knee still touched Val's. That without thinking about it she'd turned in her seat to face her, unconsciously favoring Val at the expense of her lifelong friend. And now Val playfully made fun of her landing on the ice while Jackie bubbled with conspiratorial laughter and rewarded Val with an appraising smile. Nicole shot Jackie an apologetic glance. Jackie winked and she blushed anew. *Honestly, brain...* Yet she still granted Val a smile and another nudge as she turned back to her meal. This time she meant to leave her knee where it was, and she didn't even try to ignore the sudden, furious flare in the pit of her stomach when Val didn't draw hers away either. She didn't care if it was childish. Apparently, she'd been single long enough that dubious background and inexplicable physical abilities were acceptable as long as they came in a gorgeous and charming package.

The aviator in her, however, refused to be distracted. The bright sunshine beyond the windows grew muted as they ate. Nicole pulled her attention away from Val to eye the patch of sky she could see from their spot at the bar, silently logging first wispy clouds, then a dim gray that replaced the gorgeous blue morning, one eye constantly on the evolving weather. When the blue had been completely subsumed by gray, she laid her palms on the counter. "I hate to say it, J, but we'd better go if we're going to beat the weather I see rolling in."

Jackie leaned over the counter to get her own look at the sky. She frowned. "Better take your dessert to go."

As if by magic, a paper bag appeared on the counter in front of them. "Take these and get your butts out of here," Jackie said with a smile, pushing it toward them.

Greasy spots on the bag betrayed the sinful nature of its contents. Nicole leaned toward Jackie as Val stood and moved toward the door, out of earshot. "J, are these some of your famous fritters?" *Val is going to love this.*

"Now they're *your* famous fritters." Jackie tilted her head toward Val and winked. "Use them well."

The sparkle in her warm gaze practically pushed Nicole into Val's arms. She resisted the blush threatening to rise again, happy that her best friend approved, then clutched the paper bag mischievously and followed Val out the door. Through it all she tried desperately *not* to overthink the fact that she and Val were about to be alone in her cabin again.

Val hung back to hold the door for a gaggle of locals coming the opposite direction. The last of them was a woman Nicole knew from the sightseeing cruise line, who nodded in recognition as she made eye contact. As she reached the door, however, the friendly smile she'd bestowed on Nicole simmered into unadulterated, blatant ogling as her gaze raked overtly along Val's body.

"Hey there, newcomer," she said.

"Ma'am." Val stood straighter, held the door wider, and inclined her head toward the open entryway.

An unexpectedly powerful bolt of jealousy shot through Nicole. She turned away, unwilling to see Val's hot shot swagger in the face of another woman's interest, and tried to push away the acid churn of envy. *You're exhausted.* Seconds ago, they'd been drawing closer together, touching, laughing. Their chemistry was unmistakable. Holding the door for a passerby wasn't flirting. Val was just being polite…wasn't she?

She busied herself with pulling the keys from her pocket as she approached the truck, hoping Val wouldn't see her childish reaction. Even if she had just acknowledged to J that she *wanted* to, she had no claim whatsoever over Val—quite the opposite, really, considering she'd spend her life trying to make up for shooting her. But she couldn't help resenting her burning awareness of the other woman's gaze on Val as they approached the truck. The keys trembled in her hands while she unlocked the driver's side door.

"Want me to come back later and pick you up?" she asked around a forced smile, unnerved and dismayed at the note of resentment that seeped into her teasing tone.

Val paused, a question in her silence, but Nicole refused to meet her gaze lest she catch a glimpse of the unjustified hurt.

"I believe I have a flight to catch," Val replied at last, her tone light but cautious.

They climbed into the cabin, where warmth from the sunny morning still lingered. Nicole's heart sank a little more at the reminder of their shared adventure.

"Hey." Val leaned across the cabin, inserting herself into Nicole's space until the overtness of it forced Nicole to meet her gaze. She smiled, the heat of it blossoming in the small space between them, and a squadron of butterflies took hopeful flight in Nicole's stomach. "I do not intend to let *every* woman I meet on this trip take my pants off."

A shocked laugh burst from Nicole, her jealousy retreating behind a tumultuous wave of commingled embarrassment and satisfaction. She shook her head, chuckling, and turned the key.

"Okay, Casanova."

The old truck's engine rumbled to life. She turned her attention to the road. But every fiber of her being was riveted, once again, on Val in the cab beside her. *God, I'm in trouble.*

PART IV: *DESCENT*

THROUGH SKY AND STARS

CHAPTER ELEVEN

August 5, 1996 [Terran Calendar], 1730 hrs.
Seward, Alaska

"Sure you gals won't stay the night?" Jack asked, leaning against the strut as Nicole fastened her seat belt. "I know you saw the forecast, and the pie Jackie made last night…it'll make your socks roll up and down. You could camp out on our futon!"

Nicole smiled down at him through the open door. "I'd love to, Jack, and thanks for the invitation, but the weather's supposed to go bad for a few days. Your futon's not *that* comfy. Plus," she waved the paper bag at him, "J hooked us up!"

Jack let out a theatrical sigh, closed the door, and gave it a playful pat. "Okay, kid. Fly safe!"

He gave Val a friendly wave, who returned it with a smile and nod, then hopped off the strut and strode away from the plane. As Nicole began her checklist for the fourth time that day, she passed the paper bag over to Val in the right seat. "J likes you."

Val's face was partially hidden by her cap and sunglasses as she bit into the fritter, but her appreciative moan left nothing to the imagination. Nicole busied herself with the starter to hide her satisfied smile.

In moments, they were airborne, the Beav's nose sweeping south over the water before pointing homeward up the valley. Nicole eyed the low ceilings closing in on them with a frown. A hazy mist of rain obscured the world just beyond the bay.

• 129 •

TESSA CROFT

"So, Jack and Jackie?" Val asked, the fritter demolished, her voice tinny over the radio.

"My best friends in the world. They're the lifeblood of that town. And yes, they're married. Jack is the best A&P I've ever met—I swear he could make a toaster fly—and now you know that Jackie's burgers are the best this side of the Kenai."

Val smiled and stretched out in her seat with a sigh. "After today I think I'm in love with Jackie."

An amused retort withered on Nicole's tongue as she looked out at the low clouds scudding in from the ocean. *Shit.* "This is looking pretty crappy. I thought we'd have plenty of time...but it's deteriorating fast."

Val stilled, radiating calm, and her playful mood vanished as the air in the cockpit turned serious once more. "Is there anything I can do to help?"

Nicole pursed her lips. The ceiling was lower than she'd like, but at this point the only options were to turn around or navigate through it. "Keep an eye on the river once we're over it. We only need to make it about twenty miles up it to the cabin. As long as we don't lose sight of it, I can follow it all the way home even if this shit closes in fast."

A curl of discomfort wound itself around her gut as she spoke. *Altitude is your friend,* Gramps's voice cautioned her in her memory. She checked the altimeter and eyed the clouds.

"We've still got margin," she continued, "but make sure your seat belt's tight, because this is likely to get bumpy."

She raced the lowering clouds toward the valley, the weather moving impossibly fast, clouds pressing them relentlessly closer to the slate-gray, churning ocean below. The first fist of turbulence rocked the aircraft, dropping them several feet. The rain caught up to them, first mist, then droplets beginning to pelt the canopy. She descended reluctantly, looking for her familiar waterway. The coastline reared up out of the ocean, a black-and-brown slash across the sea, until at last a meandering gray line led up into the valley.

She locked her gaze on the riverbed and let them descend out of the clouds closing in around the aircraft. The Beav began to buffet

THROUGH SKY AND STARS

and the rain picked up. A big drop made the vertical speed dial bounce and her stomach crawl into her throat.

Val's hands clenched in her lap but she said nothing.

Clouds rolled over and past them. Nicole didn't dare blink. If she lost the river she'd lose the visual reference that kept them in the middle of the valley...making it extremely likely that they'd end up like countless other bush pilots who simply disappeared into the middle of nowhere. The valley walls were close, only a few hundred feet in either direction—if she lost course, either of those rocky walls would put a swift end to both their lives. She imagined Jack searching the valley for days with grim determination, seeking even the smallest trace of red wings in the trees.

Don't think about that. Aviate.

She started to hum, the melody settling her churning nerves, and her shoulders uncoiled slightly. A cloud engulfed them.

"Damnit," she muttered, locking her eyes on the place she'd last seen the river. She pulled back the throttle and descended further. *Altitude is your friend.* Another reproach. A small gap opened and she spied her target, adjusted course. Another gap, another tiny motion of the yoke. Turbulence rocked them, playing havoc with her careful navigation. The back of her neck tingled with alarm. *This was a bad choice. Bad choices kill you.*

Then, as if on cue, the engine sputtered. A fist seemed to punch her poor bird, rattling them both.

"Val," she barked, tension edging her words, "pull the carb heat."

Val hesitated. Nicole didn't dare look away from the course, couldn't risk missing even the smallest gap in the clouds, wouldn't risk both their lives when another pilot could take care of the task. The engine sputtered again. The carburetor was clogging with ice. When it at last choked closed, cutting off the precious air the engine needed to burn fuel, she would not only be landing in the wilderness, she'd be doing it without power. The most likely result of which was a very quick end to two human lives.

"Val. Carb heat!"

Val reached uncertainly for the levers at Nicole's knee. Slow, too slow.

TESSA CROFT

"I thought you were a pilot!" Nicole leaned down, grasping sightlessly for the lever, and yanked.

The engine gave a dip, then roared back to full power as ice melted away. She breathed a sigh of relief. At last they broke below the clouds.

"We are going to talk about that," she growled through clenched teeth, glaring at the river, "when we get on the goddamn ground."

The tundra tires had barely rolled to a stop in the gravel when she ripped her headset off and leapt to the ground outside, running her postflight checklist with trembling hands. Rain lashed them both, soaking her ballcap and running in rivulets down the back of her neck as she tied down the aircraft, while adrenaline and anger pushed her through bone-deep exhaustion that threatened to suck the life out of her. The beautiful morning was gone, replaced by a nightmare of a day. The valley was nearly invisible through rain and mist, the world muted in dark grays and shuddering with cold gusts of wind. She slipped and cursed on the wet rocks of the gravel bar.

Val stayed mercifully quiet and offered a hand where she could, but Nicole accepted the help with a quiet glare. It was going to take more than that, Thank You Very Much. They were soaked through, cold, shivering and, in Nicole's case, furious, as she stormed into the cabin.

She stoked the fire, willing it back to life as she considered the similar fire boiling inside her. Water dripped and puddled around her as she knelt by the fireplace. Still, her anger burned hot and bright. The flames caught and she turned.

Val stood silently, arms crossed, leaning against the door, but her normally sharp gaze clouded with uncertainty as her eyes met Nicole's. The gray in them echoed the world outside. Her hair was plastered to her forehead and her navy tee was nearly black where it stuck to her powerful shoulders. For once her expression remained placid, the grin absent, and she waited quietly for Nicole to speak.

"Damn it, Val. I was almost starting to believe you. But carburetor heat is Private Pilot 101. You are *not* a pilot. Who are you? *What* are you?" Her eyes burned as the betrayal sank deep into her gut. She'd *known* Val was lying, had as much as openly acknowledged it, and yet…she'd wanted to believe Val was who she said she was. She wanted a friend, a…*whatever*. A confusing rush of embarrassment, disappointment, and pain catalyzed her anger. "Don't obfuscate. We nearly lost the engine because I *trusted* you to be what you said you were. So. Spill."

Even as the angry words passed her lips, while she waited for Val to say something, *anything* to justify herself, Nicole's conscience rebelled. Val wasn't the pilot in command. Nicole was the one who'd nearly lost the engine. She should have turned around the moment she'd seen that weather.

Who was she mad at? Val or herself? Val remained silent, seemingly oblivious to the guilt swirling through Nicole's anger and hurt. Her stillness betrayed a quiet calculation behind her eyes. A tiny rivulet of rainwater escaped her hair and ran down her temple. At last she said, "I *am* a pilot."

Nicole scoffed, throwing up her hands. "Please!"

"I just fly…spacecraft."

Nicole froze. The statement was so absurd that she almost couldn't process it, the words hitting her brain and sloughing off like rain from the canopy. "Excuse me?"

"I fly spacecraft. Technically, tactical insertion vehicles."

"Quit bullshitting me. It's offensive."

"I am absolutely serious."

"How am I supposed to believe that? It's the most ridiculous thing I've ever heard. And after you've been lying about everything else!"

Val sighed and her expression relaxed into acceptance. She raised her red, chafed palms in defeat.

Nicole resisted the concern threatening to dilute her anger.

"I don't expect you to believe me. That's why I was never going to tell you."

Nicole's echoing sigh dripped with frustration. Not only was Val's pilotage a lie, but she was also, apparently, crazy. Did she imagine herself some kind of sci-fi soldier? Were the strength, the courage and confidence, all the byproduct of some deep and elaborate delusion? Alarm shot through her. Was everything about this woman born of some kind of psychosis?

Even as she asked herself, though, the thought rang false—Val's competence on the ice had demonstrated genuine ability to manage life-or-death situations and spoke of real military training. Still, if she thought she flew *spacecraft*...a screw was loose somewhere. Nicole felt no outright danger at the realization, as Val hadn't so much as feigned a threat since that first night by the fire, but it was clear that she'd somehow let a delusional and lethal stranger into her life. Because she'd thought she was hot.

She mentally castigated herself as the false trust shattered between them. Conflicting shards of disappointment and mortification dug into her gut. The whirlwind of emotions ratcheted her frustration higher until it finally burst from her lips.

"As soon as this shit blows through I'll take you to meet your friends...if they even exist. Until then I don't want any more goddamn lies." She paused, considering. "In fact, since apparently I can't trust a single thing you say, you might as well not say anything at all."

She turned away, her last glimpse of Val a knife ripping open the chasm of disappointment in her heart. Val's hurt echoed in the space between them as she climbed the ladder to the loft. She ignored it, wrapping her anger around herself like a shield against her own bitter pain. It was better to pretend that she wasn't hurting too.

Val's heart twisted with surprising ferocity when Nicole turned her back. The uncharacteristic urge to reach out, to stop Nicole and ask her back, to make her understand, welled up in her with such overwhelming strength that she took a step forward, opened her mouth to form an apology. But the words hung in her throat. Her mission loomed large in the rubble of their crumbling relationship. She had to let it go. Here was the chance she needed to make a clean break, to rip herself away from this beautiful distraction and get on with the reason she'd come here. She'd already lingered too long.

But when Nicole dropped her off in the pass, it would be clear that she was—and would remain—alone. Nicole *probably* wouldn't do anything ill-advised, like head straight to Anchorage and report her suspicious presence, but Val couldn't be sure. The soldier in her whispered that the most logical answer was to eliminate the possibility. She could end Nicole's life quickly and painlessly, and no one would ever be the wiser. She'd complete her mission and be long gone, likely dead herself, before the body was ever found.

The thought turned her stomach. She was here to *protect* humanity, not kill an innocent Terran who'd done nothing but help and befriend her. And Nicole was so much more than collateral damage. She couldn't deny that what she'd felt on the ice was more than simple desire for a beautiful woman. Before the weather had soured, she'd been fairly certain they were about to fall into Nicole's bed. She couldn't, wouldn't hurt Nicole. But now, if she couldn't let Nicole know where she was going, she was well and truly fucked. Now she had to get herself to the hive without Nicole's help. Concussion or not, she'd wasted precious days in which she should have been marching.

And yet...the inexplicably powerful ache in her chest urged her to make things right with Nicole before she left. The truth might have intervened, preventing Val from openly acknowledging what Nicole meant to her, and perhaps that was a good thing. But she'd do what she could to heal this rift before she left.

She heated water over the fire, then climbed the ladder painstakingly with a thermos in one hand and a mug jammed into her pocket. Every rung demanded payment for her poor decisions. Her palms stung as she gripped them, shadows of the guide's rope burning across them, and her fatigued shoulders screamed by the time she reached the top.

She found Nicole sitting on the edge of her bed, staring at nothing, still sodden. Sadness draped itself on top of the burdens she hauled up the ladder. She'd already hurt Nicole, whether she wanted to or not. Suppressing a sigh, Val heaved herself up the last few rungs.

Nicole's face tightened in a flash of anger at Val's approach, but just as quickly softened with fatigue. Her shoulders slumped. "Thanks," she said softly, accepting the mug.

Val nodded. She poured cocoa into the mug, nestling one hand around Nicole's to hold the mug steady as she did so. The loft finally began to warm with the gentle heat of the woodstove. She picked up one of the blankets folded at the foot of the bed, shook it out, and wrapped it around Nicole's sodden shoulders. "You should get dry," she said, punctuating her words with a gentle squeeze.

Nicole looked up, the shadows beneath her eyes twisting the ache in Val's chest tighter.

"I will," Nicole said, smiling briefly. "Thanks."

Nicole reached out as Val turned to leave, catching her fingers in a belt loop, and for a brief second a gentle pull held her fast.

"Look," Nicole started, her voice heavy with exhaustion. "You know I can't just accept what you told me. It's…it seems crazy. But I'm sorry I got so angry. It's just that I really, really wanted you to be who you said you were."

Val placed one hand over Nicole's and sighed. "I wanted to be, too."

Nicole's gaze lingered on their entwined fingers.

"Your hands," she breathed, and pulled Val's palm to her.

The skin was red and raw, scabs darkening the places where the rope had chafed deep into the soft flesh, and stinging prickles danced up Val's forearms as Nicole lightly traced the injuries with her fingers. She grunted softly.

"I'll be fine," she protested, but didn't remove her hand from Nicole's soft grip.

She needed this to stop before Nicole distracted her, yet again, from her mission. Her logical mind railed as the silence between them deepened. Her heart pounded traitorously. Back at the diner she'd have said this was evolving into exactly what she wanted—a night of fun with an incredible woman. Despite her resolution on the ice, she'd let herself flirt and had taken immense, expectant satisfaction in the moment Nicole realized what was happening. The thought of a night in Nicole's bed had seemed a sort of tantalizing farewell. Her body's response to the imminent reality, though, hit Val with terrifying force. Whatever had whispered to her on the ice, it was more than the nonchalance of a casual fling. A bolt of desire and fear shot through her and she shivered, suddenly afraid of giving her emotions free rein. She could imagine it now, see it in the slight parting of Nicole's lips and the way her hands cradled her ragged

THROUGH SKY AND STARS

palms. She could almost feel Nicole's lips on her wrist, warm and gentle as Nicole herself, their touch soft above Val's own clamoring pulse. She saw herself sinking to her knees, cupping Nicole's face and pulling their bodies together, shattering the tense silence with a groan of acquiescence. The half-imagined sound caught in her throat. A tense knot formed in her center. Turning her mind from the thought felt as impossible as walking straight up into the sky, the full force of gravity resisting each step. She could let herself fall, instead, and in falling burn hot and furious as a meteor. She wanted to. The ache of her emotions pressed against her chest, a siren call of want. But like a meteor, at the end of the fall she would find a hard, iron core. Her mission, lying in the ashes, and herself no closer to averting a future in which this world burned, too, in chemical fire.

The thought quelled her rampant heart. Whatever this was between her and Nicole, no matter how many times she ricocheted from duty to desire and back again, even Nicole would elect to stop the Sh'keth if given the chance. She loved this world too dearly to choose anything else. Even without the many, seemingly fantastical reasons why this was a bad idea, Nicole was also physically and mentally exhausted. Neither of them was in a position where this should happen. Val pulled a breath deep into her lungs, withdrew her hands regretfully from Nicole's grasp, and watched the hope in Nicole's eyes cloud with confusion. Her shoulders slumped.

"I'm sorry I disappointed you," Val forced out, the words gruff in her own ears.

With every ounce of strength she had left, Val pushed the quiet invitation aside and retreated down the ladder. She had to leave before her idiot heart fucked up her mission even more than it already had.

THROUGH SKY AND STARS

CHAPTER TWELVE

August 6, 1996, 7:00 a.m.
Kenai Mountains, Alaska

When Nicole woke, Val was gone.

A fire had been laid and burned low, having warmed the cabin enough to lull Nicole into such comfortable complacency that she hadn't noticed the silence as she dressed. Now, the quiet apology of the gesture did nothing to blunt the spear of hurt and anger that stabbed through her at the emptiness of her own home. She stood lost in her own living room, staring at the place where Val's pack had rested for days. How could she just *leave*? An old, familiar pain needled into the confusion and hurt. Nicole hugged herself, suddenly cold, and stared at the world beyond her windows.

Rain lashed the panes. Wisps of cloud scudded low across the treetops, dragging through spindly spruce branches as mist drenched the world outside. The alders twisted and writhed in the wind. The Beav could go nowhere and she'd never catch Val on foot.

She could wash her hands of Val—every gorgeous, insane inch of her—guilt-free. Val hadn't just left. She'd snuck out, slinking back into the forest from which she'd emerged. On the surface she'd given exactly what Nicole had asked for—a clean break. She shouldn't care what happened to her.

But she *did*. As angry as she'd been, Nicole couldn't help the subtle tug pulling her to Val even if she *was* a stranger who'd materialized from the darkness outside her home. Despite her harsh

• 139 •

TESSA CROFT

words, she wanted Val in her life. On top of it all, no matter what Val felt or what she meant to Nicole, she was still hurt. She'd limped back to the ladder last night, and Nicole's own palms twitched at the thought of the mess of Val's hands. Not even an impossibly fit woman with nerves of steel who thought she flew *space fighters* would last long in the bush with a gunshot wound, maimed hands, and the lingering effects of a concussion. No. Whatever Val thought she was doing, Nicole wasn't going to let her just march away into memory.

She was trapped, for now, by the weather. But weather wouldn't last forever.

CHAPTER THIRTEEN

August 7, 1996, 9:00 a.m.
Kenai Mountains, Alaska, Earth

Nicole banked low, skimming over the figure kneeling in the rocky plain, and laughed ruefully as Val tried to wave her off. *Like hell, you Soviet Night Witch.* She lined up on the nearest open stretch. Her mind was made up after a day trapped between dreadful weather and the restless ache of loss, the decision firm as the mountains after hours of flying the valley, scanning for Val. Another day of rain and she'd have lost her—too many passes and ridges fractured this land into a network of glacial valleys, an ever-growing maze of possible routes into which Val would have disappeared like oil from the Beav's engine. Only the stubborn concern for Val's safety, lodged deep in Nicole's chest, and sheer luck had brought her overhead. *I am not letting you walk yourself into a ravine in a stubborn, one-legged march through the mountains.*

She threw her headset onto the seat, leapt from the cockpit as soon as the propeller surged to a halt, and tore for the last place she'd seen her.

She hadn't gone far when Val approached, running full tilt toward her.

Running? Nicole stopped, confused, and rested her hands on her knees. Her lungs burned from the uphill sprint. "What...?"

Val skidded to a halt, appearing remarkably unfazed by sprinting across the rugged ground with a pack on her shoulders. "I should ask you the same question," she said. "What are you doing here?"

"Why aren't you limping?" Nicole countered. "I *know* you weren't lying about being hurt. How are you…?"

"Good as new. They don't send a soldier into enemy territory without the best technology medicine has to offer."

Nicole stood upright, still catching her breath. "*Enemy territory?*" She propped her hands on her hips, staring at the sky in disbelief. "God *damn* it. I knew it."

Val laughed. "You only think so."

"Okay, I'm willing to accept that you are both a cosmonaut *and* a spy."

Val's deep laugh rivaled Jack's. "Case and point."

Nicole's frustration rose. "Look. I came out here to make sure you don't kill yourself trudging through the wilderness with a gunshot wound, however minor. If you're miraculously healed, prove it."

Val blinked. "What?"

"Prove it!" She sighed, pointing at Val's butt, and ignored the bemused expression Val made in response. "If you're magically healed, I'll fly away and leave you to whatever your business is out here. But I suspect you're bullshitting me again and I won't live my life plagued with worry over your disappearance. For some crazy reason, I care about you." She let her frustration spill out as a glare beside the confession. "I don't want you falling off a cliff because you're too stubborn to let yourself recover from a gunshot wound. If you're *not* fine, I'm taking you wherever you're going. No questions asked. None taken, either."

She crossed her arms and waited.

Val responded with quiet, wide-eyed incredulity.

"Val, it's nothing I haven't seen before. Remember?"

"It's not that. It's…"

She hesitated, and a furious blush flamed across Nicole's cheeks. "Val, please. I just want to make sure you'll be safe."

Val looked horrified. "No! Nicole, it's not that either. Trust me." She looked straight into Nicole's eyes as she said it. "It's not that."

Val's shoulders slumped as she relented. "You'll see."

She pulled fabric away from where Nicole *knew* the wound should be. Nicole gaped. Nothing. The wound had disappeared as if it had never happened, gone without even a scar.

"How?" she managed.

Val grinned that stupid, cocky grin of hers, and Nicole fought simultaneous urges to kiss her and sock her. "Twenty-eighth century medical marvels."

"I..." Her words faltered, the sudden, tumultuous reality of Val's words finally finding purchase in Nicole's mind. "What?"

"My... Neosporin," Val struggled with the name as if she'd never spoken it before, "is infused with medical nanotechnology that accelerates healing."

"But..." How could she respond to something so blatantly, unequivocally, impossible? *Nanotechnology?* It was something out of the novels on her shelves. The insane ramblings of a Russian spy who'd wandered from her sanity along with whatever mission she'd truly been sent on. An elaborate joke from the universe, a gorgeous woman fatally flawed. It couldn't possibly be *real...*

Could it?

She *knew* Val had been hurt. She'd seen it. Hell, Val had limped away from her in the loft just two days ago! Gunshot wounds didn't just disappear. That would take...her mind shied away from the answer, but her heart lunged for trust. For Val. She sank to the tundra, suddenly bearing the weight of two realities—one she'd known, and the other beginning to show through cracks in the first's foundation. "The twenty-eighth century?"

Val set her hiking pack aside with effortless grace and settled to the ground beside her. She crossed her legs, leaning her elbows on her thighs, and stared toward the summit ahead. As she sat, her smile dissolved, as if considering Nicole's dumbfounded question had drawn her into an eddy of darkness. Ferocity deepened the crease between her brows. Her eyes grew hard in the flat, gray light, and her lips formed a tight scowl. Whatever lay ahead of her, it filled Val with an unfamiliar rage that left a sea of disquiet in Nicole's gut. The threat in her visage was back, the bear stalking the fringes of her reality. Finally, Val nodded.

"The year 2765 by your calendar. And if we're lucky, I'm the only one left who will ever know it as it was."

The agony in her voice gripped Nicole's reeling thoughts and hauled them to a stop. Behind Val's anger was an avalanche of grief burying Nicole's confusion, her fear, even the wall of doubt between her and the universe Val described. Real or imagined, Val's pain ran deep, pulling her onward with merciless finality. The set of her jaw, the hopelessness of her tone—wherever she was going, Val expected never to return. Could someone simply hallucinate that kind of suffering? She didn't think so. Like the first blade of grass peeking through the snow in spring, Val's reality began to weave itself into Nicole's. But like the spring growth, the fullness of it remained buried. She had to dig to see more.

"Val, I don't understand."

Val met her eyes, her gray irises cold as steel. "I hope you never do. Not fully. But in a hundred and fifty years, aliens called Sh'keth will emerge from a colony they've established near here. They're monsters, Nicole, consuming everything in their path. When they emerge they will be hungry. They'll scour this valley and everything in it. Your home. Seward. Before long, the entire Earth will be poisoned in the fight against them."

Nausea rolled through Nicole. "They...eat it?" She imagined green bodies and huge eyes, antenna and multi-segmented limbs. Little green men, feasting on the plants and animals of the mountainsides. "What are they?"

Val's face twisted with disgust. "Bugs. Too big to step on, though."

"Giant bugs. That eat the plants and animals?"

That sounded...terrifying, but not evil. Val, though, stiffened. "Not just the plants and animals, Nicole. They will eat..." she trailed off, swallowing, and her face paled.

Oh. Horror shoved Nicole's nausea aside, setting off a battle between her terror and the urge to vomit. "God," she whispered, shuddering.

"It will be too late before anyone realizes how far gone the planet is. Before anyone cares. By then humanity will be too desperate to stop it, to save the Earth, and will flee aboard a fleet of starships cobbled together from stolen Sh'keth technology. And for hundreds of years, we'll fight them. Until there are only a handful of ships left. Until me."

She paused, meeting Nicole's eyes. "I'm here to stop it. To put an end to the colony before it grows strong enough to desecrate our world." She took Nicole's hand in her own, running her thumb along Nicole's palm, and a rueful smile tugged at the scowl plaguing her features. "You've shown me what I'm fighting for. The people, as well as the place." She sighed regretfully. "But I have to go, Nicole. I have to destroy the hive. Today. If I don't do it today, I..." she faltered, swallowing hard.

Val stood abruptly, leaving Nicole as bereft and confused as the day Val had walked away from her on the riverbank. Nicole opened her mouth to protest, but the battle between her heart and her mind froze disbelief on her tongue. Her hands shook. She laced her fingers together in her lap and stared at them, waiting for the shock waves to propagate through her mind.

"God." Her universe had turned inside-out. Did she actually trust Val in this? "You mean I almost doomed humanity by shooting you? I *shot* a soldier from the future sent through time to save the world?"

The statement was so ludicrous that she had to clamp her lips around a giggle. Val cast her a concerned look.

It had begun to make a strange sort of sense. But what was that theory Sagan was fond of? Occam's razor? The simplest explanation was that Val was a spy, dropped here for some kind of intelligence-gathering mission. There were countless military facilities sprinkled throughout the state, any one of which would be a prime target for a Russian spy. Or maybe she really was a cosmonaut and her pod had landed off-course. It would explain her bearing, her accent, her bogus cover story...everything but the complete disappearance of that wound. From what she'd heard, the Russians barely had enough tech to keep their space program going, let alone develop *medical nanotechnology*. On top of it all, Val had proven herself to be a terrible liar.

So somehow, despite how preposterous it seemed, Nicole believed her. Believed that she'd shot, helped, and wound up devastatingly attracted to a woman who was literally trying to save the world. She shook her head. God, this was actually insane.

"What happens now?"

Val drew Nicole to her feet, still staring over Nicole's shoulder at the pass narrowing to an apex above them. "I have a mission, and you have a life to live. Whether or not I succeed, you'll never know—the hive won't emerge until long after you're gone. If I were you I'd go enjoy this incredible planet." She smiled sadly and Nicole's heart gave a lurch. "I did, for as long as I could."

Nicole made up her mind. "Let me help you. I'll take you up to the pass."

Val scowled and crossed her arms. "They're likely to shoot you out of the sky."

"I don't think so. I've flown through this area more times than I can count, and if they're trying to keep as low a profile as you described then they're not in the business of taking out aircraft and drawing search parties to their doorstep."

"You do have a point," Val murmured as she scanned the ridges around them. "I can't believe you would fly into this in that... extremely primitive technology."

Nicole laughed, her certainty drowning the last vestiges of doubt lingering between her and Val's tale. "Done it a hundred times. Let's go."

❖

The plane dropped into the pass with a rush that made Val let out an exhilarated *whoop*.

Nicole grinned as the big tundra tires hit gravel, bringing them to a stop, but her smile faded quickly and her heart sank as the purr of the engine shuddered to a halt. This was it. The end of their time together. This was where she would watch Val walk away, most likely to her death.

"I feel like there should be more I can do," she said as they both climbed from the aircraft.

Val, nimble without her injuries, quickly opened the cargo door and pulled out her pack. "You've done more than enough," she said, hefting it onto her shoulder. "From here you'd only be in danger."

THROUGH SKY AND STARS

"At least take this." Nicole handed her the rifle she kept tucked in the rear compartment.

Val raised a brow. "Is that the one?"

"No, sorry." Nicole couldn't keep the smirk out of her voice. "If I'd known I'd have brought you that one for luck."

"Either way," Val said, "I don't actually know how to use that thing. We have...had...different tech where I come from." She handed the weapon back, folding her hands over Nicole's as she did. She gave them a squeeze. "I appreciate the sentiment, though."

Nicole swallowed, a lump rising in her throat. Two hours ago she'd thought Val was utterly off her rockers, dangerous, arrogant, and probably a spy which, when coupled with charming, beautiful, and competent, somehow meant Nicole couldn't let her go. She'd been so certain of it that she'd launched herself through the sky to keep Val from confidently waltzing into her own demise. Now nothing was clear, except that despite everything, she didn't want to watch Val walk away.

"Val, please, I..." She struggled to fit her churning heart into words.

Val's cocksure expression softened. She shifted her grip on the rifle to one hand and gently stroked Nicole's cheek, pushing a rogue strand of hair behind her ear.

Nicole leaned into the touch and closed her eyes, savoring its warmth and impermanence, before cupping Val's hand in her own and pressing a kiss into her palm. Val's skin was rough but unmarred. The rope burns, too, had vanished without a trace. She folded their fingers together and looked back up at her.

"I'm coming back for you. Tomorrow," Nicole said. "Be here."

Val smiled sadly. "I'll try."

Now she's honest. Nicole released her hand reluctantly. "You'd better."

She didn't trust herself to say anything else. Instead, she turned to the airplane that she knew and loved, picked up her checklist, and tried to distract herself with the preflight as Val's figure ascended the pass above her. As she climbed onto the strut she looked up one last time and saw Val atop a boulder, face turned back down the pass. Val waved, one hand held up stolidly.

• 147 •

Nicole held a hand up as well, feeling the weight of their short, uncertain relationship hang like a ball at the top of the arc, waiting to fall. They stared at each other for a long moment in which time seemed to hold its breath. Then Val turned and was gone.

She climbed into the cockpit. It was warm, and quiet, and so very, very empty without Val laughing in the right seat.

As the engine roared with the first opening of the throttle, she paused.

"Nicole, don't be stupid," she said to herself. But it was no use. Tears started to flow down her cheeks, the release of immeasurable confusion and anxiety, the fear for Val, the lingering memory of her touch. Grief for something gained and lost in the same breath.

CHAPTER FOURTEEN

August 7, 1996 [Terran Calendar], 1100 hrs.
First Sh'keth Hive, Earth

The ancient engine roared to life, consuming Val's regrets in a roar that filled the valley with purpose and power. Her first moments on Earth rose in her mind, the sight of Nicole and her aircraft drawing light across the sky as Val stood on the shore of that godforsaken lake. With the memories came comfort. These were the visions, the moments, she'd given everything to preserve. Even if the odds of seeing Nicole again were dismal, at least she'd be safe.

With a last sigh lost in the purr of the engine rumbling below, Val turned to the task at hand. An army of historians had dredged up schematics of the hive and briefed Val before her departure. If their research was right, an access shaft up here brought fresh air to the depths of the hive. It also, she noted with a sniff and a wrinkle of her nose, must bring stale air up from below. The hive couldn't be far.

She dropped her pack, no longer needing the survival gear, and stripped down to a black, lightly armored uniform coated in a thin foam that would deflect and confuse the Slugs' echolocation. She sheathed her only weapon—a long and deadly trench knife—in her boot, and draped a small pack, containing just enough explosive to collapse the central corridor of a Slug hive, over her shoulders. Once again, she wished for the pressure of a mag rifle's grip in her palms—a comforting weight that might have lifted some from her shoulders as she descended into the pit of enemy activity—but the

• 149 •

technology would have been laughably overt if it fell into importune human hands. So she would finish this job with simple, Terran-equivalent explosives and do her damnedest not to need the knife. A knife would be next to useless against a Protector, anyway. From here on, her mission was to stay alive long enough to destroy the colony. Stay hidden, find the queen, and drop the ceiling on her before the Slugs became the nightmare this planet didn't deserve. Simple as that.

Yeah, real *vakking* simple.

She followed her nose to the entrance. The perforated metal grate, tucked behind a pair of large boulders that shielded it from view, hung askew on corroded hinges. The cloying stench of rot grew stronger. Val coughed into her elbow, swallowed, and scowled as her throat worked around the odor. *Fuck.* It was no surprise that Slugs were disgusting—it only took one assault on an active feeding chamber to see and smell things that would haunt a soldier for life—but this was a new low even for them. It would be just her luck if the passage led directly out of their waste recycler. The place certainly smelled like it. Sadly, a respirator would've been one more item out of place here in the twentieth century… Not that being secretive had mattered much, after all.

She took one last look at the sky from which she and Nicole had descended, laughing, mere moments before. Earth had been good to her. With luck, she'd return the favor. She thought of the woman who'd embodied that goodness, and paused to hear one last murmur of the old engine. Only silence, now, urging her onward. She steeled her resolve and lowered herself into the fetid darkness.

Familiar, otherworldly architecture enveloped her along with the putrid stench of the cavern. Sh'keth runes, as finely engraved as a silken web wrought in stone, emblazoned the tall, narrow walkway that descended into the darkness of the mountain. The swirling patterns, delicate as shimmering clouds, had once seemed beautiful to her. She'd wondered what they meant and what their creators pondered as they painstakingly etched their messages into unforgiving stone. That wonder, though, had bled out onto the muddy ground of her too many missions. Now, the Slugs and their language meant nothing but death.

The corridor had clearly been abandoned for years. A dozen tiny skeletons littered the floor, detritus of small predators. Moss choked a shallow channel at its base, thinning where the last rays of sunlight met their doom in the dark passage, and a pathetic trickle of water emerged from the soggy growth to lead her downhill. The stench grew oppressive as she descended, building and souring until it felt as if she waded bodily through a rotting swamp. Val flicked on her red headlamp, moving slowly and carefully along the mold-slicked passage.

After what seemed hours of descent, long after the sun's light had faded from view, the ventilation shaft met another metal grate. She knelt, flicking off her headlamp and letting the darkness settle about her. She closed her eyes and considered what she'd been taught of the hive's layout. This was most likely the central passage of the colony, the circular hub and home of the queen, from which the hive radiated like spokes from a wheel. It should be a busy thoroughfare through which Sh'keth herded larval slugs to their dens and delivered nourishment to their queen.

Yet she heard nothing beyond the grate. Just absolute, dead silence.

Where the fuck were they?

They had to be here. A hive the size of the one that ruined the Earth took decades to grow under ideal conditions, and this was clearly far from perfect even by Slug standards. Had this section been abandoned? She scowled, imagining her access route blocked by a cave-in, then shook her head to dispel the worry. She'd cross that gap when she came to it. Perhaps hive culture had evolved in the hundreds of years between her understanding and this single, far-flung colony. Maybe they'd isolated themselves into the deeper recesses of such an unhealthy hive. Val huffed out a breath. Either way, the queen couldn't be far.

She lifted the grate painstakingly, willing the crumbling metal to allow her silent passage. *Vakking hell.* Flakes of rust coated her palms, gritty in her grasp. *This slime-fest must be even older than Nicole's plane.* The metal resisted, shuddering over crumbling hinges, but the damp coat of mildew deadened the worst of the mechanism's groans.

Slicker than a slug on ice, too. She skidded in the slime of the central passage, nearly landing on her ass when she dropped to the floor. A meager patch of moss provided just enough traction to prevent her downward spiral into the muck.

Thankfully, only echoing darkness witnessed her graceless flailing.

The corridor stretched into pitch-black overhead. Only the faint return of her own breathing, teased out of the quiet by her enhanced ears, disrupted the heavy stillness of the cavern. Not a drip, not a scurry. Nothing, alive or otherwise, moved but Val. She risked her headlamp again, curious—and nearly fell over backward as Sh'keth mandibles loomed suddenly out of the inky black.

She scrambled backward, seizing the hilt of her knife, adrenaline surging through her. Another ambush, her first and last missions coming together in perfect irony...

But the alien remained still.

Val relaxed, heart thudding in her throat. Swallowed the tight knot of fear. No fight to be won here.

She inspected the giant insect. Its jaws hung slack, pillowed on forelegs canted toward the grate from which she'd emerged. Massive, veined wings draped the brittle carapace in a blanket of mold. The huge eyes, once the shining orbs haunting her nightmares, were a sunken honeycomb of decayed tissue. Cautiously, Val pressed her fingers into the dull exoskeleton. It disintegrated under her touch.

She recoiled, shocked at the state of the carcass. *What the fuck?*

The thing had been dead for months. Far too long for this to be a thriving colony. The fact that it hadn't been cleared away spoke volumes.

She scowled as confusion sifted through her focus. Sh'keth were fastidious and wasted nothing, even dragging their own dead and wounded back to feed their growing hives. They only abandoned their dead in defeat. Here, in their home, the decrepit remains were a bellwether. What kind of catastrophe had led them to waste such a perfect meal?

She began to understand the stench, if not the story.

Creeping further down the passage, expecting to meet a living Protector around every curve in the pitch darkness, Val finally picked up the deep, thrumming notes of the living hive. Her pulse notched upward.

There you are.

The bass notes of Slug echolocation grumbled out of the darkness, inviting her to finish her mission. She paused, listening to the familiar, grotesque song and thinking of the friends for whom it had heralded death. This melody, however, was different. The notes warbled. Their pace faltered, the sounds emitting from the darkness in plaintive bursts. They're dying without my help, Val realized, heart sinking into a sea of consternation.

What the hell was she doing here if the hive was dying already?

She didn't have time to wonder.

A sharp crack reverberated through the air of the corridor, slicing through her confusion. Her blood ran cold. The thrumming of the hive quieted ominously.

She spun and sprinted back up the passage. The hive would investigate the sound, unfamiliar in the depts of the mountain, but she knew exactly what it was. She'd heard it before. *Fuck.* Heart hammering, breathless, she retraced her steps in a frantic race to beat the Slugs back to where she'd entered the colony.

She skidded to a halt in front of the desiccated Protector, crouched defensively, willing the darkness to open.

"Nicole!" she hissed into the depths.

A rustle. Nicole was there, throwing herself into the circle of red light. A storm of intertwining tenderness and fear rippled through Val at the sight of her.

"I'm sorry!" Nicole gasped into her shoulder. She clutched the offending rifle in one hand.

"You really need to work on your policy of shooting first," Val murmured into her ear, allowing a brief embrace to comfort her. "At least this time I wasn't on the receiving end."

Nicole laughed softly, pulling back. "Have I messed everything up? It looks like they're already dead."

Val held them still for a moment, listening. A dull thrum reverberated through the soles of her feet. Slugs were slow, but their Protectors would be here soon. They needed a plan, fast, if she was going to keep Nicole safe and complete her mission.

"Maybe, but I don't think they've ever sensed a gunshot before. They won't necessarily be expecting company. If we just had…" She searched the blackness around them. It did nothing but consume the light of her headlamp. Sh'keth needed no furniture, and no workstations cluttered a passageway meant for traffic. The setting left precious little opportunity for cover. Except…

She lifted one moldering wing of the dead Sh'keth. "Under here."

"Are you serious?"

Val cast her a sidelong glance.

"Carb heat," she said, and the implication was clear. *We don't have time to argue.*

Nicole acquiesced quickly but no less reluctantly, settling into the bracken beneath the wing and grimacing as the glutinous muck squeezed between her fingers. "If we live through this, I *will* exact revenge."

Val huddled down next to her, lowering the wing over them both, and flicked off her headlamp. They plunged into utter blackness.

"I'm counting on it," she murmured, her lips close to Nicole's ear as they huddled together in the small space. "Now. The Slugs can't see. They echolocate. They perceive only rough shapes, and my clothes are designed to dispel the waves further. So I'm not too worried about them. The grown Sh'keth, though, are another matter. They *can* see and they move *vakking* fast. Our only hope is that they don't see us. If we stay back here and don't make a sound, you may get your chance."

Nicole nodded into her shoulder.

The warbling bass notes drew closer; first a humming in the floor, then the chest, until even the long-dead Protector resonated with the approach of its distant kin. Val strained to hear the telltale clatter of Sh'keth legs on stone. Nicole curled against her, their bodies concealed by the decayed, lifesaving husk of a dead insect as the larvae of a new hive surged closer. Images of past combat rode the thrum of the hive into the pitch-dark void around her, slipping through the invisible darkness into her soul and pulling forth images she'd tried to forget. Scoured hives, blackened and burnt, crowded with the piled remnants of human and Sh'keth corpses alike. Human soldiers slaying larvae grown fat on the diet, only to be cut down in the next breath by diligent Protectors under the icy, timeless gaze of a watchful queen. Her thigh twinged. The resonant darkness tugged at her. Before today, such visions promised only her own death. Now Nicole risked the same gruesome fate. Nicole, who'd helped her, healed her, and now risked everything to be with her. Her heart had soared at the sight of her Terran, but Nicole's presence added another layer of consequence if she failed. Nicole deserved so much more than to die in this withering, grotesque hive. The urge to protect Nicole at all costs nearly overrode the call of her mission yet again, the pull to Nicole singing through her blood. She couldn't let her die here. Val's stomach clenched.

Breathe. She focused on her training. *Inhale.* Pine and woodsmoke cut through the stench of the cavern as she drew in Nicole's scent. She concentrated on the gentle sound of Nicole's breath, the solidity and warmth of her in the dark, the tickle of her hair against one ear. Nicole's presence stilled her rampant thoughts even with the Slugs bearing down on them. *Exhale.* She let the fear go. She was *supposed* to be here, the tip of a spear of thousands of engineers and scientists pouring their all into a last-ditch effort. She would save them *and* Nicole. Nicole pulled tighter against her. She waited, willing the deadly horde to pass them by.

A mournful call interrupted the thrumming. The slugs had arrived at the scene of their dead kin. But...no skittering, no clacking of mandibles. Only the soft hiss and slap of soft bodies along wet stone.

Val imagined what they could not see—enormous larvae, bodies pulsing as they inched along the corridor, with gaping mouths lined with hundreds of small teeth. A human nightmare in the flesh. The crumbling Sh'keth carapace rocked against her as a soft mass hit it, showering them in a dust of moldering insect. Val blinked the debris from her eyes. The Slug notes rose and fell in excited bursts. Another bump against their hiding place.

Vack. They're going to eat this thing, and us with it.

She tensed, ready to fight to the end. Without Protectors here she might be able to get them free, cut a path to the grate and get Nicole through it, at least. A Slug's bite hurt but wouldn't stop her. At least, a single bite wouldn't. Maybe Nicole could pull her through before she was overcome. She could at least save Nicole. Her fingers inched toward the knife in her boot.

One of Nicole's hands settled over hers. The other uncurled to lay a palm against Val's chest. *Wait.*

A tearing sound echoed through the hall. Shredding, ripping… Val tensed again, sure that this was the hive gorging themselves on the decayed carapace, but their shelter remained still. Whatever the bastards were eating, it wasn't the Protector.

❖

It sounded for all the world like a feeding frenzy. Nicole cringed when something tore with a cascade of fibers pulling and snapping. Soft bodies clambered about, scraping and pushing. She shivered, her breath hitching in her throat while her rational mind tried vainly to hang on to one fact—they hadn't been found. Whatever the slugs were diving into, it wasn't their hiding place and it wasn't a pair of unfortunate humans.

Val radiated hostile intent. She clearly meant to fight, seizing the distraction and making for safety.

Please don't go. She tightened her grip on Val's shirt, pleading silently for her to remain still. *They've forgotten about us.*

The shredding ceased abruptly. The crescendo of slug voices began to fade away. Val relaxed against her as silence descended around them. The thrumming song fell to a hum, then a vibration, then stillness. Her terror subsided with them, slowly retreating into the darkness beyond their hiding place. Her shivering ceased. She became aware of a trickle of brackish water seeping under her jacket and shifted, trying to escape it. Val wrapped a protective arm around her.

"Just a little longer," she whispered in Nicole's ear.

She sought comfort in Val's embrace.

At last, the invisible clock expired. Val switched on her headlamp and they both peered out from their hiding place.

"What?" Val murmured, climbing out from under the wing.

She held it up and away from Nicole as they emerged, sodden, from the muck, but she eyed the grate through which they'd entered. She frowned, her brow etched by deep shadows.

The area had been scoured. No mold, no slime, and no trace of the moss that once coated the ground beneath it. "They ate the *moss*?"

Val scowled at the scene for several seconds, arms crossed, while around them the cavern waited in pregnant silence. Nicole watched her shoulders rise and fall, slowly, with a series of long breaths. This was a Val she hadn't seen—the side Val had tried to hide, buried beneath the distraction of flirtatious bravado. Now, half-invisible in the blackness of the cave, she was the full picture of a soldier, her muscular, armored body radiating confidence even as she frowned at the mystery before them. She was beautiful and terrifying.

Val was here to bring death and she looked the part.

Nicole shifted and hugged herself in the damp darkness. After several long seconds, Val's gaze shifted to Nicole. It gripped her as firmly as a hand. The steel in her eyes shone bright and hard in the light of her headlamp. "I'd send you right back up that damn tunnel if I had any faith you wouldn't just pop right back out of it."

Nicole grinned at her. "You'd have to waste a lot of time carrying me bodily back to the cabin. Let alone disabling my plane while you were at it."

Her levity faltered as Val held her gaze unrelentingly. Silence stretched between them, heartbeats passing in the dim, silent cave. Tension coiled in Nicole's chest. At last Val dropped her gaze.

"Fuck." She kicked at the now-dry ground at her feet. "You realize we're probably both going to die."

A protective fire burned in the depths of Val's eyes. "I want you to live a full life, flying to your heart's content between Reggie and Jack and Jackie and eating those goddamn incredible fritters for the rest of your days, appreciating a thousand perfect skies, not dying in this *vakking* horrible shit show of an alien hive. This isn't your fight. You don't need to be here." She stepped closer. "I want you with me, but I don't want you here. You understand that, don't you?"

"Of course I do," Nicole said, willing herself to forge ahead. "But how could I enjoy those skies, how could I live in the shadow of this mountain without always wondering what had happened to you? Every time I looked up, I'd be reminded of letting you march to your death while I stood by and did nothing." She took a deep breath, willing her fear to subside long enough to get the words out. "I told myself I wouldn't abandon you. That's as true now as it was when I picked you up from the ground outside the cabin."

"You don't owe me this for shooting me."

"You know that's not what I mean." She stepped closer, grasping Val's hand and entwining their fingers. "I don't know what this is, or *why*, but I can't just let you go."

"Nicole," Val sighed, her military mask cracking, "I feel it, too, but it's not worth you dying."

"Can't I be the judge of what is or isn't worth my own life?"

Val held her gaze, searching, and Nicole held her breath as the contemplation stretched endlessly into the dark and silence of the cave.

"Okay," Val said at last. "Yes."

The grip around Nicole's heart snapped so abruptly that she blinked back tears. She hadn't realized, until Val relented, that she'd been deathly afraid of being sent away again, of being denied the chance to see this through to the end. Of being denied the chance to spend every, imperfect second she could with Val, even if it was her end. She probably *was* going to die, but if so it would be while helping this mysterious warrior she couldn't seem to let go of.

"Thank you," she said breathlessly, and kissed her.

For the briefest of moments Val stiffened in surprise. Then Val's arms were around her, pulling their bodies together, and Nicole sensed in her grasp the same sudden, furious desperation that drove her own actions. It was the last thing they should be doing, deep in an enemy lair with death hanging over their shoulder, but this intangible, relentless pull, strong enough to draw her into the darkness beneath a mountain and freed by her relief at being allowed to stay, took rein. Her heart lifted just as it had the first time she looked out the window, alone at the controls, and watched the ground fall away from her airplane. The same release, shot through with adrenaline, burned through her. The sensation was wild and powerful and somehow, despite the unfathomably inappropriate setting, also completely and unutterably *right*. Whatever befell them in this dark, dying realm beneath the Earth, she'd made the right choice. She would face this with Val.

Val smiled as their lips parted. Her eyes sparkled within the shadows cast by her headlamp. "*Not* rescuing you is already infinitely better."

Nicole laughed softly into their lingering embrace. She could go on kissing Val forever, enemy lair be damned, until the whole thing crumbled around them. Even as she thought it, though, Val stepped back. The chill of the hive rushed back into the space between them as the soldier reasserted herself. Val's expression hardened. "I'd love to carry on, but we *absolutely* need to focus now."

Nicole nodded, the words quelling the flutter in her chest with a new wave of anxiety. She squeezed back against Val's grip and willed her hands to still. She had to trust the soldier behind that grasp to lead them if she had any chance of making it back up that tunnel. If *they* were going to make it back up the tunnel.

"We need to locate the queen. Then, we place this"—Val lifted a shoulder to indicate her pack—"where a blast will collapse the cavern around her."

Oh God, we're going to blow ourselves up. Nicole's heart skipped a beat.

"No queen, no hive, no swarm. You'll have to stay back and cover me. If you see I've been spotted by a Sh'keth, you'll probably get one shot before it's on me. It'll be fast as fuck." She gripped Nicole's shoulders. "They're armored, so you have to shoot it in the head if your rifle is going to do any good. Even if you're not sure the shot is clean, go for it. I can survive a gunshot," she arched an eyebrow wryly, "but not if a Sh'keth lays me open first."

Nicole nodded again, trying not to imagine Val dying a horrific death before her eyes. Then what would she do? Fight? Flee? There wouldn't be much point in the latter if what Val had said about a Protector's speed was true. The visceral image of giant mandibles closing around her sprang into her mind. An involuntary tremor surged through her body, betraying the terror that surged up from her belly at the thought.

Val gripped her shoulders. "You have to shoot. I trust you. Okay?"

"Okay," she whispered, unsteady.

"I'll signal for you to wait when we find the right spot. If there's cover, take it, but if not just hang back in the darkness. The Sh'keth won't see you, and the slugs won't feel you unless you make noise."

"Okay," she whispered again.

Jesus. Was she really doing this? Another tremor paralyzed her. Her teeth chattered as her body shook. What the hell was she thinking? She wasn't a soldier. Maybe she should just let Val do her job—Val laid a calming hand against her cheek, breaking the spiral of Nicole's terror. The gesture took her back to the mountainside where she'd sat, alone in her airplane, while the lingering warmth of Val's presence slowly dissipated from her life. Her inexplicable pull to this mysterious, beautiful woman made the thought of walking away horrifying. No, she needed to be here. But God, if something happened to Val…her shoulders rose and fell in a jerking shudder.

"Nicole," Val murmured, waiting for Nicole to meet her gaze in the darkness. "I'll be right there. We're doing this together. We're going to save the *vakking* world, okay? Just you and me. But first we're just going to go for a hike down this cave and see where it leads."

She winked. Nicole laughed feebly.

"You're s-such a jock," she forced past a tremble, but the gesture loosened the noose of fear around her guts. She took a deep breath to steel her resolve.

"Okay," she said steadily, finding the calm at her center, closing her eyes and imagining the calm of a perfect blue sky and a roaring engine waiting to take flight. "Let's save the…vakking world."

Val laughed quietly and squeezed Nicole's shoulder. "I feel right at home."

She moved like a predator on the hunt as they crept farther into the depths of the mountain. The stench rose around them, filling Nicole's nostrils with death and decay until she nearly choked on the putrid air. The heat of the Earth enfolded them, growing as they tread slowly and carefully into the heart of the mountain. Unnatural stillness draped itself over every inch of the crypt-like tunnels.

THROUGH SKY AND STARS

Val ghosted ahead, nearly invisible in the darkness but for her dim headlamp, providing just enough light for them to find footing as they went. The hum of the hive grew louder.

Nicole focused on Val's indistinct silhouette and on putting one foot in front of the other. She gripped the Ruger like a lifeline to still her trembling fingers. Fear leaked through despite her resolve. *Follow Val.*

At last, when she thought she might suffocate in the ghastly heat of the cavern, Val stilled. Something shifted in the dim light ahead. The thrum of slug conversation expanded. She sensed the corridor ahead opening, the walls vanishing from the meager field of Val's light. Val hardly moved but for the rise and fall of her breath, her head cocked and listening. Nicole heard nothing but the labored throb of the giant larvae's weak calls.

Val laid one hand gently but firmly against Nicole's chest. "*Stay,*" she mouthed.

Nicole nodded. *Please come back.*

The light of Val's headlamp danced across the open space ahead. Grotesque white forms reared up in its light, larvae miraculously unaware of the human presence between them. She tried to count the formless, white hulks looming out of the darkness, but the indistinct alien bodies blurred in the bobbing light. Too many, but nothing firm. No giant mandibles, no buzzing of giant wings or clacking of pointed forelegs. Her grip on the Ruger relaxed infinitesimally.

Nicole listened to the voices of the colony as Val made her way across the vast expanse. If she closed her eyes, suppressing the urge to shudder at the sight before her, they sounded...*pathetic.* Sad. Their sonorous tones crested and fell as if they drifted on some miserable, hopeless sea. Her subconscious seized on the notion, thoughts snagging on a tenuous recollection, until recognition surged through her. They sounded like *whales.* Like a pod of melancholy humpbacks drifting in a cold, heartless ocean. She blinked, the familiar context ripping away the picture of vicious alien killers in a heartbeat, and with a start she realized that *nothing* she'd seen so far suggested these creatures would harm her. What she'd seen and heard were starving beings, desperate for a meager meal, lamenting a pitiful existence as the colony died around them.

• 161 •

Val reached the far wall and knelt. Removing her pack in one swift motion, she installed the explosives with cool efficiency and turned back toward Nicole, in whose gut a remorseful foreboding was settling like lead. These creatures didn't deserve to die. They were nothing but the last gasps of a faltering outpost abandoned by their kind. She couldn't—

Val stopped halfway across the room and flicked her headlamp to a higher setting. Nicole's breath caught on a surge of adrenaline, fight ready to triumph over flight, but Val merely turned, casting the bright beam in a slow survey of the great chamber. Nicole stifled a gasp as the scope of it unfolded in their vision. Hundreds of larvae shuffled slowly about the vast room, humming their aquatic songs, chorusing their misery into the unforgiving darkness.

Val's headlamp lingered on the pitch darkness of a gaping opening in the far wall of the chamber. Nicole's heart lurched at the sight of massive cocoons flanking it, easily thirty feet long and wreathed in resinous fibers as thick as pine roots, the implications of their horrific scale warring against the tide of pity rising in her heart. Yet even she could tell that no monsters would emerge from these; the fibers were spotted and scarred with dark mold while foul, black liquid seeped between them and dripped to the floor in glutinous puddles. Val stood for a moment, studying the scene with hands on hips, then turned and resumed her careful return.

Nicole jerked at a twitch of motion in the corner of her eye. One second, Val was making her way across the cavern, unfettered, and in the next a black shape heaved itself from the gloom with a screech like a thousand locusts bursting from the earth. Nicole's breath froze in her lungs, a wave of terror paralyzing her as the monster fell upon Val. The sea of larvae writhed spasmodically away from the fight as they dispersed like oil on water, opening a gap around the combatants. The cavern erupted in a cacophony of low, anxious keening. *Jesus, it's fast.* Val leapt to the side and rolled away from the thrashing mandibles, coming up with a knife in hand. *That's it???* Nicole's mind railed at Val. *You brought a knife to fight a giant fucking alien ant!*

The beast darted in, Nicole hardly able to follow its rapid movement, and Val let out a pained gasp as a red gash opened in her forearm. The sound ripped Nicole from her terrified stupor.

THROUGH SKY AND STARS

She raised the rifle and tried to take aim. Her rifle wavered, bobbing in the darkness, and frustration burned through her. The thing never stilled, rearing and prancing as Val ducked and rolled, unable to get past the flashing blades. The vague forms of Val's kata were visible as she wove between the alien limbs. Her knife arced out, slicing through the air in a lethal flow, but deflected harmlessly off alien armor.

"*Shit*," Nicole hissed as she willed an opening to form. *Shit, shit, shit,* if she took a shot and missed, she'd have given away her position for nothing. It was clear, though, that Val wouldn't last long against the thing. She just needed it to *stop*. She needed to see it fully. It just needed to—"Stop!"

The command rang out of her lungs almost before she realized what she was doing. *And it worked.* Val froze. The giant fucking alien ant froze. And then it turned its multifaceted eyes on her and *flew*.

She had maybe three seconds before it cleared the distance. Val's headlamp, behind and below, lit Nicole's impending doom in a terrible spotlight. It *was* wearing armor! Val cried out and launched herself into an all-out sprint toward the cavern entrance. But now Nicole had a clear shot, a clear view of the gaps in the armor, of the blades glinting on its forelegs, and the blur of its wings as they battered the air. She pulled the trigger.

A screech rent the cavern and it fell. It landed with a gut-wrenching *crunch* of crushing carapace, shrieking, and Val fell upon it, leaping onto its back with her knife held high. She raised her fist in the killing blow.

And stopped short as a guttural rumble shook the cavern.

The larvae flowed toward the opening in the far wall with a groan like an ice dam bursting. The Protector's angry shriek tumbled into a low, gritty growl as its struggle abruptly ceased. Val herself settled into a defensive crouch as her headlamp landed on the far wall like a spotlight.

The queen.

Nicole gasped, the fear and adrenaline of the fight swept away like so much dust as the mother of the hive emerged ponderously from the darkness. She was *beautiful*. Her huge, purple eyes swam with opaline swirls and her deep, indigo carapace, easily thirty feet in length, was painted in lovingly intricate, white runes that circled and danced in patterns incomprehensible and stunning to human eyes. Her small wings, tucked up against her body, fluttered like silken kites that sparkled in the bright light of Val's headlamp. They twitched in agitation as the great body rose laboriously from her resting place. Her eyes stared as she approached, but Nicole sensed no malice—instead a weary, aggrieved plea was nearly palpable in the great gaze. As she came closer Nicole noted vast, dull patches of her beautiful body were worn thin, the runes faded and the shell mottled with black, creeping scars. A leg emerged from one of the diseased regions, dragging pathetically behind the otherwise magnificent body. Nicole's throat tightened. *She's dying.*

The queen's warrior offspring slunk down, forelegs washing themselves nervously, looking for all the world like a child caught misbehaving. Nicole could clearly see, now, where her bullet had struck its head, leaving a dark streak from which a thick, yellow fluid seeped. Val stood over the creature, knife clutched in her right hand, blood dripping from the fingers of her left, her eyes bright with the suicidal fire of a final sacrifice. She hunched like a cornered wolf coiling her power for a final, killing strike.

"Val," Nicole said, "*Wait.*"

Val turned her head toward Nicole, but her eyes never left the alien queen. Her shoulders heaved with rapid breathing. "We have to do this."

"No," Nicole said simply, calmly, her fear dissolving into a sea of certainty as the Protector lay quietly at Val's feet. "We don't."

Val growled like a caged animal. A universe of pain Nicole could never imagine rippled in the air between them. The struggle between mercy and vengeance played out in stark shadows and trembling muscles. Val's knife rose slightly, then stopped. The muscles in her jaw stood out in the vicious shadows of her headlamp.

"You don't understand," she ground through gritted teeth.

The queen stopped several long paces away, her forelegs stretched wide, her great head tilted to the floor. The larvae had gone quiet. The cavern was still, silent, echoing with possibility. "Val, *look.* She isn't going to hurt you, or us."

THROUGH SKY AND STARS

Val's fingers flexed on the hilt of her knife but she remained where she stood. A drop of blood fell from the fingers of her left hand, a black diamond arcing to the ground in the dim light.

"Look at them, Val. They're dying without your help. They're *miserable*. What if...what if we help them, instead of killing them?"

Val sputtered, her eyes leaving the queen long enough to cast scornful knives at Nicole. "Are you insane? This hive will destroy the Earth."

Nicole took a deep breath. "No. This hive will destroy the Earth *if we do nothing*." The words poured from her as fast as her racing mind could form them. "This is the turning point, Val. If you kill them the war starts again when whoever left them here comes back to find we've murdered a struggling hive. Violence begets violence. What if, instead, they come back to find allies? Friends? Then it's not war. It's peaceful contact."

"No," Val spat, but the word fell from her lips almost as a sob. The stern set of her jaw wavered.

"Val, *please*."

Val shook visibly as a violent tremble took her. Her voice was ragged. "I sacrificed *everything* for this, Nicole."

"I know."

"What if you're wrong?"

Nicole took a deep breath. "Then war is inevitable, and no amount of quantum heroics will change that."

"That's not good enough."

I know. She fought despair. Her eyes danced across the scene, desperate for inspiration. The queen stared patiently back at them, unmoving, almost as if she could understand the words passing between the two humans. Val's labored breathing echoed in the darkness. Violent anticipation poured from her, straining the air around her like the ground before an earthquake, ready to rupture with killing power. Nicole took another calming breath and made up her mind.

She knelt, set the Ruger at her feet, and rose on steady legs that carried her to stand in front of the queen. Val cursed softly behind her. Nicole held her empty hands wide as she approached. Her breath wavered as the sheer scale of the queen loomed up in front of her, but the enormous, morose eyes watched her calmly. The whisper-thin wings lay still upon the queen's back. *Do you miss taking to the sky?* Nicole wondered as she knelt, stretched out one hand, and gently laid it upon a massive foreleg.

She nearly jerked back in surprise when her palm met the warm, leathery shell. She'd expected cold, hard carapace, not a body radiating heat. Despite the desperate state to which her realm had fallen, the alien queen radiated life.

A giant leg rose slowly, ponderously, and came to rest, paper-light, on Nicole's shoulder. The purr of an incomprehensible language filled the cavern, one wizened voice joined by a hundred young ones, a song that rose, and rose, into an endless crescendo that permeated first the air, then the rock, then settled into her soul. Hundreds of voices rose in a harmony of welcome, of *hope*. Nicole lost herself in the oceanic tide as it rose ever onward, and as the song crested, Nicole looked up into the massive, ancient face and realized that her cheeks were wet with tears.

A rustle punctuated the fading notes of the chorus as Val appeared at her side, the tension sloughed from her body, her skin pale in the dim light. Her gloveless hand lay atop Nicole's. Their gazes locked. The moment held, fragile, the violence dispelled like a puff of snow bursting into bright sunshine. Tentative hope permeated the air.

"It was you," Val whispered. "You're the reason why this time and place were important. Not because it was when I would succeed…but because it was when I *wouldn't*."

Val wavered. She dropped to her knees. Then her eyes rolled back in her head and she crumpled to the ground with a barely audible sigh.

PART V: *STALL*

THROUGH SKY AND STARS

CHAPTER FIFTEEN

August 7, 1996, 1:00 p.m.
First Sh'keth Hive, Kenai Mountains, Earth

"*Val!*"

Anguish roared through Nicole when Val folded to the ground like a ragdoll. She forgot the queen, forgot the hive, forgot the reason Val was injured in the first place—her world collapsed to the sight of Val sprawled, lifeless, in the darkness. Her heart constricted in terror. Nothing mattered but Val. Nicole fell to her knees beside her, visions of their first night by the cabin skittering through her memory. "Oh, Val. Please. Val."

Her fingers glistened red as she lifted Val's wrist. She'd seen the Protector's brutal slash from afar, but Val's strength and rage had hidden the severity of the awful wound. The gash was neat but deep, Val's lifeblood leeching from it to dribble onto the unforgiving stone beneath her. The reflections of Nicole's frantic movements flickered in the pool already gathered beneath Val where she lay. "Oh, God."

Panic threatened to freeze her in place. There was already so much blood. Val's skin was clammy and pale. She looked almost— No. Nicole wouldn't think about that. She could prevent that. She just had to stop the bleeding. But her first aid kit was in the plane... she shook her head, dispelling the fog of terror. She could do this.

She threw her jacket aside and ripped off her flannel, then folded the end of a sleeve into a makeshift bandage. She pressed it to the wound, then tied the rest of the sleeve around Val's arm as tightly as she could. Val groaned softly, eyelids fluttering. "I'm here," she whispered. "I've got you."

With the bleeding stanched—temporarily—she considered her next move. Dread settled into her gut as she realized that putting pressure on the wound had been the easy part. Everything else required getting Val to the airplane. Up the tunnel. Up a long, dark, slope slick with algae. Nicole looked toward the passageway they'd come down, invisible in the blackness beyond the circle of the headlamp, and imagined the long trek. Her heart fell. Following Val down the passage had seemed to last hours. Simply carrying Val for a few minutes, that first night when she'd moved her into the cabin, had taken most of Nicole's strength. "Shit," she whispered.

This was going to hurt.

She didn't have a choice.

She donned Val's headlamp, put her jacket back on, and lifted Val into her arms.

The injured Protector skittered back as Nicole stood. Her fear long exhausted, Nicole simply paused as the giant insect shifted restlessly in front of her. The blades it had used to fight Val were gone, disappeared while Nicole treated her. Now its wings shimmered, vibrating as they rose and fell in a deliberate, measured pattern. Was it trying to say something? It danced back and forth anxiously, then paused, head canted, and stared at her with dark, gleaming eyes. A drop of amber fluid dripped from the wound she'd inflicted. Shame cut through her. She looked away. "I'm sorry for hurting you," she said, even though it couldn't understand.

She started up the path, muscles already burning. Giant larvae lumbered around her, rolling into the circle of her light only to fade back into the shadows like whales sinking into the depths of the sea. Their songs echoed in the chasm. The Protector raced ahead of her like a shepherd, herding the huge creatures out of her way. *Helping her.* It was almost invisible, flickering in and out of view as it efficiently cleared her path. Only the thrum of beating wings and the occasional clattering of pointed legs on stone revealed its position. Nicole, herded as well as the larvae, followed the path the Protector created.

Her arms screamed. Her legs shook. By the time she reached the decaying carapace of their earlier hiding place, her breath came in ragged gasps. Sweat stung her eyes. She looked at the grate, several feet off the ground, and whimpered at the impossible thought of lifting Val into the opening. Frustrated tears welled up, hot and bitter, to burn a path down her cheeks. "Val, wake up," she whispered, hoarse. "I can't carry you out of here."

Val's head rolled against her shoulder.

She stumbled, then halted, lowering Val to the ground with trembling limbs. She groaned in relief as she let go of Val's weight. "Val," the name came out as a sob, "please."

The last time they'd stood here, she'd accepted that they may never make it back to this spot. Expected it. But for one brief, shining moment of unadulterated joy, she'd thought that they would make it out together. They'd averted catastrophe. *Together.* In that blink of an eye she'd thought they might have the chance to share more than that one, abbreviated kiss. That they might make a life together. Now here they were, back where that kiss had crystallized her feelings for Val, and she may still lose her after all.

"Val," she pleaded again, but Val remained motionless.

The Protector appeared, startling Nicole as it zipped into the bubble of light around them. It settled next to her and leaned close, wings trembling. Nudged her shoulder with a foreleg. Gestured.

A ray of hope shot through Nicole. "Yes!"

Summoning the last of her strength, she lifted Val onto the giant creature's back.

"Thank you," she whispered to it. She lay one hand on the carapace, amazed again at the warmth that met her touch. The giant wings settled. The creature lowered its head and knelt, slightly— almost a bow. Then it straightened, opened the grate to the tunnel beyond, and headed toward the pinprick of light gleaming in the distance.

"One more push," Nicole told herself, then followed as fast as her bedraggled body allowed.

When she at last knelt over Val to properly dress the wound in the warmth and stability of her home, the slow seep of blood had ceased and Val still breathed.

It seemed a dream. A nightmare. A confusing wash of elation, horror, fear, triumph…tears welled up, buoyed by worry and pride as she looked down at Val's strong features, soft in sleep. Her insides knotted as she tried to sort her emotions into some tidy bin of human comprehension. There was too much. And still more to come.

Nicole tucked the blankets around Val with weariness that urged her to simply lie down on the floor and let unconsciousness sweep her away. The adrenaline and fear faded slowly, leaving weak tremors in their wake, and she was afraid that if she tried to climb the ladder to the loft she'd end up breaking her neck.

Val moaned softly, almost whimpering, in her sleep. Nicole cupped her face with one hand. "We did it," she whispered. "You can rest."

She dragged herself to the woodstove and lit enough of a fire to warm the cabin, hauled her aching body to the medicine cabinet and downed a double dose of ibuprofen. Her reflection stared back at her from the mirror, eyes red-rimmed, face caked in black grime, loose strands of hair falling in every direction. She looked like she felt. Unable to face the prospect of a ladder, she lay down next to Val and fell into dreamless sleep.

THROUGH SKY AND STARS

CHAPTER SIXTEEN

August 7, 1996, 8:00 p.m.
Kenai Mountains, Alaska, Earth

Nicole rose slowly back to consciousness with the blanket tucked warmly up to her chin. The fire popped. Its heat suffused her body with a delicious glow. A wordless sigh of pleasure escaped her and she stretched...then instantly regretted it as every muscle in her body screamed in protest. Her contented sigh turned into a groan of bodily ache.

Quick footsteps crossed the floor. *Val.* Relief surged through her. Nicole opened her eyes as Val dropped to her knees by the couch, the fingers of her left hand tracing Nicole's chin, her gray eyes dark with concern.

"I'm here. Are you okay?" she murmured.

Nicole smiled and grasped Val's hand, pulling it against her chest. "Yes," she said as relief washed through her. "I pulled every muscle in my body getting you back here, but God am I happy to see you up and about."

Val's answering smile was small. Her eyes dropped to the floor guiltily. "I'm sorry."

"Don't be," Nicole murmured. "But..." The events of the previous day surged back as her sleepiness faded. "How are you... okay? You lost so much blood. Val, I thought—" she broke off, running one hand along Val's forearm to the clean bandage. She'd cleaned and rewrapped the wound while Nicole slept. "How did you survive that?"

• 173 •

"We—" Val broke off sharply. "*I* have nanites in my bloodstream. They drive clotting to keep me from bleeding to death if I'm wounded in battle. They're not as strong as the salve—it takes different nans to close a wound, so we need to go back for my pack before I'll be able to use this hand much." She grimaced, looking down at her handiwork. "They did exactly what they're supposed to, though, which is keep me from dying. And they've accelerated rebuilding my blood volume to some extent. But I expect I lost a good deal of them, so I can't count on them working too well in the future."

"So a different…flavor of your magical Neosporin?"

"Essentially."

A small laugh escaped Nicole. "I don't know if this will ever stop feeling insane."

She looked Val over. Though she moved with purpose, her normally rich, bronze skin was pale. Dark circles under her eyes belied the surety of her touch. They were both filthy with the grime of the cave, layered beneath the sweat and mud of her ordeal on the mountainside. When Nicole lifted her own hands, the nails were crusted with grit and traces of Val's dried blood. She shuddered. They needed to go back up there, but they needed to heal a bit, first.

She sat up and groaned as every muscle in her body protested violently. Meanwhile, her stomach threatened to consume her from the inside out. Val held out a steadying hand, her grip strong as ever. "How the heck are you not keeling over? This is so unfair."

Val's gaze was serious as she looked Nicole over. "You wouldn't think so if you'd also been through this kind of thing before. But I also ate all of the Pop-Tarts while you slept."

Nicole considered her pantry with a straight face. "All eight boxes?"

She stood, creaking like an old crone, and Val enfolded her in steady, strong arms. "Only seven and a half," she said blandly into Nicole's shoulder as they embraced. "I saved you two."

The halfhearted reply hardly tempted her to joust back. She was content to let it lie, wrapped in Val's arms and leaning into her impossibly solid presence. She rested her face against Val's neck and let relief surge through her. They were here. They were back, together. They'd lived. Val had given everything of herself to set events in motion that, Nicole was sure, had averted the disastrous future from which she'd come. She was fiercely, irrationally proud of someone she'd known for such a short time. They'd *won*. She thought back to their desperate, abbreviated kiss in the cavern, when they'd both expected it to be both first and last. Her breath caught as the feel of Val's lips roared back into her memory.

"Val, we did it," she murmured, pulling them closer, and pressed a kiss to the skin of Val's throat.

Taut muscle tensed beneath her lips. Val's embrace tightened, pulling a murmur from Nicole as strong fingers dug into her back, and her rational mind dissolved into every excruciating inch over which their bodies touched. She ran her fingers into the soft hair at the back of Val's neck. *Yes. This.* The inkling had drawn tighter with each second since she'd watched Val walk away that first day on the riverbank, had wound within her until it pulled her into the darkness beneath a mountain, and the chord between them had been a glimmer of hope in the blackness. Always Val's mission had stood between them, first in omission, then in purpose. But the mission was over, the barriers gone. Nicole pressed into Val's firm body, relishing the solidity of her presence, and let herself want the mysterious woman who'd materialized from the wilderness a lifetime ago.

For a moment Val stilled, arms wrapped tightly around Nicole, and her eyes squeezed shut as a breath rose and fell. A muscle twitched in her jaw as Nicole traced it with her fingertips. Her lips parted as Nicole kissed them, softly, exploring, and a soft breath trembled out.

And then Val moved.

Nicole gasped. She lifted her, pivoting, and corded muscle flexed beneath Nicole's hands as Val pushed her roughly against the wall. Her hips pinned them in place, an avalanche of need crushing their bodies together. Val's thigh threaded between Nicole's legs, insistent, and she arched into the contact with a cry of surprise and pleasure. "God, Val—"

Her words caught on a breath as Val rocked into her. Val dipped her head, nipping at the skin of Nicole's neck, and she grunted softly as Nicole threaded her fingers into her hair. Val tugged the clasp of her jeans open and slipped her hand inside.

Nicole hardly recognized the moan that escaped her as Val's touch grazed bare flesh. Caught in the frantic rush of heat pouring through her body, Nicole struggled to keep up with the faultlines rupturing between them. Every nerve in her body cried out for the feel of Val's hands. Wasn't this what she wanted? Yet somewhere, a warning bell rang. Val wouldn't meet her eyes. Her touch, explosive as it was, was targeted and efficient, a calculated drive toward pleasure alone. The muscles in her shoulders rippled with tension when Nicole ran her hands across them. Worst of all, she was silent, her ragged breathing the only sound as she worked beneath soft fabric. Disquiet writhed through the searing want in Nicole's belly.

"Val—" the name was half plea, half gasp, her head falling back as Val touched her. Another second she'd be lost in the dip of Val's fingers.

She cupped Val's face, desperate for an anchor, and her blood chilled at what she saw. Confirmation settled in her gut. Val's brow was furrowed, eyes screwed shut, and the sharp lines of her jaw were rigid. She looked at war.

"*Val,*" Nicole forced out, sharply, and Val's eyes flew open.

The emptiness in them ripped Nicole from the fog of desire. She stilled, gripping Val's firm jaw in one hand, and traced the line of Val's agonized features with her fingertips. "Val," she whispered, gently, as if beckoning a scared animal from hiding. "Come back."

Val blinked and shuddered. Storm clouds swirled in her eyes. She shook her head, looked down, dropped her chin as if to capture Nicole's lips in a rough kiss. "No. You—"

"*Val,*" she repeated, insistent, and tightened her grip on Val's chin.

Val stilled at last. They hung together at the inflection point as Val's ragged breathing cut through the silence of the cabin.

Nicole recognized the anguish that had haunted Val since that first morning by the fire. It railed against the cage of Val's stiff shoulders, her clenched jaw and trembling breath. Nicole traced Val's brow with her thumb, smoothing the harsh lines etched there. "I won't do this without you."

THROUGH SKY AND STARS

Val trembled. Her eyelids fluttered closed, droplets gathering on her lashes, and her lips parted in a pained gasp. "Nicole," she breathed, "I'm sorry. I need…I can't…"

"It's okay," Nicole murmured, wrapping her arms around Val's shoulders as they heaved with a tremulous breath. "It's okay."

Val's fingers drifted to the simple chain around her neck, where Nicole had assumed dog tags hung beneath her shirt, but Val's touch lay across three metal rings, interwoven, a short chain of interlocking finish glinting in the firelight. A necklace. Given to Val by someone else, somewhere else, in a universe she could never return to. The token of her life *before,* a tiny object imbued with an entire lifetime that Nicole would never know, left behind to save a world and a people *she* had never known. The memories lay naked over Val's heart at last, cool beneath Nicole's fingers as she laced them between Val's, and Nicole finally understood the immeasurable grief that had lain dormant beneath Val's smile. *God, the cost.*

Val jerked at the touch but didn't pull away. A muscle jumped in her jaw. She'd hidden the single, simple reminder of home so well, shrouded her grief and loneliness beneath bravado and purpose, but she could no longer hide the torment. Devastation spilled across her features through the spreading cracks in her facade.

Nicole's heart constricted with guilt. How could she have failed to see it? "Val, I'm so—"

"*I erased them,*" the anguished words burst from Val's lips, her walls crumbling before Nicole's eyes. "I *erased them,*" she sobbed, crumpling back into Nicole's arms.

Nicole held her tightly, helpless as shuddering sobs shook them both. The grief she'd glimpsed before came roaring free, thundering past whatever barriers Val had used to hold it at bay, and raw suffering spilled from her like the blood she'd shed mere hours before. Her weight sagged into Nicole's embrace. They settled slowly to the floor, Val clinging to Nicole like a lifeline in a storm.

Powerless against the tide of anguish, she simply held Val and rocked her slowly, murmuring soothingly into Val's hair. She couldn't stop the flood, couldn't diminish its power, but she could be a harbor against which the storm crashed and broke. She rubbed Val's back, tracing gentle, unconscious circles across her shoulders, and waited for the hurricane to pass. She thought about the first night Val lay here, unconscious, lit by the firelight and full of mysterious, dangerous potential. How could she have imagined what lay beneath the purpose and power in those eyes? The depth of her grief was unfathomable. Nicole would never comprehend the utter finality of the tragedy that had befallen her—just as she could never comprehend the infinite expanse of creation, she could never fathom its loss. Yet as she sat there, she wished desperately to draw the hurt into herself, to pull the darkness back from Val's soul.

At last Val quieted, curled against Nicole's chest, one hand clutching the buttons of her flannel. A log shifted in the fireplace with a pop and hiss. Val's breathing softened to a gentle whisper, the rise and fall of her chest the only movement as the last of the flames sank into embers. Nicole stroked the soft hair on the back of her head. "I'm sorry," she said softly, afraid to disturb the tentative reprieve in Val's emotions. "I'm so sorry, Val. I would fly to the ends of the Earth and back again if I could take this pain from you."

Val sniffled, stirred and released her grip on Nicole's shirt. She circled her arm around Nicole, instead, and settled her face into the dip of Nicole's shoulder. "It's better with you here," she said softly.

A lump of bittersweet happiness rose in Nicole's throat. She swallowed thickly. "I wouldn't be anywhere else."

Cautiously, she asked, "Are they really gone? You said it was uncertain."

Val tensed in her arms before exhaling a shaky breath. "If I'd saved them…" her voice broke. A breath hissed through her teeth, her fist clenched at Nicole's side. "If I'd saved them, they'd tell me. Signal me. Somehow. They sent me with an entire ship…they must be able to send a message. But there's nothing."

Nicole filed the mention of a ship away for later reference as hot tears slipped from Val's chin. They traced a silent path of anguish down Nicole's skin. "Fucking *statistics*. Models. Who the hell knows whether they were right? Was I ever going to save them? Maybe Astrey made it up. Maybe it was always impossible."

"But you stopped the war."

"Did I?" Bitterness poisoned Val's tone. "How will we know? We'll both be dead long before the colony vessel returns."

THROUGH SKY AND STARS

"You did it," Nicole said firmly. She had to shut that line of thinking down fast. "You saw the queen. She greeted us peacefully. And that Protector helped me bring you back." She shook her head. "We're allies. They helped us, we'll help them. That, I won't question."

Val fell silent, either unwilling or unable to argue. Nicole tightened her embrace. One slow breath at a time, Val's anguish evaporated into the stillness of the cabin. Nicole reluctantly disentangled their embrace.

"Come on," she said, and Val followed their joined hands as they climbed to their feet. "You'll feel better without an inch of grime coating your body."

Val hesitated, then leaned into her, folding her arms between them and settling her face against Nicole's neck. Nicole enfolded her in an embrace, content to let Val move at her own pace. Eventually, Val released a long sigh into her shoulder. "I'm so tired, Nicole."

"It's okay," she said softly. "You're allowed to be."

Val relaxed into Nicole's touch before drawing a deep, shuddering breath. Nicole tightened her embrace. "One day at a time."

Val nodded into her shoulder. "I know."

"One foot in front of the other."

Val murmured wordless assent.

"One Pop-Tart at a time."

Val paused. Then she scoffed, softly, and the small laugh against Nicole's neck was the greatest victory in the world.

· 180 ·

Chapter Seventeen

August 8, 1996, 7:45 a.m.
Kenai Mountains, Alaska, Earth

Nicole woke the next morning with Val pressed against her back, one arm curled protectively around her middle. Neither of them had wanted to be alone at the conclusion of a day wrought with physical and emotional fatigue; they'd collapsed side by side into Nicole's bed and fallen promptly to sleep. Now Nicole lay as still as possible, fully aware that Val would awaken as soon as she even *thought* about moving, and savored the closeness. In their days together Val had unfailingly awakened before her, always up with the dawn and her kata. As much as Nicole relished waking up snug in a warm loft, she would gladly trade a thousand warm cabins for the heat of the body next to her. She smiled and, succumbing to her own weakness, wrapped her hand around Val's and pulled the muscular arm tighter around herself.

Val stirred, snuggling into Nicole's back as she murmured sleepily into Nicole's hair. "Pop-Tarts?"

"Oh my God," Nicole laughed, warmth spreading through her at the realization that Val had been lying similarly awake and still. "Do you ever think about anything else?"

Val's chuckle vibrated through them both. "Sometimes," she said as her hand separated from Nicole's. She ran her hand along Nicole's side, settling in the curve of her hip. Her fingers played lightly across the small expanse of exposed skin she found beneath the hem of Nicole's shirt. The playful caress turned Nicole's bemused chuckle into a sharp intake of breath.

"But I've been awake for a while," Val murmured, "with nothing but my thoughts and my stomach to distract me."

Nicole rolled over and traced the hard plane of Val's abs with her fingertips. They tensed beneath her touch. She thought about the morning, a lifetime ago, when the sensation of being pressed against those very muscles had been more arresting than the threat of walking into a mauling. Val's breath rose and fell beneath her hand.

"Your stomach *is* very distracting," she managed with a smile.

This time she felt the impending kiss like the first, imperceptible drop of a wing before a stall, the promise of imminent release to an inevitability she'd been holding back. When their lips met, the simmering longing in her gut unwound with a rush of breath. Val pulled her close with a soft, satisfied groan and buried her fingers in Nicole's hair. The reverence in her touch sang through Nicole's veins. *This* was the Val she wanted, the woman beneath the mountain of control.

Val rolled on top of her, their legs entwining as her weight settled over Nicole's hips. God, she was an avalanche. An impossibly hot, sexy avalanche. The absurdity of the thought bubbled through her pleasure, a soft laugh mingling with her gasp as Val's lips touched her throat. Val paused to quirk an eyebrow over bemused eyes.

A flush warmed Nicole's face. She smiled sheepishly. "Sorry," she said. "I...may in fact be getting carried away by how fantastically buff you are."

The answering sparkle in Val's eyes portended mischief. "You're saying you want a demonstration?"

She raised herself into a plank and lifted the delicious pressure of her body away, hovering with a teasing gleam in her eyes.

"Jock," Nicole murmured with fond exasperation. "I'm very impressed, but that's not quite what I had in mind." She wrapped her legs around Val's hips and attempted to pull her back down on top of her. Instead, she lifted herself out of bed with a surprised laugh.

Val chuckled in return and relaxed her arms. They fell back to the mattress in a tangle of limbs and laughter. "I'm glad you're feeling better," Nicole said through her giggles.

Val paused. Her smile was small, ghosts of sadness at its edges, but her eyes were clear as she looked down at Nicole. "Always, with you."

She dipped her head and captured Nicole's lips in another kiss, drowning the moment of tenderness in a swift rise of heat. Nicole let her hands wander, exploring the hard planes of Val's back, and luxuriated in the ripple of muscle beneath her touch. Val was gorgeous, and she needed more. More touch, more skin. She slid her hands beneath Val's shirt, tugging it to her shoulders. Yes, this was—she touched warm metal at the nape of Val's neck. The links shifted, breaking free of friction to slither over Val's shoulder, and the necklace dropped into the space between them. The metal rings landed with a soft clink against Nicole's chest.

Val jerked and her breath caught in her throat. Her eyes closed. She stilled, shuddering, and visibly struggled against a sudden riptide of emotions.

Concern overrode Nicole's desire. She wrapped both arms around Val and pulled her into a tight embrace.

"It's okay," she whispered fervently as Val's breath hitched. "It's okay."

Nicole held Val until her ragged breathing calmed. "I'm sorry," Val eventually whispered.

Nicole shook her head. "Don't be. You have nothing to be sorry for."

Val shifted against her, hugging her tight. "Fuck," she hissed. "I can't control this. One second, I'm fine, and then something makes me think of Kass and it just *hits* me like a goddamn freighter. It feels like I should be able to turn around and see her there. To me, she was just there. And now I'll probably never..." her words trailed off. A tear dropped against her skin, cool.

"Sorry," Val repeated, hoarse.

Nicole tightened her embrace and turned the new name over in her mind. In time, she'd ask. "Never apologize for missing them."

Val sighed, a long breath seemingly laced with a hundred memories. She shook her head into Nicole's shoulder. "You're incredible."

A gentle, incredulous laugh burst from Nicole's lips, although she couldn't help the warm glow of happiness that coursed through her.

TESSA CROFT

"Your whole life has been turned upside-down," Val continued, "and yet here you are, unfailingly worried about *me* and always setting your own needs aside."

Nicole made a soft, incredulous noise. "My current 'needs' are about as meaningful as a snowball in hell relative to yours, Val."

Val propped herself up on one elbow. The tenderness in her gaze made Nicole's chest tighten. "It's not just that," she said. "You went out of your way to make a wounded stranger welcome in your home. Even when you were pissed as hell at me, you dashed off in the Beav to make sure I was safe. You saved my life even though you were scared half out of your wits in the hive. And then you stopped me from repeating the disaster I was sent here to avert, simply by caring about the creatures I thought I was supposed to kill." She paused, lowering her gaze as she chose her next words. "You have an unbelievable capacity to care."

Nicole averted her eyes, embarrassed by the litany. "You don't get by in the bush without looking out for others. That's just how it is."

Val pushed a lock of hair back from Nicole's face. "Somehow I don't think everyone who lives in the bush would follow a soldier from the future into a cave to destroy a hive of alien monsters, then empathize with the queen of said aliens and end up helping them, instead."

Nicole didn't know what to say to that, so she simply closed her eyes and tilted her face into Val's shoulder. The reality of the last twenty-four hours would take a lifetime to process. Val trailed her fingers idly through Nicole's hair. Her smile faded. "We need to go back up there."

Nicole nodded. "I know. But…what do we do? It's clear they need help, but what? Do you know?"

Val's expression turned inward. "I wasn't exactly at my best, but from what we saw of her, I think we need to fix the ventilation."

"The ventilation?"

"The discoloration of her carapace. The dark, dying patches."

Nicole stared blankly in response. "I don't think I know enough about giant alien ants to understand how you're getting there."

"Sorry." Val leaned in for a quick kiss, sweet enough to dispel Nicole's confusion, fleeting enough to avoid setting her libido on fire again.

Nicole hummed appreciatively as Val leaned back. "I forgive you. Now, you were saying?"

"Have you ever noticed that bugs don't breathe?"

Nicole tilted her head, considering the apparent non sequitur. "I...guess. I never really thought about it."

"They have tubes all over their body that pipe air into their organs. It's not very efficient, since it relies on oxygen diffusing straight into their bodies, so they're highly sensitive to reduced oxygen concentration or any contamination of their air."

Nicole digested this for a moment. For a woman who dealt in the mechanical—carburetors, gears, and spark plugs were more her bailiwick—*oxygen diffusion* was a bit outside her usual realm. "Okay," she said at last, "So if we fix the godawful air down there, she might actually get better?"

Val nodded. "I think so." She paused. "I don't know what happened to the rest of the mature Sh'keth, but they normally maintain the hive. My guess is that something killed most of them off, maybe disease, and the systems fell into disrepair. You may have noticed that I lasted more than ten seconds against that Protector. It wasn't at its fighting best. And if it really is the only one left, it's no wonder the infrastructure of that place is completely *vakked*."

Nicole smiled. "What does that even mean?"

"What?" Val asked, raising one eyebrow.

"*Vakked.*" She said, "You knew it wasn't a word I'd use—you tried to hide it. But you're obviously used to saying it all the time."

Val chuckled. "Well, spacers abhor a vacuum. As slang I guess it's somewhat synonymous with fucked. But without the...potential positive connotations."

Nicole raised a bemused eyebrow. "I see."

"But you know, sometimes I use it as a noun," Val said slowly, as if analyzing the word for the first time. "So I guess it's a word of many uses. But generally bad ones."

"Well," Nicole said, interrupting her contemplation of the curses of the future, "I'm *vakking* hungry. Breakfast?"

"Vakking yes," Val said, then screwed up her face as she realized she'd used the word positively. "Damn."

Nicole smiled and whacked her playfully with a pillow. Val sputtered, chuckling, as Nicole glanced out the small window at the apex of the A-frame. "The weather's foul again," she observed, eyeing the wet, gray patch of forest she could see. "We both need rest. So today, we'll recuperate. After that, as soon as the sky lets us, we'll head back to the hive."

The thought seemed to drag Val back into melancholy. She nodded absently, gaze as cloudy as the weather, and stared sightlessly out the window. Nicole touched her cheek. The shadows fled and Val met her eyes. "I'll be with you every step of the way," she said softly.

Val entwined their fingers. "I'm glad."

CHAPTER EIGHTEEN

August 10, 1996 [Terran Calendar], 1100 hrs.
Kenai Mountains, Alaska, Earth

The foul stench of the cavern grew thicker, slowly congealing around them like a rotting stew as they descended again into the depths of the mountain, and Val relished the toxic air as it invaded her body and mind. The still, dense air whispered of suffering, of death, of battle lost, and her fists clenched around it as the vakking *wrongness* of walking unarmed into the alien cavern skittered up her spine. The runes etched into the walls pulled ghosts from her subconscious. For Nicole's sake she tried to push them back, to trust the woman who'd carried her out of this cave alive and relax into the tenuous peace Nicole's actions had granted them, but five minutes of fragile truce meant nothing against a lifetime of loathing. It surged up in her now like a beast from the darkness, and the barely-healed gash in her wrist burned with it. Her fingers twitched with longing for the solid weight of a mag rifle.

As much as she wanted to resist the hatred as it bubbled up in her, Val drank it in like a desert pauper stumbling upon an oasis. The familiar hatred dulled her grief, gave her tortured heart something other than misery to gnaw on, and offered relief from the days she'd spent struggling to find her way back to the comfort of waking with Nicole in her arms. No matter how hard she'd tried—and *vack*, she'd been trying—she couldn't reclaim those fleeting moments basking in the warm joy of Nicole's affection and the barest hint of satisfaction at an improbable success. When Nicole looked at her she *wanted* to throw herself into this new world. She wanted to give Nicole what they both knew was there. But that trickle of happiness pried open the floodgates of grief, making way for the price of her victory to rip through her chest like explosive decompression, and she wouldn't let the furious tidal wave of anguish eviscerate her again. So she took a step back and put up walls as best she could, even if it was like hiding under a tin roof while a hurricane raged outside. Gingerly, she backed away from that wall to a safe, muted core. She let herself hover at the bottom of that deep, dark lake, suffocating in a world of muted color, caught on the event horizon of a grief that threatened to drown her soul in utter, breathless emptiness.

Part of her knew she'd have to deal with it eventually. The riptide was too strong, the source too cataclysmic, for her to simply lock it away and never look back. She was self-aware enough to know that no human could simply ignore the sort of trauma she'd not only endured, but *caused*. She was guiltily aware that Nicole suffered alongside her, patiently waiting for Val to wrestle the demons she'd wrought, and that alone was reason to pull herself together.

She would, eventually. For now, though, her mission remained incomplete. She swallowed the rage and anguish, wrestled them down beneath the flimsy hatch battening the murky abyss she shied away from, and focused on *why* they had returned to the hive. *One step at a time.* They had a job to do.

The Queen's chamber opened around them in the darkness, invisible but audible as the sound of the larvae resonated through the massive space. The darkness nearly swallowed the beams of their headlamps as the walls spread away from them. Val looked down, half expecting to see a pool of her own, dried blood on the floor, but there was no sign of her anguished final moments in the cavern. Just the warm sea of air and the sonorous rise and fall of alien voices. Val tried not to think about the white bodies surging into the circle of their headlamps before slithering away into the darkness.

"Is that normal?"

Nicole's voice broke into the symphony of alien sound, and the slugs nearest them shifted and shied away from the unfamiliar sensation of humanity in their midst. Nicole swept an arm out, indicating the cocoons flanking the dark recess from which the queen had emerged. The putrid, rotting husks had to be responsible for most of the stench; evil, black liquid oozed from them, pooling on the smooth rock of the floor. Val grimaced, trying hard to suppress the part of her that rejoiced in the sight of death where life ought to flourish.

"Absolutely not," she said. "It's a sign that the queen is too ill to care for her young. Those two will never emerge. The Protector I fought...the one who helped you...I think it's the only one."

Nicole shuddered and crossed her arms, hugging herself against the horrible reality. "And she can't even muster the strength to remove them. How awful."

Chittering erupted in the darkness. Val turned, spotlighting the Protector in question as it approached, and her heartbeat surged ahead of her rational mind. The sight opened a bottomless vessel of nightmare images that poured through her consciousness like water spilled across the deck, scurrying across the surface of her mind to fill every corner. Her own friends' mangled bodies, cut to unrecognizable heaps of flesh and fabric. The screams of humans mowed down like so much chaff. In her mind's eye this creature, this *thing* wanted nothing but to kill her, to run her through just as the one in her nightmares. Cold fear gripped her chest. Panic shot through her as her fingers closed around empty space where her knife should be. This was suicide. This was—Nicole laid a hand on her forearm and squeezed gently. Val blinked. She closed her eyes and drew a long, shuddering breath, forcing herself to release the tension grinding her teeth together. This Protector had helped Nicole drag her unconscious body out of the hive. She owed it her life. *This Protector is your ally.*

The thought couldn't stop the flood of nightmare images. But if Nicole, who'd never met a sentient, alien species could empathize with those dark, reflective eyes...Val could work to replace the awful images with different, better ones. She could *try*. She opened her eyes.

It had stopped several feet away, forelegs spread wide and massive head tilted to the floor, wings lying still against its long,

• 189 •

glistening carapace. A bare carapace, she noted, devoid of even a single rune. In the still light of her headlamp, she took in the scuffs in its armor, the frayed straps and missing fasteners, the poor fit and patchwork of it. Its foreleg blades were retracted into sheathes through which she could see the blades in worn, shabby patches. *It's a child playing soldier in hand-me-downs.* An unexpected pang of sympathy lanced through her distrust.

The Sh'keth's posture was intentional, almost ritual, as it paused before them, but neither she nor Nicole quite knew what to do in response. Seconds passed as the Sh'keth held its pose. Nicole's brow furrowed over thoughtful eyes, her lips pursed. "The queen did this, too," she said slowly, and took a cautious step forward.

Val clenched her fist to quell the urge to reach out and stop Nicole as she gingerly extended a gloved hand. Nicole laid her fingers gently against one extended leg. The Protector relaxed, clearly receiving the acknowledgement it sought, and the shadows beneath it thickened as it dipped its head in a final bow before raising its gaze back to them. Its wings flicked once, twice. The mandibles clicked a rhythmic, expectant beat. Waiting.

Nicole held one hand up, palm out, and the Sh'keth inclined its head. Nicole leaned forward to inspect the gunshot wound she'd inflicted. "I'm sorry," she murmured to the creature. Then, to Val, "It looks like it's healing alright. Must have only been a glancing blow."

It was an incredible shot, Val wanted to say, thinking back to her horror as the Sh'keth came within seconds of ripping Nicole to shreds, but she pushed the memories of the fight away. "Lucky for both of us," she said dryly instead, "glancing shots seem to be your specialty in the heat of the moment."

Nicole cast her a reproachful glare from under her eyebrows, a small grin belying the threat with a playful smolder that momentarily surprised Val out of her own dark thoughts. Nicole was *happy* getting to know a Sh'keth Protector. Val shook her head, a small spark of amusement flickering in her. She shouldn't be surprised. Of course Nicole's endless capacity for care extended to alien life. "Is that so, Lucky?" Nicole turned back to the Sh'keth, whose wings shivered in the darkness. "Do you think he knows I'm talking to him?"

THROUGH SKY AND STARS

"It seems like she does, but I doubt she understands human speech. The hive has been isolated here."

"She?"

Val shrugged. "If I had to guess. Most Protectors are biologically female. I don't know, though, whether Sh'keth even differentiate between genders. As far as I know, even the term *queen* is a human label derived from similar Earth organisms. Perhaps *they* would be most proper."

Nicole crossed her arms, digesting the new information. "Huh," she said, before her smile brightened. "Well. Already learning new things from the aliens next door." She let out a soft laugh. "Yep. Still crazy."

Val smiled halfheartedly as she pulled a notebook from the pocket of her pants. They'd planned for this. *Find the failure.* Regardless of her discomfort, her mission would not be complete until they'd assured the queen's health. She held the paper out and Nicole took it, her grip lingering long enough to press Val's fingers between her own as their eyes met across the beams of their headlamps. She smiled. Val nodded. "Time to find our shared language."

The Sh'keth—*Lucky*, Nicole elected to name them—grew more excited as understanding unfurled between species. Val had detailed knowledge of the hive, thanks to her endless studying in advance of her mission, that could be put to repairing the hive's systems. Nicole had years of keeping engines in flying shape and keeping herself alive in the wilderness. Lucky had passable knowledge of the hive they'd grown up in and how it *ought* to work. Images, diagrams, and pantomime eventually led them to a theory. By the time they were elbow-deep in what appeared to be the control room for the hive's power generator—a cleverly-engineered geothermal system nestled in the heart of the mountain—dread had stopped parading up and down Val's spine. Her loathing slowly dissipated into their shared goal. Each time she recognized the excited flurry of Lucky's wings, some new message understood, a small bolt of joy nibbled at the mountain of her distrust.

They followed the chain of cause and effect through the hive's degraded systems for days. They restored power, bringing light back to the caverns. Lucky came and went, indicating the need to hunt to feed the larvae growing slowly larger in the central chamber. They found the ventilation system and began working their way through the layers of fans, pumps, and valves. Val and Nicole camped on the mountainside, the gentle quiet of the pass soothing Val's aching heart, and she tried not to think about the relentless days crawling by. Did they matter, at this point? She wasn't sure. What she could control were their hours in the hive, searching for answers. Their slow and steady progress. They would save the queen. And *then* she would let herself grieve. Not a second before. She had to hold herself together.

Two weeks in, they came to a dead end.

Val pulled the shoebox-sized component out of a bank of fans that pulled clean air in from the outside world, frowning at the dull face of it. It looked fine, but Nicole's voltmeter said that somewhere in its guts, a circuit was broken. She held the box out toward Lucky and pointed at it. "Spare?"

The Sh'keth's wings fell, drooping against their body, and Val's own mood echoed the gesture. Her heart fell like the *Soyka* falling out of the sky. *Fuck.*

Nicole, however, reached for the box. She turned it over in her hands. "You said it's a motor?"

Val nodded. She scowled at the damn thing and tried not to let defeat curdle her insides. "I guess it's time to find out if the hive has an electronics shop. But I should warn you: I'm fucking useless when it comes to electronics."

"Hmm."

When Nicole met Val's eyes, the smile growing on her face felt like the first, warm ray of sunshine breaking open a riotous sunrise in Val's heart. "Please tell me you're a wizard with a soldering gun."

Nicole's eyes sparkled. "No, but I know someone who is."

PART VI: *LIFT*

THROUGH SKY AND STARS

CHAPTER NINETEEN

August 22, 1996, 11:00 a.m.
Seward, Alaska

Nicole walked through the open hangar door to Jack's shop, Val at her side, with their critical payload clasped firmly in both hands. She stepped carefully over the door's runners. After everything they'd done to find it, the last thing she needed was to trip, drop the thing, and damage it even further. It would be hard enough to get an alien motor repaired *without* adding structural damage to the list.

She raised the shoebox-sized component like a trophy as she approached the partially-disassembled airplane in the middle of the hangar. Jack bent over an open cowling, back to them, with his hands buried in the guts of the engine. He hummed along with his radio, classic rock echoing through the large space, and Nicole raised her voice to be heard as they approached. "Please tell me that the best A&P this side of the Yukon can fix this thing."

"Of course I can!" Jack said, extracting his hands from the project. "Never met a piston engine I can't—" He turned, wiping his hands on a greasy rag, and stopped short. His eyes bulged as he took in the unfamiliar block of metal in Nicole's hands. "What in the hell? That's not from a plane."

Val and Nicole laughed. Jack looked at them askance, crooking an eyebrow as he scratched at his scruffy beard. Then he looked at his oil-slicked hand with a grimace and stepped closer with an outstretched hand.

• 195 •

Nicole offered the trophy up. "Careful," she said, handing it over gingerly. "It's a motor from an…air conditioner."

"Air conditioner? Looks like an alternator from hell," Jack grumbled, frowning down at the thing in his hands as he turned it about, peering into the crevices he could inspect without a screwdriver.

"But can you fix it?"

Jack frowned at Nicole. "I'm offended. How long we known each other?"

He set the small machine on his workbench and popped open his toolbox. An engine roared to life on the taxiway as he set to work, and Nicole turned to watch as a Piper Cub taxied past, its yellow wings bobbing in the slanting, crisp sunshine. She wrapped an arm around Val's waist as they stood side by side.

"Now *those* are fun," she said, breath puffing into the cold air. "I love the Beav, but those little guys can land on a twig. Some day we'll have to take one for an adventure."

Val returned the squeeze. "Maybe some day I'll take you up in *mine*."

"*Oh.* I forgot that you mentioned a ship! I guess I assumed you just…I don't know. Magically appeared out of nowhere. Where is it?"

"You know where it is. You saw me the day I got here."

Nicole's mind raced. "Saw you the day…" A memory surfaced of a person standing on the shore of a lake, waving up at her. "Cooper Lake? That was *you*? But that was the same day… You ran *thirty miles* that day?"

Val frowned playfully at her. "I will slowly cure you of that archaic unit so that we may someday speak in the godlike tongue of kilometers. But," she continued as Nicole poked her playfully in the ribs, "it was about fifty kilometers, yes."

Nicole shook her head in amazement. "Every time I think I've got you figured out, you set a new bar for insanity."

She pulled her eyes away from Val's grin as the Cub roared a short distance down the runway and leapt into the sky, nimble as a chickadee. It sailed overhead and dipped its wings, disappearing over the trees to the north. They turned in unison as Jack grunted behind them. He had a penlight clenched between his teeth and had already removed the casing from the motor.

"I see your problem. The primary windings are shorted. Give me a couple of hours to fix 'er up and you'll be good as new."

He squinted at the sky outside the hangar. "Prob'ly means you're stayin' with us tonight, ladies. I don't want you haring off into the mountains at night."

Nicole thought about the last time she'd turned down Jack's offer of hospitality and shuddered. That was an experience she'd not soon forget, but a lifetime had passed since then. She struggled to put herself back into the shoes of the Nicole who'd been oblivious to Val's mission and the alien world just north of her home. The mountain of experiences since that afternoon could fill a hundred lifetimes. They had plenty still to do, but she smiled at how easy it was to feel hope for the queen, dwelling even now in her deep, dark castle. This motor was the first piece of the puzzle that would restore her health.

"You fix this thing and you've got beers for life, on me."

He looked at her quizzically. "Must be gettin' pretty hot in your place if you need an air conditioner fixed so bad." His eyes gleamed as he deadpanned, "What've you two been getting up to?"

A blush heated her cheeks as a surprised laugh burst from Val's lips.

"Jack," Nicole tried to discourage him over the sound of Val's mirth. "Seriously?"

He chuckled. "I'm just sayin'."

He fiddled with the motor for a moment longer, letting Nicole stew in her own mortification. Never mind the fact that they *hadn't* been getting up to any such thing. Val's tenuous emotional state had only wound tighter with each day spent in the hive. Nicole, who vividly and frequently recalled the effects of Val's hands on her, was rather proud of her ability to patiently tamp down on her desire. But she certainly wasn't going to extend the conversation by telling *Jack* that.

Mercifully, the siren call of an unknown machine drew Jack's attention back to his workbench. "You gals ought to head over and see J. She'll get a kick out of seein' you while I focus on this bad boy for a bit. Meet you for dinner."

They reconvened as Jackie finished her shift at the diner. The four of them walked the few blocks to the couple's small home, where Jack's pickup sat in the drive and the frame of a Piper Super Cub took up the garage. Jack had been promising to make it airworthy for most of a decade, much to Jackie's chagrin, and she never missed an opportunity to get in a pointed remark about how the garage would be the perfect place for a woodworking shop, "or, you know, a *car*," she said as they walked up the drive, relaying her eternal, loving gripe to Val with a smile.

"You'll thank me when I take you out to see the orcas in it!" he protested.

Nicole smiled as Jackie said, as if reading a script purely for Val's entertainment, "If I can even see them, withered as my eyes will be with old age."

Jack blustered. "Well, I'd make more progress if Baker here didn't bring me the weirdest damn fixer-uppers in the universe. I could've spent two whole hours on it today if she hadn't brought me some kind of space age technology to fiddle with!"

Val caught Nicole's eye as his comment skirted the truth. Jack caught them.

"You two," he said, "got something up your sleeves." He eyed Val's biceps. "And it's more than just those guns."

"Oh God, Jack, don't encourage her," Nicole blurted, laughing, although she unconsciously laid a hand on the muscles in question.

Val quirked an eyebrow, leaning close, and whispered, "You don't like them?"

Her eyes sparkled with mirth, spreading a warm glow through Nicole's middle. Val's happiness had been painfully scarce for days after their first, tumultuous descent into the hive. Seeing it return—with gusto—gave her hope that the torrent of Val's pain was finally subsiding. She gave Val's arm another gentle squeeze. "You know I won't complain."

Jack scratched at his beard. "Seriously, though—that thing wasn't too hard to figure out, but I don't recognize the model. I've seen enough DC motors to know it ain't actually from any HVAC system on this continent. The windings are a weird gauge. And it's got some kinda writing on it that I've never seen. So, spill. What's it for?"

Through Sky and Stars

A knot of uncertainty tightened in her gut. Bringing the part to Jack had made this conversation inevitable, but she wasn't sure how she was going to relay all that had happened without coming across as a raving lunatic. Would her friends accept the admittedly fantastic tale? She remembered all too vividly how she'd responded to Val's first attempt. She tried not to think about what would happen if her friends thought she'd gone certifiably insane.

Val swept in. "That will be an excellent story for dinner."

The reprieve was short lived. Val wasted no time, leaping into the deep end the moment they'd settled around the table.

"I was born in the Terran year 2733."

Jack coughed, sputtering, an interrupted drink spilling onto his beard. Jackie froze with her fork halfway to her mouth, confused. "I'm sorry?"

"By your calendar, 2733 AD. I was born and raised on Luyten, a desert planet about twelve light years from here."

This momentarily distracted Nicole from her anxiety, too—Val hadn't started quite so early in her history when she explained her mission on the mountainside. But across the table, Jack looked like he awaited a punchline and Jackie, unusually, was stone-faced. The mood at the table suddenly seethed with the uncertainty of stepping onto thin ice with a fifty-pound pack on. Despite her enthusiasm for Val's backstory, Nicole took a deep breath. Val charged ahead onto the ice.

"I was born to be a soldier. We all were. Where I come from, there was nothing else. Grow, fight, reproduce, keep humanity alive one more day. My training began almost as soon as I could walk. We'd been at war, on and off, for six centuries by the time I was born, and every single one of us was needed as quickly as possible. We were losing. The best analysts estimated a century, at most, before humanity was exterminated." She laid her palms flat on the table and stilled, staring at them. Her jaw clenched. Nicole laid a supportive hand on her thigh. Val inhaled deeply. "That changed shortly before I left."

Val explained Lieutenant Haskell's invention, leaving Nicole just as confused as their friends across the table. Val claimed not to understand it, either, but her frame of reference, coming from an age when such technology was even *possible*, was so far beyond the

• 199 •

others at the table that Nicole doubted Val grasped how fundamentally incapable they were of following even her simplistic explanation. Jack scratched his beard, frowning and skeptical. Jackie sat with arms crossed, index finger tapping in the crook of her elbow. Damn, she had a poker face. This was harder than she'd imagined. Neither of them had said a word, but they looked like they were about to call a psychiatrist and have them carted away for observation in a small, padded room. Thankfully, Val ignored their looming skepticism and laid out her mission. She eventually turned to Nicole, threaded their fingers together, and squeezed. "Fortunately, it didn't quite work out the way we'd planned."

"Wait," Jackie broke her silence, holding both hands up. "I... Nicole, I love you, but this is the craziest thing I've heard since Hobo Jim drank himself under the table at the Night Watch last summer."

Jack grunted. "Damn straight."

Disappointment plummeted through Nicole's chest. Had it been a mistake to offer up the truth? They couldn't come up with a backstory. It suddenly seemed foolish to unload it all and expect them to buy in. She'd had the chance to get to know Val, to see her gunshot wound erased from existence without a scar, and still hadn't quite grasped it all until she'd followed Val into the hive and come face to face with the dead Protector. How the hell were they supposed to convince her friends, who'd known Val for a few, scant hours? She'd hoped to broker her decades of friendship for a bit of trust, but the set of their shoulders told her that they'd take more than social capital to win over.

As Nicole's thoughts spiraled, Val leaned forward and extended her left arm. She laid it on the table between them. A faint line remained where the Protector had cut her, the scar a reminder of their descent into the hive, but the wound had healed in seconds once Val had applied a dose of her magical Neosporin. A bolt of alarm shot through her at the thought of Val's seemingly magical ability to heal her own wounds. She reached out, placing her hand lightly on Val's arm. "You don't need to bleed to convince them."

Val, taken aback, looked at her askance. "Interesting thought," she murmured, "but don't worry." She laid her hand across Nicole's, skimming a reassuring touch over her knuckles. "Watch."

THROUGH SKY AND STARS

She swept the fingers of her right hand over the inside of her left forearm.

A map sprang to life on her skin.

Nicole gasped.

Jack and Jackie leaned forward with harmonic cries of dismay. Val sat patiently as they all clambered for a view. It looked like a tattoo—black lines on her light-brown skin, a map of Seward bordered in a thin, inky line—but a clock counted in the corner nearest Val's thumb, clearly showing that the image was in motion. Beneath it sat a set of coordinates and a cluster of unfamiliar script. More unreadable characters labeled various points on the map.

"*Val,*" Nicole mock-scolded her, surprised but no longer shocked by the technology Val wielded so casually that she often forgot about it. "When were you going to tell me that you had a computer in your *arm?*"

"A computer?" Jack had leaned in, dark eyes shrouded beneath his eyebrows as he frowned at it. "Where's the whatchamacallit? Motherboard?"

Val tapped behind her left ear. "Somewhere around here."

"What?" Jack's face scrunched up further. He craned his neck to see. Val turned her head. Nicole couldn't even see a scar.

"No way," Jack countered.

"I know it's hard to believe, but computers are going to get very, very small. Pretty quickly, actually."

"And turn your arm into a...screen?"

Val shrugged. "That part's actually quite simple. The array of nanites has only to activate the right pigment when commanded."

Jack sat back in his seat, befuddled.

"What does it do?" Jackie asked.

Val tapped out a pattern on her arm and the map disappeared, leaving a simple menu in the foreign script. Nicole shivered, both impressed and utterly weirded out as Val casually navigated through the examples by touch. Val swept through the list indifferently, revealing different images and text, as if having the equivalent of a television screen embedded in one's arm were the most ordinary thing in the world. "Position and navigation data, service manuals, a link to my HUD, a link to my ship—"

"Your ship?" Jack exclaimed. "You have a—"

Jackie shushed him. "One thing at a time, hon."

"She can also heal quickly," Nicole added, "thanks to other technology inside her body. The cut that made that scar probably would have killed one of us. She got it in the hive, when we finally made it down there. One of the Sh'keth tried to protect its queen."

She seized the opportunity to resume the story, describing her own decision to follow Val into the hive. Jackie tut-tutted, disapproving the dangerous choice, but her admonishment gave Nicole hope—it revealed that she was focused on the sequence of events, not doubting it.

Tears sprang to Nicole's eyes as she relived the queen's arrival. "She's… God, it's hard to describe. I expected to be terrified if I saw her, but she moved with such *grace*. Her skin is gorgeous, despite her illness, but she was so clearly suffering…" she cleared her throat, struggling to describe the depths of her soul into which the queen's call had reached. "It was obvious that they needed help. And equally obvious that fighting them would only lead to more bloodshed. I just knew…"

She trailed off, at a loss to describe the utter surety of her knowledge that compassion, not violence, would prevent the rift between races. Val swept in, voice soft. "It turns out that my mission's timing had more to do with meeting Nicole than with the state of the hive."

Jackie smiled. "This one's always been good at putting others before herself."

Nicole blushed, looking anywhere but at her friends, and shrugged. "Anyway. We've been working to fix their systems, make it healthy to live down there. This motor we brought you, if we repair it, could be the key. And if we save them, we build a bridge between our races. We prevent the war by turning conflict into friendship."

Silence fell as their tale ended. The grandfather clock in the next room loudly punctuated the silence. Nicole looked to Val, desperate for a face reading anything other than disbelief, and Val gave her leg a reassuring squeeze under the table.

Jack visibly shook himself. "Jesus, that's a lot to handle."

Next to him, Jackie shook her head, then sighed and rubbed her eyes. "It just might be the wildest thing I've ever heard in my life," she said, "but not even my fritters have enough crack in them to make you both have a trip like that." She raised her head, spearing Nicole with a friendly, but firm, glare. "So when are you taking us to this hive?"

Val chuckled and the grip of uncertainty released Nicole's stomach. She breathed out slowly, tentatively, dipping a toe in the relief washing through her. "You want to go up there?"

"Yeah, kiddo. How could we not? Plus," Jackie winked, "visible proof is the surest way to let us know you're not batshit crazy."

Nicole laughed uncertainly. Jackie leaned across the table and gripped her hand, giving it a gentle shake. "I'm kidding, Nicole. But it *is* a lot. It's going to take me time to process what you just told us." She shrugged. "But you don't seem crazy, and your girlfriend has a computer in her arm."

Before she could respond, Jack grunted. "Wait. So, I get all of the stuff about the giant alien bugs in the mountain. Okay. Weird as hell, but okay. What I want to know is, how in the heck did you two end up together on this?"

Nicole cringed. Val assumed a theatrical air. *Oh, no.*

"Well," she began conspiratorially. An embarrassed groan escaped Nicole's lips. "I was simply trying to ensure Nicole *hadn't* been murdered by bloodthirsty aliens…when she *shot* me in the *ass.*"

"You scared me!" Nicole looked at her friends hopefully. They looked even more surprised than they had at the revelation of aliens living in the mountains. "She ran around the side of the cabin in the dark."

"She *shot* me."

Jack looked at Jackie. Jackie looked at Jack. And they both burst into uproarious laughter that went on and on as Nicole sank lower and lower in her seat, hiding her face behind one hand. At last Jack, wiping his eyes, said gleefully, "That's why you were limping!"

Val stopped Nicole from completely disappearing under the table by wrapping an arm around her waist and pulling her close. Her eyes sparkled with a warmth that held nothing but fondness. "Fortunately, I have that medical technology under my belt—"

"Literally!" Jack exclaimed, then guffawed at his own joke.

The evening descended into laughter and gentle interrogation as their hosts sought the remaining details of the adventure under the mountain. Val downed more dessert and cocoa than any human had a right to, Jack burst into uncontrollable giggles whenever something even remotely skirted the topic of butts, and Jackie delved into concern over the family of beings struggling to survive in the depths of the mountain. Nicole waited for their incredulity to rear itself anew, dropping like a curtain to cut off the unbelievably good-natured reception of their story. But as the evening went on, the comfort of unwavering acceptance surrounded her as tangibly as one of Jackie's effusive hugs. Maybe she had traded in on a lifetime of friendship—and Val's near-magical technology—but they'd not only accepted the truth of the adventure, they'd welcomed Val as Nicole's partner without question.

As they made their way to bed at the end of a long evening, though, Jack stopped in the doorway of the guest room. Nicole paused in the middle of throwing a quilt over the unfolded futon. "Good night, Jack."

"Good night, ladies," he said, then lingered in the doorway with a thoughtful expression.

Nicole raised an eyebrow, waiting for him to spill whatever question he was dying to ask about the hive.

Finally, he pointed at Val and gave her his best big-brother smile. "You break her heart, and I'll kick your ass so hard you'll *volunteer* to jump out of my plane without a chute. Okay?"

Oh, God.

Nicole buried her face in the pillows with a groan.

CHAPTER TWENTY

August 23, 1996 [Terran Calendar]
Seward, Alaska

Despite the camaraderie of the evening, the satisfaction of finding the malfunctioning component and her certainty that Jack's mechanic's skills would soon have the hive back on its feet, sleep eluded Val. Nicole lay against her, head resting on her shoulder, and the weight of her urged Val's restless thoughts to settle. For the most part, it worked. Nicole's mere presence had an uncanny ability to quiet her tumultuous thoughts. She ran her fingers gently through the golden strands of Nicole's hair. Savored the slow rise and fall of Nicole's breath against her body. Wanted to be at peace.

And yet.

Nicole shifted with a sleepy murmur, snuggling closer, and her fingers came to rest atop Kass's necklace. Val stilled. The now-familiar ache blossomed from the point of contact, the loss that lingered beneath the surface of her soul revealing itself like the pain of a healing bruise beneath her skin. Each time she touched it, the pain grew a little fainter. Each gust of grief was slightly weaker than the last. Still, although she recognized the slow healing, the sting of it remained sharp enough to dispel the tentative comfort that had taken root in her heart.

She sighed and let go any thought of sleep. She lifted Nicole's hand, kissed her fingertips, and eased herself gently from Nicole's warm presence. She pulled on clothes, boots and jacket, then slipped

• 205 •

out the back door. Cool air filled her lungs. Her breath clouded in the sharp chill of impending winter. She looked up, following the burst of breath skyward, and blinked back the sudden tears threatening her vision.

The gibbous moon hung low in a sky purpling with incipient dawn, but a few, bright stars still shone through the brightening atmosphere. With sudden, insistent clarity, Val's memories rushed in to fill the space between them. She imagined her old life, skimming through those tiny points of light. The thoughts began in safe, neutral territory: the gunmetal walls of her quarters, the neat rows of uniforms she'd left pressed and folded in her wardrobe, the major's pips bright on the deep black collars. She thought of the briefing room and its scuffed chairs, aging terminals, and the eternal scent of burnt, day-old coffee. She let her teammates fill those chairs in her mind's eye, gingerly peeling back the shutters from the shelter she'd thrown up around her memories. Could she hold the memories close while accepting that their subjects were lost forever?

She had to. Weeks had passed since she and Nicole descended into the hive, since Nicole had changed everything, yet there'd been no sign from her former life. She didn't know what she'd expected—some kind of miracle sign, dropped from the sky like the *Soyka* to land at her feet with a triumphant *thud*? A letter magically downloaded to her implants? The ideas were preposterous, but Kass would send her *something* if she'd escaped the apocalyptic roulette. Wouldn't she? To leave her alone, endlessly wondering…not even the military brass, focused on mission above all else, would be so cruel. Right?

Her heart broke and mended itself, over and over, in the merciless silence.

A soft sound brought her back to Earth. The screen door squeaked open. Familiar footsteps crunched across the frosted grass behind her. Finally, Nicole slipped her fingers between Val's and squeezed briefly in the gentle suggestion of an embrace. In her other hand she carefully clasped the handles of two, steaming mugs.

"You okay?" Nicole murmured.

Val leaned into her presence, silently acknowledging the question while she accepted the proffered mug, but she struggled to form an answer. Instead she stared down into the cup for a long moment, watching swirls of tiny bubbles on the dark surface. Her emotions were as opaque as the chocolate, which was thick and rich—Jackie's specialty, nearly guaranteed to put a smile on Val's lips despite her disheveled thoughts. Nicole took a sip from her mug, seemingly content to wait Val out. Val smiled at her feigned nonchalance. It was sweet, if obvious. "I'd never had cocoa as good as this before you brought me to the diner."

Nicole shifted slightly, as if preparing to tack against the nonanswer.

"Nothing aboard ship ever came close," Val went on. "It was always fake, the kind of stuff you'd give kids to shut them up." She smiled. "Though to be fair, in a lot of ways we were a bunch of kids, and we probably did need to shut up."

Nicole chuckled and cast a sidelong look her way, barely visible in the predawn shadows. "You know, I've met a few of that type flying through here, going to and from the military bases. Seems to be a theme with hotshot aviators." Her lips quirked in the hint of a smile. "They like to brag."

Val was silent a moment, thinking about the bluster and bravado of the mess on a good day. "Usually too much bragging, not enough flying."

Nicole made a soft sound of agreement and bumped their shoulders together. "You don't strike me as that type."

Val shrugged. "By now I've…seen enough to know my limits."

The quiet of the morning enveloped them again, the whispering of birch leaves interrupted only by the distant caw of a raven. The memories resumed their restless push against her mental walls. Nicole had seen her scars, and she understood the toll of the life Val alluded to. She'd seen the spiritual wounds, too, when they tore open in the cabin—raw and deeper than any in her flesh—and she'd patiently supported Val as those, too, healed. Shouldn't she feel safe, letting her memories roam free in Nicole's presence? She took another drink of cocoa, fighting the sudden sinking in her chest. She grimaced at the trembling in her hands. It wasn't Nicole she was afraid of.

"Do you miss them?"

TESSA CROFT

Val twitched, her gaze leaping skyward involuntarily, and she felt Nicole holding her breath in the wake of the careful question. Her memories surged forth, pressing against her careful walls, but the bravery of Nicole's question captured her attention. *Vakking* hell, would she be able to ask a question like that? Probably not. She'd barely been able to tell Kass goodbye. Since that day in the cabin, even the most tenuous reminders of her old life had sent her soul flinching back as if from a flame. Yet Nicole had just asked a question that must feel awfully like leaving the airlock without a safety tether. The bravery of it reached into Val's heart and pulled out the answer before her mind could catch up.

"Yes."

Nicole drew in a long breath. Val didn't miss the slight tremble in their joined hands, though it was quickly suppressed by another gentle squeeze—this one longer than the last.

"Do you want to talk about it?" Nicole asked.

She hesitated.

"I…do," she said honestly, then shook her head. "I do, Nicole. But," she swallowed thickly. "You know what it did to me, last time."

Her words trailed into a hoarse whisper. She *did* want to talk about it. Desperately. The words were already clamoring for release, a logjam of memory and grief begging for freedom, but loosening her stranglehold before had utterly broken her.

Nicole took a long drink from her cup, thoughtful.

"What if you told me about your last day? Before you left." She smiled, gently loosening the vise grip of sadness in Val's throat. "What did you have for breakfast?"

"Ha!" The surprising question successfully derailed Val's melancholy. "A protein drink." She shrugged. "Bland. Military. I wish I could say it was something more interesting, but we were deep in preparation for this mission, my brains were leaking out of my ears, and I couldn't stomach much else. I think…" She scowled thoughtfully. "We had an early briefing on the local flora. What record we had of it after eight centuries, anyway." She sighed. "And fuck if my stress level wasn't high enough to blow the seals off an

• 208 •

airlock, so I didn't remember one iota of it. We had to review it again, that evening."

"We?"

"Kass and me. Kass is," she gulped, then pushed on, "was my best friend. She was also my backup on the mission. Though they said the odds of her succeeding were significantly lower." She cast a sidelong look at Nicole and forced a grin past the sudden threat of tears. "Not as charming, I guess."

Nicole scoffed and took a drink, but it didn't hide the blush creeping up her cheeks. "I'm not sure what I think about that, honestly. This whole thing seems pretty dependent on...you and me."

Val raised an eyebrow, smiling as she imagined Kass trying to impress Nicole with her surgeon's ego. "Kass can be a charmer when she wants, but I suspect the circumstances would have been quite different." She dropped her voice to a grumble. "She probably wouldn't have gotten herself shot in the ass."

Nicole sputtered. "I'm going to be sorry forever."

"Don't be." Val leaned in and kissed her. "The outcome has been more than satisfactory."

Nicole laughed softly. "Were you lovers?" she asked teasingly. As soon as the question left her lips, she cringed. "Oh, God, Val. You don't have to answer that. I'm sorry I asked."

Val soothed her worry with a squeeze of their joined hands. "I don't mind. But no. We slept together occasionally, but I loved her only as a friend. The way I felt about her wasn't anything like—" *the way I feel about you.* She caught herself before she said it. Paused. It was true, though she wasn't ready to admit it. "It wasn't that kind of love."

Nicole raised one eyebrow as if hearing the words unsaid. "Okay," she said simply.

"Kass was more like my...counterpart." She faltered, tears springing to her eyes again. "She saved my life more times than I can count. We kept each other sane. We..." her voice caught and she swallowed, abandoning the thought. "Sorry."

She pulled a breath in through trembling lips, fighting for control against the grief surging forth. Nicole released her hand, bringing her palm to Val's cheek, and closed the distance between their lips. Val sighed into the kiss, ignoring the tears that slipped down her cheek to meet Nicole's palm. "You're not broken," Nicole whispered. "You're allowed to grieve."

"I know." She trembled, touching her forehead to Nicole's. She did know. Understood with every bit of her rational mind. And yet her heart constricted with the words.

"Kass would be proud of you."

Val let out a short laugh, half sob, and smiled despite a renewed surge of tears. "She'd tell me not to get soft, then throw me around the dojo for an hour."

"Either way, I think she'd understand a few tears."

She let out a long breath. "Yes."

Morning had crept in around them, heralded by a few brave chickadees chirping in the brush at the edge of the yard, and as she listened to their merry cavorting Val realized that her shoulders had relaxed. Her head was clear. Nicole, once again, had soothed her anguished heart.

"Thank you," she whispered.

She closed the distance between their lips again. This time she tightened her grip, pulling Nicole closer, and was rewarded by a soft gasp as their bodies pressed together. Maybe she'd never be free of the memories, of the grief, but maybe she could live her life despite those chains. Nicole accepted her, all the broken pieces of her, and didn't seem to mind the imperfect whole. Maybe she would be safe, falling into Nicole at last.

Nicole's fingers tightened in her hair, a tingle of sensation that obliterated her doubt. Val groaned. Nicole bit her lower lip. Val melted. "I need—"

"You two scandalizing the neighbors?" Jackie's voice cut through the screech of the screen door opening.

Nicole jerked back, a furious blush reddening her cheeks even before she met Val's eyes with a soft laugh. Her emerald gaze was dark. Val, still holding Nicole close with one hand, spread her fingers possessively across the small of Nicole's back.

"To be continued," she murmured, quietly enough that Jackie wouldn't hear.

Nicole drew in a sharp breath. Her blush deepened, but she held Val's gaze for a long, burning second. Oh, *vakking* hell... Val struggled to draw a breath. "I hope so," Nicole whispered.

Jack had joined Jackie in the doorway, smile showing through his beard. "We going flying, or what?"

CHAPTER TWENTY-ONE

August 23, 1996, 12:00 p.m.
First Sh'keth Hive, Earth

Nicole sighed, looking around the dusty guts of the ventilation system, and wrinkled her nose as yet another unearthly smell assaulted her. She tried not to think about what it was or where it came from. They'd restored power and lights to most of the hive, but the smells—and their sources—still permeated the network of tunnels within. She'd stepped gingerly around a few of them just getting to this room. "This place still has a long way to go, doesn't it?"

Val, kneeling next to an open access panel with the newly-repaired motor in her hands, looked up at her. "It does." She shrugged, returning her focus to the motor, and deftly maneuvered it into its receptacle as she continued, "But recruiting Jack was genius." She glanced meaningfully across the room, to where Jack was up to his elbows in an open Sh'keth toolbox. "Once he comes back down to Earth, anyway."

Nicole chuckled. The sheer glee in Jack's eyes—and the mild worry in Jackie's as she watched him pull yet another alien gadget from the bin—tugged at her heartstrings. She shared a bit of Jackie's worry that Jack would inadvertently hurt himself playing with God-knows-what, but she couldn't blame him. She and Val had enjoyed their own voyage of discovery through the same pile of unfamiliar tools. She was *pretty* sure there wasn't anything explosive in there. "True. *If* we can get him to focus, we'll be done in a week."

Jackie, however, had reached a new level of desperation. "Hon, do I need to bribe you with Cub parts to get you to leave that stuff alone?"

Val laughed. "J, he's lost in a fog of unadulterated, mechanical bliss. Pure heaven. Good luck."

"What if he blows himself up and takes all of us out with him?"

"Pfft!" Jack feigned offense, frowning and waving an unrecognizable metal object in front of him. "See? It's harmless! Plus, these two already got to look at this stuff. I'm just gettin' started! What if we need somethin' for the repairs?"

"They already removed that motor, hon. Don't you think they have what they need to put it back in?"

Jackie's logic was futile. The clatter of parts drowned out Jack's reply as he dove back into the cabinet of wonders.

Val returned to her task, smile lingering. Nicole's heart melted at the sight of her relaxed and happy. This morning's peace had survived their descent into the hive, the inkling of joy finally emerging from beneath Val's battered surface, and the effect was stunning. Her smile was brighter, her face more expressive, her movements sure and steady. Nicole, left without an official duty for the moment, stood back to appreciate the change. *God, she's gorgeous.* She smiled, certain Val would eventually look up and catch her, and knew she'd blush furiously when it happened... but she didn't care. Val continued to work, unaware for now. She retrieved the Sh'keth screwdriver—yes, from the exact toolbox Jack now raided—and fastened the motor in place, then began deftly connecting the harness of wires around the box. "This is almost—"

Furious chittering shattered Nicole's mooning. She jumped, dodging Lucky as they burst into an excited flutter and flew across the room with an agitated buzz, and gaped as they seized an unrecognizable tool from Jack's hands before he could blink. They gently placed the item back in the toolbox, looked Jack squarely in the face, and pointedly shut the lid. Jack stared back, stunned. The room hung in dumbfounded silence.

• 214 •

THROUGH SKY AND STARS

Nicole broke it with a laugh. Her glee bubbled past Lucky's rebuke and Jackie's disappointed glare, ruining their scolding with merriment. "Jack, I think you're being sent to your room!"

Jackie harrumphed, crossing her arms. "See? The alien agrees. You were gonna blow us up!"

"Now hold on, I—"

Val stood, bringing the banter to a screeching halt. All eyes turned to her.

"It's in." She grinned, wiped her hands on a rag, and pointed at the control panel. "Who's doing the honors?"

As if anyone other than a Sh'keth could read the myriad labels scrawled across the panel in runic script. Nicole gestured to it, inclining her head as she met Lucky's huge, ebony gaze. "Please."

Components whirred to life as switches and buttons clicked. Somewhere in the depths of the hive, a low thrum began, deep vibrations felt in the soles of their shoes. Hope rose slowly, invisible as the fresh air working its way into the hive to displace the lingering traces of death and decay, a potential cure seeking release. Nicole stared at the reinstalled motor, willing it to work. Praying that when it did, the rest of the systems would behave. *Come on.* The little motor kicked on, humming in concert with its big brother below their feet, and a valve behind it slid open with a soft *thunk.*

A breath of cool air ghosted across her face.

"Yes!" Val pumped a fist in the air, her smile bright as sunlight burning away morning mist. Nicole turned her face to the source, drawing a deep breath of cold, fresh air pulled into the hive from the outside world, and smiled. She took Val's hand. "We did it."

Val tugged Nicole into a tight embrace. "*You* did it." Her voice was low, her lips soft against the skin of Nicole's neck as she spoke. "Thanks to you, Nicole, we did it."

When they emerged from the hive, shielding their eyes at the bright sunlight glinting off the canopies of the two aircraft parked in the valley below the entrance, they were sweaty, smelly, and stained by the muck in the chambers below. Yet happiness had buoyed them up the long climb out of the cavern. Happiness and a gentle, insistent breeze that had eased their passage. The ventilation was active, pushing the stagnant air out of the cavern, and the air in the

• 215 •

hive had already begun to improve. They still had a ways to go, but the hive was truly on the road to recovery. Nicole breathed easily as she stepped out into the sunlight and slid her sunglasses on, smiling.

Val, emerging behind her, had just wrapped up her version of Nicole's appearance in the hive. She blushed as Jack's laugh boomed into the open valley.

"You're a threat to humanity with that thing!" he hooted.

"You could have left out the part about me shooting the one that was already dead." Nicole feigned indignation, turning long enough to give Val a gentle jab to the shoulder, and their eyes met over shared smiles. Val winked, her eyes twinkling, and a rush of warmth surged through Nicole.

Jackie tut-tutted and shushed her giggling husband, although her shoulders, too, shook with laughter. "Don't worry, kiddo. We won't forget about the part after that where you saved the world."

Nicole turned back to the path ahead as Jack's tone turned thoughtful. "We've still got a bit of work to do to make sure things are ship-shape down there, though," he said. "Are we sure the heat works? The weather's gettin' awfully chilly…"

He and Val fell into discussing technical details, their conversation punctuated with grunting and grumbles about machinery, and Jackie caught up to Nicole. "You think while he's distracted with this, I can set up a wood shop in the garage?"

"Don't you dare touch my Cub!" Jack exclaimed, not missing a beat before resuming his technical conversation with Val.

Jackie, snickering, threaded her arm through Nicole's as they approached the parked airplanes. Her tone dropped low, conspiratorial. "Your stranger seems a bit lighter today."

Nicole flicked her gaze over her shoulder. Val looked up, meeting her eyes as if she'd sensed Nicole's gaze on her. She smiled. Nicole's heart lifted. "Time and the healing properties of your cocoa."

"Hmph," Jackie huffed skeptically, then raised an eyebrow as Nicole's attention returned to her. "I saw you two talking this morning. I think you're good for her."

Nicole blushed. "Right before you, ahem, *rudely* interrupted us?"

Jackie laughed and squeezed Nicole's arm. "I think you'll live."

She raised an eyebrow at her in mock reproach, but her insides did a small flip at the thought of being alone with Val. She flashed back to their abbreviated kiss. Was it only this morning? The fire of it still lingered in her veins. The possessiveness of Val's grasp. The heat of her lips. God, that body against hers. The thought made her cheeks heat further. Suddenly at a loss for any appropriate response to Jackie's gentle kidding, she turned to their destination.

"Oh, good, we're almost there."

Jackie chuckled.

Jack and Jackie loaded into their Cessna, waving as they took off down the valley on their way back to Seward. The sound of the engine faded slowly, seeping into the moss at Nicole's feet as she conducted her own preflight, until the quiet of the mountainside enveloped them once again. She paused, staring into the pass above her head, and the reality of their task rushed into the stillness. A surge of pride lifted her. They'd saved the queen. Someday, the Sh'keth colony vessel would return and find their outpost strong and healthy. *First contact.* She shook her head, still unable to grasp the enormity of it. It would feel like a dream to the last of her days.

Val came around the nose of the aircraft, searching, one eyebrow raised questioningly. Nicole grasped her hand and pulled her close. Val snuggled up behind her against the chill, wrapping her arms around Nicole's waist, and settled her chin against Nicole's shoulder. The silence of the pass settled over them, nothing but the wind whispering between the boulders.

"I've never been anywhere so quiet," Val murmured eventually, voice barely audible.

Her breath tickled the back of Nicole's neck, sending a shiver of want racing down her spine. She took a deep breath and willed her body to be patient. "At first, it was unnerving." Val continued, arms tightening. *Not helping.* Nicole's pulse ticked upward. "And then I met you, and the quiet didn't feel so empty."

Nicole chuckled, leaning back into Val's embrace, and focused on the sweetness of Val's statement as she prayed for the patience to survive the heat it elicited. "You're such a charmer."

Val's lips touched her neck. Her breath caught. So much for patience. "Did it work?" Val asked.

Val pulled aside her collar, trailing kisses into the soft hollow of her shoulder, and Nicole let her head fall back with a groan. She smiled even as her knees went weak. "You know it did."

Val chuckled, kissed her again and undid the top button of Nicole's shirt with her free hand. And then another. Nicole turned in her arms. "We're going to end up in the airplane if you keep that up," she said breathlessly.

"So?"

Nicole fought to form coherent thoughts as Val pressed their hips together. Her fist tangled in Val's shirt. Val's voice was low, almost a growl, and she made no move to release her hold. "I haven't stopped thinking about you since this morning."

A small sound escaped her throat, half plea, half moan, and she bit her lower lip.

"Val," she whispered, unsure how to voice the question tangled up in her desire. It *felt* like Val was truly comfortable, body and soul, but was she pushing too hard? She pushed away slightly, needing air for rational thought, and laid a hand on Val's chest as she breathed the cold mountain air deep into her lungs. "Is this…," she stumbled. "Are you…?" A heartbeat of silence followed. "I'm sorry, I shouldn't—"

"Shh." Val stopped her gently. "Thank you for worrying about me," she said softly. "For caring, and setting yourself aside."

"I'm not im—"

"Nicole."

The quiet confidence in Val's voice stilled the swirl of anxiety in her chest. Val trailed her fingers along Nicole's jaw, searching her gaze, and lifted her chin. The softness in Val's touch washed the uncertainty away in a heartbeat. Her gaze was clear. She was fully present, unfettered by the weight of loss. "I'm okay, Nicole. We're okay." The corner of her mouth quirked upward. "Okay?"

Nicole blew out a breath, freeing her worry to dissipate on the wind. "Okay."

"Good." Val's kiss was possessive, her strong hands digging into Nicole's hips as she pulled them together. Oh, God, they were

THROUGH SKY AND STARS

going to end up in the plane. She was five seconds away from throwing Val in the back of it, comfort be damned. "If you don't want to do this in the airplane," Val murmured, reading her mind, "I suggest you fly us home..." She traced her lips along Nicole's jaw, into the soft skin of her throat, and continued in a whisper. "Right..." she nipped at Nicole's ear, sending a hot shiver through her body. "Now."

She'd never been more motivated to achieve a perfect landing.

PART VII: *GO-AROUND*

CHAPTER TWENTY-TWO

August 24, 1996, 6:15 a.m.
Kenai Mountains, Alaska

Val jerked awake with the echo of her own scream ringing in her ears. *The fuck?*

She'd been dreaming again. That goddamn battlefield on Piscium-b, the mud and blood and screams. The scene that now reeked of regret along with her guilt, Val's subconscious rebelling against the senseless killing that had ground the souls of two races to bitter, black dust. But this time, as her rifle quit and her whimpers died away, she'd looked up to see Kass standing over her. Kass, face twisted in disgust, staring down at her with the hilt of a Protector's blade clutched in her hand.

You failed me, she'd said, then struck the killing blow.

Cold sweat prickled Val's forehead. Dread and horror thrummed in her veins, the pain of the words echoing in time with her heartbeat, and tears threatened. Would she ever be free of the horrible certainty that she'd wiped her best friend from existence? Why couldn't she just let herself believe that they'd all made it? She had no proof. No way of knowing. And yet her heart refused to hope. She cursed her own, tortured thoughts.

Nicole murmured softly and shifted in her sleep, and all at once, Val's entire being refocused on the warmth of the naked body stretched against hers. A surge of memories dispelled the lingering effects of the dream as if she'd opened an airlock and blasted them into space. Warmth pooled in her center. The sounds, the tastes, the touch...the *intensity* of intertwined physical and emotional connection. She hadn't anticipated the sheer joy of letting herself fall into Nicole. The echoes of it lingered in her heart, resisting the melancholy clawing at her.

The sun had risen, the first rays spattering the treetops just visible through the tiny window at the cabin's apex. Nothing moved but the flickering shadows in those boughs. Even Nicole's breathing, deep in sleep, was barely audible. The fire had long burned to embers. Not even the logs creaked, the cabin itself apparently content to wait for its occupants to awaken.

It was too quiet.

Her hackles rose, enhanced senses leaping into overdrive.

No birds greeting the morning, no Reggie on the hunt for food. Something had stilled the small creatures that usually cluttered the background of her heightened senses. Perhaps bears passing through...but the silence persisted. The unnatural tranquility tugged at Val's instincts.

She slipped from Nicole's embrace—Nicole stirred with a discontented murmur, but dropped quickly back into sleep—and collected her shirt from its haphazard crumple on the floor. The ladder creaked softly as she descended. She peered out the windows into the darkness beneath the trees, hoping to see the grizzlies returned to trundle across the clearing, but there was nothing. Her skin prickled. The tangle of tormented emotions evaporated into the deadly calm that preceded a fight. She didn't see anything, but her instincts told her something wasn't right...and she wouldn't let anything threaten Nicole.

She stepped outside, hyperalert, attuned to the smallest sound reaching her ears. Frigid air forced goose bumps up her arms. She fought the urge to settle into a defensive crouch.

A familiar, self-satisfied chuckle shattered the silence. She whirled, years of combat response driving her motions even as the sheer, impossible, improbable recognition flared through her chest like a supernova. Her breath lurched in her throat.

"What the *fuck*, Koroleva? You defeat the Sh'keth in your panties?"

Kass.

Val stood wide-eyed, her breathing shallow and tentative, her mind turning endlessly on a single note: *alive!* Her friend was haggard, despite the satisfied smirk—her cheeks were gaunt, her eyes haunted by dark shadows in her pale skin, and her uniform, while neat, was threadbare at the knees. This wasn't the healthy Kass of her memories, holding up bravely against the uncertainty of Val's departure, but she was *here*. Impossibly, wonderfully here, sauntering up to the railing and standing there with arms crossed as she waited for Val to respond.

When she didn't, Kass barked a laugh. Her eyes were bright despite the fatigue written in her features. "Slime-fucking Christ. Did you lose your mind in the hive? We could tell you made it—we had to give Haskell a moment alone with the data, it got him so hot and bothered—but I figured you'd have gotten out of it with your wits intact."

Finally, Val stammered, "You survived…?"

She couldn't seem to make her brain engage. She'd yearned for this. Grieved this. Longed for the sight of Kass standing there. And now she couldn't form a single sentence! Kass shrugged. "You did it, Koroleva. You fucking rearranged the universe. And now I am here to shower you with praise. Astrey wants to give you a medal."

Val rubbed her temples. The reality of Kass, standing there, sat on her consciousness like oil and water. She was afraid to accept the sight as reality, afraid she'd fallen into a crevasse of guilt-riven insanity. Maybe the sex literally had blown her mind. Maybe she was having a stroke. "I…why didn't you get here sooner? I waited. I thought…." The bedraggled state of her friend registered, sending chills down her spine. "What aren't you telling me?"

Kass looked away and shrugged. "It's complicated, Koroleva. The fucking Slugs couldn't just stop hating us the moment you disappeared. Something about symbiotic quanta and multiverses and a bunch of shit only Haskell understands. They sent me as soon as they confirmed that you'd succeeded." She took a deep breath and looked Val dead in the eyes. "But we're still fighting."

Val's expression collapsed in disappointment, the emotional landslide echoed by her sagging shoulders as the news hit home. Her emotions teetered again on their shifting foundation. "I succeeded…

but you're still at war? I don't understand. Haskell said that if I succeeded, it would stop the war in every human existence."

Guilt, despair, failure—each rolled through her chest in waves. Her chest tightened, making it a sudden feat to draw a breath. Kass saw it on her face and plunged onward, "Time's weird shit, Val. Haskell says what you did changed everything else. He's been boring us all to death about goddamn statistics, and how you fixed an infinite number of *other* universes—which, apparently, we weren't sure existed before you left—and even though all of the versions with Slug wars branched from this point, the...stem, I guess you'd call it, couldn't just be cut away, or *you* would never have existed to fix all of the other ones." She shrugged. "Sorry, I'm not a fucking genius. I can't explain it all. But according to Haskell, you *did* succeed, and now you live in one of the many, perfect universes where humans and Slugs don't murder each other. Those of us you left on the *Al,* though, are stuck in the original, shitty one because it has to exist so that you would exist." She paused and a crooked smile slid across her face. "Don't let it get to your head. And call me selfish, but I do find this preferable to having blinked out of existence the moment you left. Even if the world's been a vack-sucking slime fest since you left."

Mind reeling, Val fought to digest what Kass was telling her. "Wait...how long has it been?"

"Two years. As I said, time is weird shit."

Two years of death I didn't stop. Kass leaned patiently against the railing, which creaked under her solid, *real* weight, while Val struggled not to let the insidious tide of failure sweep her under. Kass's sympathetic expression wasn't helping. "Don't worry, slug brains. Haskell said *you* would fix every timeline. So Astrey wants—" She broke off as the door opened behind Val.

Nicole stood there, hastily dressed, wide-eyed gaze full of questions. She looked at Kass standing at the railing, took in the unfamiliar fatigues and the pack on her shoulders. Realization cascaded across her features. "Oh, my God. Is this...?"

Kass burst into excited chatter at the same time. "You fucking spacer!" she said excitedly to Val in their native tongue. "I thought you were *joking* about the sex thing, but—"

THROUGH SKY AND STARS

"Suck vack," Val said in English, casting her a glare. Then, to Nicole, "This," she took an incredulous breath, "is Kass."

Kass visibly smothered a smartass reply as Nicole's mouth fell open in a shocked *O*. "My apologies," Kass said, and Val recognized the thickness of her own accent as the unfamiliar words rolled off Kass's tongue. "I am, indeed, Kassandra Volkova. Pleased to meet you...?"

"Nicole. Baker."

Nicole's expression evolved as she, too, processed Kass's presence. The initial surprise faded to a cautious edge, the subtle straightening of her shoulders in the face of a threat, whispers of her command presence on the ice sheet taking root. A fresh chill, wholly unrelated to the cold morning, sliced through Val as she watched Nicole's face. Kass *scared* her, and though Val felt like her own brain was dragging through the sludge of the hive, struggling to accept the enormity of Kass's presence, she knew why. "Kass...why are you here?"

She didn't need to hear the answer. Kass, here, could mean only one thing. She was alive and in front of her, but the price... the impending loss threatened like the Protector's slice in her arm, an escape of blood with an inevitable end. Hurt dampened Kass's fierce grin. "Seriously, I thought you would be happy to see me, Koroleva."

Fuck. Of course she was. She took a deep breath. "Kass, I'm sorry. I...I am. I just have to wrap my head around the idea that you're actually here. I thought I had—" she faltered, throat working around a complicated lump of dread and overwhelming joy.

Kass's expression softened. "I know," she said. "Trust me, I about pissed myself the moment the *Soyka* disappeared from the scanner, thinking it was the last second of my life. But," she held her hands out, "as you can see, it wasn't."

Before Val could ask another question, Nicole cleared her throat. "Why don't you come in?"

Kass beamed. "Thank you," she said before hopping over the railing, pack and all.

Val cast a reproachful but affectionate glare that dissipated as Kass stood upright in front of her. Kass, real and alive. "*I'm so*

• 227 •

vakking glad you're alive," the words burst past the thickness in her throat, tumbling from her in their common tongue despite her earlier admonition, and she wrapped her in a fervent hug that would have made Jackie proud.

Kass held it just long enough to betray her own deep relief, then pushed Val back to arm's length. "Good. Now for fuck's sake, Koroleva, put some pants on so I can take you seriously."

❖

Nicole had landed on wet ice and entered an uncontrolled skid. She could see the immediate change, even if Val couldn't. Val's steady relaxation into her old life began before Kass even set foot inside the cabin. Hell, before Nicole even considered referring to Val as her *lover.* Had she lost her already? Val's eyes followed Kass relentlessly, as if afraid she would disappear. They murmured in words and phrases incomprehensible to Nicole, unknowingly, until Val reverted to English—each time with an apologetic smile that simply worked the sting deeper into Nicole's gut. They occupied one another's space with utter familiarity. The closeness settled like a weight on Nicole's heart. She and Val had hardly set out on their journey together, yet already she could see her soldier from the future sliding back into the life she'd mourned that very morning. She'd said that she and Kass were simply friends. It was obvious to Nicole that their bond was vastly deeper than the simple word implied.

At the same time, Kass's presence had lifted an immeasurable burden from Val's shoulders. The lightness in her step, the easy way her grin lit her eyes when Kass made her laugh, made clear the relief in Val's soul. For all intents and purposes, Val's best friend had returned from the grave. So she felt awful for the resentment worming through her, but it grew nonetheless. It wound around her chest, entangling with the fear following Kass like a malicious shadow, working its way into the seams of their happy reunion… because Kass wasn't here to stay. If anything, she was desperate to return. Oh, she was quick to exchange jabs that gave Nicole a new respect for the creative use of invective, and it was clear that

Val would *never* live down the moment in which Kass had caught them, but Kass's eyes darkened when Val looked away. Her gaze was frantic, hungry. She looked at Val like she held the key to life itself. *Maybe she does.* There was a reason Kass was here.

She blinked back from her thoughts when Kass demanded, incredulous, "The *fuck* is this?"

Kass stared down at a Pop-Tart in her hands. Val glanced at Nicole, eyes sparkling with mischievous glee as Kass's dark, skeptical brow rose. Her nose wrinkled. "This looks like something you sat on in the mess, Koroleva."

She took a cautious bite. The ensuing assault on Nicole's Pop-Tart supply threatened to leave her penniless. Despite her anxiety, she was glad to bring a little joy to another careworn soldier from the future.

Kass chased the pastries with black coffee as she related how the engineers in their time had watched data pour in after Val's jump, how their shock at surviving had rapidly faded into abject awe as they measured the aftershocks of the scientific feat they'd carried out through Val. The second ripple of incredulity as they realized that Val hadn't destroyed the Sh'keth but *helped* them, making not just peace, but friendship a near-certainty in every Human-Sh'keth future.

Val met Nicole's eyes as Kass spelled out the slice of history, and a small, private smile quirked her lips.

"That wasn't me," she interrupted her, keeping her gaze tied to Nicole's. "It was Nicole. She stopped me from killing the queen." She looked to Kass and Nicole felt the loss of her gaze acutely. "She deserves the medal, not me."

Nicole blushed as bright green eyes appraised her with newfound respect. "You went into the hive?" She looked back at Val incredulously. "You *let* her come into the hive with you?"

Val laughed and wrapped her arms around Nicole's waist. Her expression was soft with pride as she said, "She made it pretty clear that she was coming along whether I 'let' her or not."

Hope rose in Nicole as their gazes lingered together. *Maybe—*

Kass huffed good-naturedly and rolled her eyes. "Should I leave you two alone for a while?"

Val spared Nicole a quick smile before letting her expression fall into a friendly scowl at her friend. Kass sighed and set down her coffee cup. The soft thud resonated in sudden silence. "Right."

Val stiffened in her arms. She released their embrace and turned slowly toward her. The inevitable shoe held over the room, waiting to drop.

"Valentina, you know I'm under orders to bring you back."

Kass said it gently, but Nicole's heart plummeted as if she'd punched her in the gut instead. A wave of nausea rolled through her. *No.*

Val hung her head. "*Vack.*"

They stood by the Beav under a perfect blue sky, the type they would have raced into together, and the thought of taking off into it *alone* pressed down on Nicole like a fist grinding her happiness to bits. The pieces settled to the ground like the leaves drifting down from the trees, coating the otherwise beautiful riverbank in a decaying carpet of yellow and brown. She buried her face in Val's neck and let her arms enfold her. Her eyelids were heavy with tears.

"I know you have to do this," she whispered into Val's shoulder. "I understand. But I…it's…God, Val, it feels so unfair."

Val murmured wordlessly and tightened her embrace. "I wish I could stay, too," she said. "And I don't care what it takes, Nicole. I'm coming back."

Nicole's heart soared with hope, but she cautiously pulled back on the throttle. She shook her head. "Don't make promises you can't keep."

Val released a low, wordless murmur, but she didn't argue.

"You're going back to war. You could be injured or killed." She sighed. "You won't turn away from that danger. So as much as I want to believe you…if something happens to you, if you never come back… I can't spend the rest of my life wondering, grieving." She had to say this. What if it was her only chance? "Val, I love you. And because I love you, I have to let you go without expecting you to return."

Val tightened her embrace. "I love you, Nicole," she whispered. "I will do everything in my power to come back to you. I *can* promise that."

"Please." Nicole squeezed her eyes shut, leaning into Val, and tried to memorize the feel of her arms, the rise and fall of her chest. "Please come back."

They fell silent, the whispering of leaves and the soft gurgle of the river punctuated by the occasional birdcall. Nicole wished futilely for their embrace to go on forever. She tried not to think about Kass, back at the cabin, waiting for them to say their goodbyes so she could whisk Val away. She wished they'd simply stayed in the pass overnight, leaving the cabin cold and empty, leaving Kass to pass them by. Even if Kass's presence soothed a gaping wound in Val's soul, she had also come to take Val away—a sin that Nicole's anguished heart was unwilling to forgive as the harshness of the reality battered her.

Footsteps crunched down the path from the cabin. Nicole's shoulders stiffened, her spine tingling as if in threat. Val pulled her into a last, fervent kiss. Then Kass was there and the end of their time together loomed like a guillotine.

"What happens now?" Nicole asked as they separated, grasping for details to pull her mind away from the furious resistance in her heart.

Kass lifted one hand, indicating a device at her wrist that looked no more remarkable than a simple watch. "I signal for pickup."

Nicole blinked. "And then you just…disappear?"

It was absurdly simple for something so incredible.

Icy dread trickled through her as Val turned to her, compassion in her gray eyes. "I don't think you want to see it happen, whatever it is."

Nicole nodded, as did Kass, who pointed to the riverbend downstream. "That's why we're going to take a little walk, Koroleva."

Kass turned to Nicole. "I know what I'm doing to you, and I'm sorry. But we need her."

Nicole nodded but looked away, unwilling to meet her gaze, and swallowed back an angry retort. No amount of rationalization would make this better. She needed Kass gone. Wanted to forget she'd ever arrived. Except—Val squeezed her hand. Kass shifted uncomfortably. "I'll go ahead," Kass said at last, then turned and sauntered downstream.

Nicole raised her eyes to Val, hopelessly aware of each second slipping away on the wind. "This isn't like the hive," Val said regretfully. "You can't follow me. But please, just wait. I'll be back."

As if she'd do anything but wait. Forever, if she had to. Try as she might, she'd never forget the woman who'd fallen out of the sky and into her heart. So she threw her arms around Val, drew in the scent of her, and said into her neck, "I'll be here. Today, tomorrow, and every tomorrow after that."

With that, she forced herself to let go. Val smiled sadly, picked up her pack, and turned to leave. Once again, Nicole stood alone by her plane and watched Val walk away, but this time she had no choice but to remain behind. When Val reached the bend in the riverbed, she turned back and waved—one hand held high. Nicole waved back. Then Val stepped into the trees to join Kass. Nicole strained to keep her in sight, unwilling to miss a single glimpse. Two indistinct shapes met in the trees and stood for a moment in the shadows, their silhouettes ghostly suggestions against the backdrop of leaves.

She blinked and they were gone.

The river rumbled past, the wind tousled the leaves and gusted through the wilting fireweed, the world around her cabin went on as it always had. But Val's absence rang in the air, the intangible loss of a presence, an energy that had come to define this place more than the place itself. She leaned against the solid skin of her airplane and let the reality cut through her, eyes closed and cheek pressed to the cool skin, as the scents of metal and engine oil soothed her aching chest with comforting familiarity. As much as she wanted to let Val go, to absolve her of responsibility for Nicole's fate, she couldn't help clinging to the tenuous hope coiled in her chest. She'd give Val the chance to come back.

"Please come back."

Only the river whispered in reply.

PART VIII: *LANDING*

CHAPTER TWENTY-THREE

Year 601 Post Diaspora [2767 AD, Terran Calendar]
UHM Cruiser Alexei Leonov, *Lunar Orbit, Sol System*

Another departure. Barely five minutes and she was traveling again, head still vaguely spinning with the suddenness of General Astrey's pronouncement—which had been less a pronouncement than a need for Val to follow like a duckling as he made for the docking slip at a pace that would've made the Beav jealous. She watched the *Alexei Leonov* fall away through her window. The familiar hum of engines percolated through her, so different from the earth-shattering roar of the Beav's radial engine, as the shuttlecraft whisked them away from its mother ship. The *Al* filled her vision just as she'd imagined while standing in J's backyard, looking up into the sky while the mountains emerged beneath stars that seemed insurmountably remote. And now here she was, in exactly the same place, with exactly the people, whose loss she'd mourned that morning. She blinked to dispel the thought. That grief was irrelevant now; everything had changed. And nothing. She was back and she had orders.

General Astrey cleared his throat softly, bringing Val's attention back within the shuttle. He watched her quietly. His presence filled the cabin around them, fifty years battling the Sh'keth having draped him in myth as sure as his authority, and Val fought the urge to drop her gaze as his dark eyes held her fast. Instead she stared back, willing him to see her loyal still, and tried to ignore the storm of unease gathering in her heart. "Major." His voice ratcheted

• 235 •

the noose of tension tighter around her chest. "We know you did *something* that averted the war in every existence but this one, but Captain Haskell's data suggest that you did not, in fact, destroy the hive as you were ordered to do."

Val resisted a sudden urge to pull at the rigid collar of her dress uniform. The tension seethed again, straightening her spine as it gripped her, but she faced his intensity with a level gaze. "That's correct, sir."

He sat silent a moment longer, iron gaze boring into hers. A bead of sweat formed between her shoulder blades. His index finger tapped once, twice, three times against his armrest. The fabric of his uniform stretched taught as he took a slow, deep breath. The ribbons on his chest flashed as he abruptly lifted a broad hand, palm up. His bushy eyebrows rose. "Well then, what *did* you do? Report, soldier."

The story poured out of her. She told him about the avionics failure that had forced her crash landing, coming across a Terran's home in the forest—she may have simply stated that she *injured herself and required assistance*—and Nicole's subsequent hospitality as she recuperated. She faltered as she described Nicole following her into the hive, then Nicole's recognition of a struggling colony and her argument to help rather than destroy. Sitting in front of a man whose orders she'd disobeyed, wearing a uniform in which she'd sworn to fight the Sh'keth with her dying breath, she couldn't help the sickening descent of her heart. *Fuck.* It wasn't just crazy, it was *treasonous*. She'd let an untrained civilian follow her into a *vakking* Sh'keth *hive* with nothing but a primitive rifle, then let that woman convince her not to execute direct orders. The more she shared, the more obviously her irresponsible, reckless decisions had endangered them both along with her mission. Worse, her actions constituted blatant disregard of orders. She was, in effect, admitting to an offense worthy of court martial. The literal fate of humanity had hung in her hands, the existence of this *entire universe,* and she'd disregarded orders.

When it was over she waited, breath held, for the guillotine to drop.

The general remained silent, one finger beating a steady tap, tap, tap on his armrest, face inscrutable as he processed her words.

He stared at the drab seatback in front of him. Val curled her hands into fists to stop their shaking. "Sir, I—"

"The Sh'keth know only that you left on a mission to destroy them." He cut her off with a raised hand. "The claim that you prevented war in multiple timelines is proof, to them, that you killed their ancestors and decimated infinite Sh'keth futures. They cannot imagine a soldier such as yourself doing anything but killing." He held her gaze unflinchingly. "You are their foremost target, and they will stop at nothing to murder you."

She let the knowledge settle into her gut. As a human soldier in this war, the Sh'keth were always out to kill you, but it was an impersonal hatred, the faceless killing of one dehumanized soldier by another. Since the start of this mission she, specifically and personally, had been marked for vengeance. In a way, nothing had changed. After her time on Earth, though, their hatred sent a chill down her spine. The old Val had turned her disquiet into anger, relishing the prospect of throwing the Sh'keth hatred back into their expressionless faces, but she now felt only regret. She knew the seed of pain from which their hatred grew, and that it should have been different; that she might yet extend Nicole's capacity for care to this one, last universe in which humans and Sh'keth still fought. A personal killing or an anonymous death in battle…either way, her mission remained unchanged. *She* was the one who was supposed to stop the war. In *every* existence. She couldn't control whether the Sh'keth blew her shuttle out of the sky or murdered her in her sleep. She couldn't even prove that she *wasn't* a mindless brute who'd executed her orders to a T and annihilated untold Sh'keth futures. But she could try. She could control her own response to the hatred, could combat it with the compassion Nicole had taught her. She would do anything, pay any price, if it brought that peace to this last, brutal version of human existence.

But you promised to come back.

She almost turned at the murmur of Nicole's voice in the back of her mind. The regret in her chest shifted form. It wasn't fair to Nicole. It could never be. Nicole had been thrust into this war unwittingly, unknowingly, whether she was here to grieve the consequences or not.

TESSA CROFT

The general's voice severed the thread of her thoughts yet again. "The council needs to hear what you did. The *Sh'keth* need to hear it, in your own words, from you personally." He frowned distastefully and shifted in his seat, eyes dark, and his fist tightened in white-knuckled frustration. "We've both spent our lives fighting them, Major, so I know you understand that every irrational fiber of my being wants to crush them decisively, militarily."

He met her eyes steadily. She saw the same fury in them that had consumed her in the hive, the groundswell held at bay by the miracle of a Terran woman extending her hand in peace. "But," he continued, "we can't. We're losing this war, Major, and every *rational* corner of my mind knows it. You must convince the Sh'keth that peace is possible. Whatever you did, do it again. *Show* them that it was all a mistake. Or in a hundred years, maybe two if we're lucky, humanity will be exterminated."

It's worse than I thought. Val fought her shoulders' increasingly strong urge to droop toward the curl of guilt winding through her chest. *Everything is worse.* "I'm sorry, sir."

He scowled back, confused. "For what?"

"I failed," she said, the words bubbling up from the disappointment in her heart. "No matter what I did, you've all still been here, fighting and—"

Astrey held up a hand.

"As far as I'm concerned, Major, you succeeded. You executed your mission within the parameters as you understood them. True, you didn't do exactly what I told you." He inclined his head. "But that's why I sent an officer, not an automaton. If we really wanted to, we could've just programmed the *Soyka* to blow the smithereens out of that mountainside. Would've been a hell of a thing for the people who witnessed it, but it would've destroyed the hive no questions asked. Instead we sent you, with a brain, and you did one better. You couldn't have known about the multiverse or symbiotic timelines or whatever the hell keeps Haskell up at night, so do not"—he pointed a finger at her—"berate yourself for something none of us knew or expected."

Val nodded again because she had to; anything else was out of the question with Astrey's hard gaze locked on her own. But the

• 238 •

sense of failure still slithered through her insides, a viper waiting to strike.

Light shifted within the cabin as a new object appeared in Val's window. She turned, curious, then blinked as the bright sphere of Luna filled her view. And beyond it...

Earth.

She should have expected it. She should have been ready. But it had never *occurred* to her to prepare for a sight she'd seen countless times. She'd seen the poisoned seas, the mottled land, the thick soup of angry clouds enshrouding a world embroiled in ecological disaster. This was what remained of a broken world, clinging to life, clawing its way back from utter devastation. Before, she'd viewed it as a challenge. The rallying cry against the Sh'keth. A broken planet symbolizing everything they'd stolen from humanity. A problem to be solved. But before her time on Earth she'd only *understood* what it had been. Now she'd lived it. She'd breathed its pristine air, seen the array of lifeforms crawling, swimming, and flying across its surface. She'd flown through the clearest, bluest skies imaginable and looked down on clean oceans and a living world teeming with possibility. She *knew* it now. Dammit, it was *hers*. It was *Nicole's*. The planet had permeated her soul and the loss of it ripped her open as thoroughly as magshot to the chest.

She raised a hand to the window, pressing her palm to the glass as the reality of the cataclysm gripped her. A growl of anguish caught in her throat. Her eyes burned at the tragedy. An entire planet scuttled in a colossal debacle. A habitable world wasted. Their *home*, wasted. For what? Ignorance, fear, and pure, stubborn anger set ablaze by weapons. Her anger rose to the thought like magma from a dormant volcano, squeezing through the cracks in the careful peace she'd built between her past and the Sh'keth. The lifetime of rage simmering beneath the delicate construct strained for release, begging to flood her mind with white-hot ferocity. How *could* they? She drew in a shuddering breath and fought the riptide of accusation. *All of them*. Not just Sh'keth. Alien and Terran alike had wrought the abomination she now gazed upon. Her hands curled into fists. Below her lay a world upon which Nicole Baker had lived, and loved, and *died* long before Val ever existed. Before the war. Before everything she knew and loved fell victim to unconscionable, unquenchable fire. Nicole's world, ruined. The gash in Val's wrist sang as the pressure of her fist tightened, pulling her attention away from the window to the memory of Nicole's hands gently pressing the wound closed, her touch soft and sure, her eyes full of compassion as she shepherded Val back from the precipice of her grief. Val closed her eyes and let the memory wash over her anger, quelling the fire of hatred, and clung to Nicole's humanity as her heartbeat slowed. Nicole was the key. She brought her gaze back to the planet below, surety quieting the unease in her chest. Nicole had never been given the opportunity to save this Earth. But perhaps, through Val, she still could.

"The Sh'keth are here, too." Astrey's tone cut through Val's emotions. "They have agreed to a meeting. Just one. On Luna. With you. We *must* convince them of your authenticity, Major, and of our intention to forge peace." He sighed. "It will be difficult, knowing that many of our own people remain to be convinced, as well."

He was right. Val had done the one thing no human soldier would understand. She'd returned to a ship saturated by anger and suspicion, the atmosphere charged with fear and desperation, and the fuse of a devastated planet simmered beyond every window. She'd returned to an anvil, with the hammer coming down to crush her between unstoppable forces. How in *vakking* hell was she supposed to change anyone's mind when *that* floated in the darkness outside their ships? The first hive, murdered. Humanity's home, destroyed. Of course her former colleagues were suspicious. Angry, even. She probably would have been, too, if the roles were reversed. She'd never have made the same decision without Nicole. But that was just it. The math, the models, the endless probabilities had somehow found the exact moment when Valentina Koroleva would meet Nicole Baker and change everything. Humanity had thrown its weight behind those results, thrown Val across time, and now she had to leverage that faith. She didn't know how, yet, but she'd figure it out. She had to.

The shuttle passed abruptly into the pitch darkness of Lunar night. Beneath them, a carpet of orange, yellow, and white lights spread away in every direction, the sea of Greater Tsiolkovsky rising steadily toward them as the shuttle sank toward the Lunar capital, humanity's first refuge beyond Earth. Astrey leaned in, peering past her at the riot of white and gold streaming by in the darkness, and shadows flickered over his face as the city sped by beyond the window. Would she die here, murdered by the Sh'keth over a monumental misunderstanding, having changed nothing for the people she gave up her world to protect? What could she possibly do here that hadn't already been tried? *Kass should have brought Nicole back with her, not the soldier who almost started everything over again.*

❖

The negotiations crumbled even faster than she expected.

Val followed on the general's heels as they marched toward the looming edifice of the Council of Greater Tsiolkovsky, the black stone rising at the apex of the city's central dome like a temple reaching for the stars beyond. In full sunlight the stars were invisible, drowned out by the bright reflections off even the darkest stone, and only the Earth hung morosely above the horizon with its pallid countenance staring down on human and alien alike as they scurried across the terrazzo toward the seat of human governance. Everywhere Val looked, her mind shied from the jarring contrast against the verdant, fuchsia-limned valley surrounding Nicole's cabin. Everything here was sharp edges and precise, engineered lineation cut from kilometers of pure rock, bored into the subterranean protection of the lunar surface. After the openness of Earth's unadulterated past, Val recognized the lunar colony—ancient and impressive as it may be—for the bunker it was. The air within Tsiolkovsky rumbled with hundreds of nearby human voices reflected between angular walls. The sights and smells of humanity pressed in around her even as they emerged from the maze of walkways into the open space before the council chambers. Across the terrazzo of polished stone, Val's unsettled gaze at last fell upon a shape that had become surprisingly familiar.

The Sh'keth delegation carved an intersecting path through the sea of humans. Their bulk rose above even the tallest of the crowd, wings stiff and still in disciplined control. Human military

TESSA CROFT

police, ostensibly to assuage nervous humans in their path, formed an awkward vanguard as people cleared the open square of their own accord, hastily dispersing from the alien delegation as it, too, marched for the council.

Astrey scowled. The armored officers at Val's shoulder stiffened, fingers alighting on the pistols holstered at their hips, and she was suddenly, vehemently glad for the regulations forbidding high-powered weapons within the station. Terrible as mag-weapons were on the field of combat, they were infinitely worse if unleashed in the fragile bubble of a dome. Tsiolkovsky's dome *supposedly* employed every modern engineering safeguard against catastrophic failure, but human history had proven time and again the inevitability of an Achilles' heel. At least in this case, the station managers were smart enough to ban the sort of powerful, kinetic weapons specifically designed to blast holes in supposedly indestructible things.

Which was precisely the thought going through Val's mind when her enhanced hearing caught the whine of a charging mag rifle slicing through the din of the crowd. "Down!" she barked, tackling the general a half-second before the column between them exploded in a bright burst of shards and melted rock.

Stinging barbs of flying debris peppered Val's face and hands as she crawled into the meager cover afforded by the remnants of the architecture. A cloud of pulverized rock choked the air, shielding their attacker as another round slammed into the wall, and she coughed as the powder snaked into her nose and mouth. Stone crumbled and fell like ice calving into a fjord, crackling and groaning before giving way to tumble free of its carefully-engineered bounds. Screams rose above the sound of toppling debris as panicked civilians fled the war zone sprung to life in their midst. *What the vakking fuck is going on here?* The Sh'keth would have relinquished their magweapons as well. *What slug-brained imbecile is*—her thoughts dissolved as the popcorn of small arms fire erupted around her.

A shudder of realization slithered down her back as a Sh'keth battle cry shrieked in response. Someone *wanted* a fight. She let loose a stream of invectives that would've made Kass blush. The idiots who'd opened fire in the plaza knew exactly what they were doing. They'd thrown a lit match onto a lake of volatile rage. This would nip the armistice in the bud, the delegations tipping over the edge into their own, violent habits.

The whine of the rifle was gone now, replaced by cresting waves of smaller, but no less deadly, rounds embedding themselves in the stone of Tsiolkovsky. The haze of dust began to settle. Val looked at the general, who knelt with his hands curled into fists, eyes hot with rage she recognized. Her fingers itched to hold a rifle of their own, to return to what she knew, to *fight*. But she had nothing—no weapons, no power, no command—as this world collapsed back into the very pattern she'd sacrificed everything to break. *Dammit*. Just a fucking helpless human cowering behind a rock while the world around her spiraled into chaos, the epicenter of the war hanging in the dark sky above. Couldn't they see? She just needed them all to *listen*. To put down their goddamn weapons for two *vakking* minutes and just *listen*. She needed them to—"Stop!"

The command rang from her chest unbidden, drawn forth by the memory of a woman hundreds of years gone and yet immeasurably present. "Cease fire!"

Somehow, incredibly, they obeyed.

Astrey looked at her in shock, eyes wide and shoulders heaving. The soldiers to either side hesitated, pistols quiet in trembling hands, and looked to the general for guidance. The Sh'keth weapons trickled to a halt as the counterattack dissipated. Paper-thin silence engulfed the square.

Val stood. Astrey locked eyes with her, the fire in his gaze singing to the loathing she'd left behind on Earth. She stared back, relentless, aware of both Sh'keth and the unknown instigators watching her through their gunsights, and waited for the bloodlust to fade to embers in his eyes. *Trust me*, she demanded. He nodded once, sharply.

She faced the Sh'keth. Stepped from the cover over the stonework. Listened to the sound of her own footfalls echoing across the plaza as her boots crunched over the debris of the firefight, grinding the polish from the ancient stonework. Human faces crept into her peripheral vision, curious and terrified as they peered from cover, and whispers stirred the eerie quiet hanging over the plaza.

Enough.

TESSA CROFT

The solitude of the deserted square split open to reveal familiar, armored forms and inky wings shimmering in the harsh sunlight. A few, mirroring the shocked humans at her back, fluttered with surprise and curiosity. Others whirred in angry reflection of Astrey's barely-controlled fury. And then, inevitably, they recognized her and the host of body language united in loathing. Vengeful shrieks eviscerated the silence as they reared up, triumphant, and surged from their cover with terrifying speed. Glistening, ebony armor filled her vision with the crimson traces of intricate, fierce battle runes. She'd almost forgotten the terrifying grace of Protectors in their prime—the tremulous, lonely youth of the First Hive, with so much to learn, rose in awkward contrast in her mind's eye. She almost grinned at the thought of the well-meaning, juvenile Protector's haphazard enthusiasm, staring down the approaching horde without malice. For the first time in her life, she stood still and watched fully trained Protectors approach. They were stunning.

She waited. They circled her, foreleg blades glinting and wings twitching in agitation. Low, gravelly rumbles escaped their throats, a growl of victory as they secured their prize. Fear pricked at her certainty as the razor-sharp weapons surrounded her. *This was a bad plan, Koroleva.* She focused on her breath. Thought of Nicole, reaching out to thank a Protector for saving her. Nicole, who had accepted without question that the Sh'keth were beings with full lives, deep and complex as any human. Nicole, who had helped Val see the Sh'keth as equals caught in the inertia of endless war and distrust.

Val waited. The human crowd, sensing death, drew cautiously closer, ringing the confrontation like spectators in an arena. The whispers faded into collectively held breath.

The final Sh'keth approached. This was no soldier; their body blazed with the same deep violet as the queen. Flowing, intricate runes danced and swirled across their carapace in clean, ivory strokes. They stood tall—not the awe-inspiring bulk of the First Queen of Earth, but dwarfing the Protectors arrayed around them. The ambassador, leader of the delegation, approached Val with unhurried grace and purpose.

Val closed her eyes and breathed the silence of the plaza into herself, willing it to condense into calm in the center of her being,

• 244 •

and sank slowly to her knees. She lowered her head, tilting her gaze away, and spread her arms wide, palms up. It was imperfect; as close as a human could get to the bow of respect she'd seen bestowed upon Nicole by the Sh'keth, but it would have to do. *Please, let it be enough.*

Murmurs rumbled through the crowd, which grew thicker as the danger constricted into the tight circle around Val. Jagged shards of split rock dug into her knees. Her thigh twinged in ragged reflex. She breathed and waited.

A computerized translator ruptured the silence with the toneless indifference of a machine. "Should we not slay you where you kneel, world killer?"

"If you do," Val pitched her voice to carry across the plaza, willing every ear to listen, "you will end the only human who has seen our two races work together for a better future. You will cut the thread of peace before we can weave it into silk."

Gasps, now, cascading through the assembled onlookers as the sea of humans processed her appeal for peace. The Protectors, sensing the unrest, took up their low growl again. She pressed on. "Our races cooperated to save the First Queen of Earth. We can cooperate again."

Silence from the ambassador before her. She longed to see their posture but dared not raise her eyes. This was the element of trust, deliberately crippling her senses as she knelt, disadvantaged in the exchange even as the Protectors shifted restlessly beyond her line of sight. Her spine tingled as she pushed a lifetime of training and instinct beneath the fresh memories of Earth. *Not everything can be calculated.*

"Do you have proof of such a claim?"

No. Despite everything, she had no answer to this inevitable, fundamental question. "Only that I kneel before you now as a friend."

The growl of the Protectors faltered.

Emotions swirled through the crowd around them. Divided human opinions washed over her in agitated, disbelieving, even ecstatic waves. Horror and bloodlust permeated the air as she gave voice to her treason, set it alight on the wind to let the Sh'keth do as they would, set herself in their path in a show of peace and respect. She pushed their restless murmuring from her mind and willed the Sh'keth to accept. Even one ambassador, even one shred of hope... *Please, let it be enough.*

A soft touch alighted on her shoulder and her heart soared. She raised her eyes at last.

"Traitor!" a haggard voice ripped her out of the fragile moment of peace.

Her HUD snapped her focus to the weapon emerging from a coat. *Magshot,* and the woman's fingers already halfway to the safety. Her eyes were wild with suicidal rage, her cheeks flushed, her hair scattering in a frazzled halo as she threw back her coat. People around her flinched back in a shock wave of horror rippling out from the weapon in her hands. The whine of a charging weapon split the air. "If you won't kill these *fucking* slugs—"

Val lunged at the same moment an ear-splitting shriek signaled the Protectors' lethal energy unleashed. Her palm hit the barrel of the weapon as the woman pulled the trigger, sending the shot arcing wide above the crowd, which erupted in screams around her. Strangers fell away in every direction. Val moved on instinct, arcing through a familiar deflection, blending her motion into the attacker's so that she could wrench the gun free of the woman's hand, until a ruthless explosion of pain jerked her to a halt. She gasped as it seared through her abdomen, frozen face-to-face with the wide-eyed attacker, and through the blinding fire of her own pain she perceived a Protector's polished blade vanishing into the woman's chest.

A blade that had passed through Val to get to her.

She looked down at the blade emerging from her own body, incredulous despite the agony shredding her consciousness, her very soul rebelling against the utter devastation she saw and felt. Two birds with one stone; even as her vision faded, the soldier in her dimly appreciated the elegance of the Protector's single strike.

Nicole... I'm so sorry.

She slipped into darkness.

CHAPTER TWENTY-FOUR

August 24, 1996, 8:00 a.m.
Kenai Mountains, Alaska, Earth

Nicole drew in a long, slow breath, willing her heart to settle. She followed it with a second. Then a third, as time marched on. If she closed her eyes she could still feel Val's arms around her, could tell herself that the lingering warmth of the aircraft's skin was the heat of the woman she loved, and could pretend it was all a horrible dream. She'd just come down here to check on the Beav, and when she returned to the cabin Val would be there, leaning against the bookshelves with a worn paperback in her hands, and her eyes would light up when Nicole came through the door. That goddamn charming grin would welcome her home and into her arms.

The wind gusted fretfully. All at once the warmth abandoned her and she shivered against the fuselage, feeling more alone than ever before. Val had dissipated on that wind like a ghost.

She'll come back, Nicole told herself yet again. She couldn't let go of the hope, even at the risk of devastation, even if there were a thousand reasons why she might not. A long sigh escaped her. What if she didn't come back? Anything could happen to a soldier in a timeline plagued with war. The fact that they'd sent Val here in the first place—even the things Nicole had seen of Val in their brief time together—suggested that the woman had a habit of getting herself into dangerous trouble. She thought of the scar bisecting Val's left thigh. *I don't even know how that happened.* She shuddered. To leave a scar like that, when technology could make a gunshot wound

• 247 •

disappear without a trace… Cold dread pooled in her gut, an icy anchor threatening to weigh her down until Val returned.

She looked up at the sky. A few thin wisps of cirrus traced across an otherwise unbroken expanse of brilliant blue. The valley had turned a rich amber in the autumn light, the fuchsia waves of fireweed having finally relented to the press of fall. The alders on the riverbank swayed gently in the steady wind blowing in off the bay, a perfect headwind that the Beav practically begged her to take off into. They would have flown today—how could you ignore a sky like that?—but the leaden chill in her soul grounded her more firmly than the worst weather. She patted the fuselage sadly. "Not today, old girl."

Slowly, reluctantly, she walked the path home. The lonely path reminded her of the first time she'd returned after Gramps's funeral. Then, too, she'd known the cabin would be empty and braced herself for it, but she'd also known that the only path led forward. Gramps was gone—the only option was to embrace the life he'd taught her to live and care for the airplane he'd taught her to fly. Now, not knowing whether Val would ever return…foreboding settled in her chest as she thought of the sheer, ominous emptiness of the cabin before her. Before Val she had come to relish it; her personal, private haven tucked into the wilderness. *Before Val*, she turned the thought over, poking at the sharp edges. Would her life be forever divided into *before* and *after*?

A board creaked ahead of her.

Her eyes shot up, hope burning away the fog of sadness as it tore through her heart and soul, and *she was there.* Val stood on the porch, leaning against the threshold with a small, uncertain smile on her face. "Hello, my light."

Her despair burst into a thousand tiny shards that evaporated into the wind as Nicole ran the remaining yards and threw herself into Val's embrace. Val let out a soft *oomph* as they came together, but her arms wrapped around Nicole and she reveled in Val's deep, appreciative inhalation against her neck. "I missed you so *vakking* much," Val said huskily, her voice cracking.

Nicole kept her face pressed into Val's shoulder as she asked, "How long were you gone?"

Through Sky and Stars

Val sighed. "Thirteen months, eleven days, and four hours."

"God, time travel is weird." She leaned back slightly, tracing the line of Val's chin. The look in her eyes evoked the first glimpse of a runway after an endless flight, of spying the break in the clouds that heralded good weather ahead, of coming home. Relief and hope. But Val had *aged*. This close, Nicole could see strands of gray working their way into Val's ebony hair, and new, weary lines belying the reassuring smile. The sparkle in her eyes was tempered, touched by an uncertain shadow wholly unlike the woman who'd walked away just moments ago. She pushed a blond strand over Nicole's ear, her touch lingering. "Long enough to doubt whether I'd ever see you again, and to wonder whether it was all just a dream."

Nicole brought both hands to Val's face, cupped her chin and kissed her with every ounce of the relief and happiness surging through her body. "It wasn't a dream," she murmured, "I love you. And I'm so glad you're back."

She paused. "But—How long have you been standing here?"

That grin—*that grin*—melted her heart even as Val said, "Long enough I had to try not to run into myself. Ran into Kass, though. I forgot she hung back."

She gasped as a bolt of anger shot through her. The knowledge that Kass had let them part in uncertainty, letting them suffer when she'd *known* Val would return—was standing just a few feet away, for God's sake!—formed a hot bubble of rage that rose up in her as she blurted, "How *dare* she? She could have told you, told *us*, that you'd be—"

Val cut her off with another kiss, enfolding Nicole in her arms until the spark of protest died, forgotten. When they parted Val smiled gently, one hand caressing Nicole's cheek. She held Nicole in a close, comforting embrace until her hurt dissipated. "Don't be angry with her, love. I thought the same thing, at first, but ultimately I told her not to tell me—" A new protest coiled to strike, and Val arched a meaningful eyebrow to quiet it. "Because we couldn't affect what happened. What we did, what I did. It was too important. I'm sorry I put you through it, though."

"Oh, Val," Nicole breathed, "I'm not angry for my own sake. I lived without seeing you for what, five minutes? You lived in

• 249 •

uncertainty for…a year? Really?" She wrapped her arms around her and buried her face in Val's shoulder, savoring the reality of her even as she lamented the aching uncertainty Val must have endured. "I'm sorry."

A year. "What happened?"

A deep sigh shook them both as Val relaxed against the railing. "You're not going to like this story."

Nicole took Val's face in both hands and kissed her again. "It ends with you coming back here, so I think I'll manage. But," she said with a smile, "it sounds like you need some cocoa to help you get through it."

She practically bounded to the door—*she came back!*—before stopping abruptly. Val pushed herself away from the railing slowly, stiffly, as if she had to consider each movement of her body. The forced motion was so at odds with the graceful woman who'd walked away minutes ago that a sick dread settled into Nicole's gut. Val met her eyes as she limped forward, grimacing as she put one hand to her back. "I told you that you weren't going to like it," she said, but she waved Nicole through the open door as she straightened. "I'll be fine. And I would *love* some cocoa."

Despite the attempt at reassurance, Val sighed with obvious relief when she set herself down on the couch. Nicole brought her a mug and sat beside her, concern churning in her stomach, and she set her own mug aside without taking a sip. Val took a deep drink, eyes closed, and the murmur of appreciation that escaped her was so achingly familiar that Nicole couldn't help but smile. "Thank you," she said, leaning back against the cushions, eyes closed, with the mug clasped in her hands.

"Please tell me that you didn't have to hike here like that."

Val chuckled, eyes still closed. "Fortunately not. Haskell continued to get the fields more and more precise. He probably could have dropped me into bed."

She opened one eye and wiggled her eyebrows at Nicole, who smiled and gave her a gentle shove. "No changing the subject."

❖

THROUGH SKY AND STARS

She shifted to face Nicole, still as frustrated by her body's sluggishness as she had been the moment she finally swung her feet out of bed six months ago, and sighed as she looked down into the depths of her cup. Sitting here as if she'd never left... She *felt* different—her body constantly reminded her that she had to work to make it obey her, and she could never erase the memories of her time away—but the cabin, Nicole, even the day itself were utterly unchanged from the moment she'd left. She had known, intuitively, that everything would be exactly as she'd left it. For Nicole it had been mere minutes. But the shock of opening her eyes, kneeling in the meadow behind the cabin, with the sun slanting through the trees and the same, gentle breeze blowing through the leaves, the sky laced with the same, diaphanous clouds—it was like having a bucket of snow, fresh off the glacier, dumped over her head. Like bursting from a deep dive to gasp fresh air into her lungs. She'd blinked in the sunlight, breathed in the wondrously clean air, and let the creeping distrust of her diluted memories whisk away in the perfect reality of the time and place. And to see Kass...the paradox of seeing her friend as she'd been that morning, blissfully unaware of the trial lying ahead, had strained Val's ability to protect the sanctity of foreshadowing. Kass had hardly blinked, seeing Val walk around the side of the cabin. Even then, she'd known Val would manage to return. Kass, a year older and wiser, hadn't exactly been happy with Val's decision to leave, but she'd made peace with it long before Val made the final jump. *For God's sake*, she'd said, shooing Val toward Haskell with a suspicious glistening in her eyes, *get out of my face and go eat a Pop-Tart*. Val smiled ruefully around the dim ache of goodbye.

When she looked up at Nicole, however, she was filled with overwhelming certainty that she'd made the right choice. She resisted the urge to throw the cocoa aside and pull Nicole back into her arms. Nicole returned her smile, blissfully unburdened by the weight of lost time, and unconsciously pushed one flannel sleeve up as she waited for Val to continue. The gesture was so achingly *Nicole* that her heart unwound a bit. Her subconscious tentatively released its stranglehold on incredulity. *You're really back, Koroleva.* A chuckle rose up in her chest. "Sorry. I know to you I was just here...but it's so *vakking* good to just look at you."

Nicole laced her fingers through Val's. "I'm not going anywhere," she said with a gentle squeeze, her thumb playing across the faint line of the scar on Val's left wrist.

Her hand rose to Val's arm. "You're wearing it," she said with a soft note of surprise.

Val laughed. "You should have seen the look on Astrey's face when I showed up to wish him goodbye. Definitely not proper uniform, but by then I didn't care...and there was no way I'd leave it behind. I was impressed, and touched, by your sneakiness."

Sometime between Kass's pronouncement and Val's departure, Nicole had managed to slip the flannel into her pack. And thank fuck. When she'd lain in the med bay, desperate, lonely, and terrified as her body refused to obey her, the disconnect between that life and Nicole's world seemed an insurmountable gulf. Without a tangible talisman of Nicole as a living, breathing, *real* person, it would have been all too easy to slip into the idea that the whole thing was a wonderful hallucination. Especially when she'd lain in a hospital bed half-crazed with painkillers and the side effects of regenerative therapies that had every nerve and synapse firing wildly throughout her body. On those nights she'd clutched the fabric close, even when the scents of pine and woodsmoke were only a memory. "It anchored me when I...when I thought I wouldn't be able to return."

Nicole leaned against her and their hands folded together in Val's lap. A few blond strands, escaped from her braid, tickled at Val's chin as she tucked their shoulders together. One arm wound tightly around her middle as Nicole waited for her to continue. "Please tell me," Nicole whispered.

Val shivered, wishing she could spare Nicole even the echoes of the memories lurking behind the joy of her return, but Nicole needed to know. "You saved the world again and you weren't even there," Val started with a small smile. "But I almost died."

Nicole shot upright, her face a stark mask of horror. "*What?*"

"I *almost* died."

"*Almost?* Oh, God."

Val opened a few buttons of her shirt, revealing a white line in the center of her chest, just below her sternum. She still shuddered to look at it. Still saw the Protector's blade vividly in her mind's eye. Saw

THROUGH SKY AND STARS

the look of shock on her assailant's face as the Sh'keth ran them both through. Saw her own fingers turning crimson as she stared down at them, clutching the wound. It was an absurdly tidy scar for the utter devastation of mind and body the injury had wrought, testament to the skill of human and Sh'keth technology that had saved her life. *"Val,"* Nicole faltered, drawing her fingertips across the scar.

"The Sh'keth delegation on Luna was attacked during the peace talks. A terrorist, trying to disrupt the negotiations by triggering a fight between the races. I stopped her, knocked her gun aside and sent the shot wide...but the Protectors were already in motion. I was, literally, caught in the middle."

The Protector's blade had severed her spine, paralyzing her from the waist down as it sliced through nerves and tissue and muscle with surgical precision. A killing strike, honed through decades of Sh'keth warfare, that nearly slayed Val along with the attacker. "It would have killed me, but by stepping in front of that gun I'd risked my life to save the Sh'keth ambassador. It put action to my words. Showed them that humans could stand with, not against, them. So the *Sh'keth* kept me alive in those first, critical moments. Stopped me from bleeding out right there in the street. Then they helped Kass put me back together in the operating room."

She remembered nothing of the moments after she'd been cut down—her mind mercifully disconnected from the devastation of her body—but she'd learned later that they'd somehow kept her alive long enough for paramedics to stabilize her. She shook her head, still amazed by, and a little terrified of, the delicacy of the operations required to rebuild her nerves. The process had been a feat of both races' technology, yet Val had no memory of the surgeries themselves.

"The next thing I remember is waking up in the med bay four months later." She spared Nicole the details. Her reawakening had been only blinding, nauseating pain through which she could do nothing but moan and retch. Nurses and doctors had moved her body for her for days. She was barely there, hardly able to grasp the razor-thin precipice between herself and death, and weeks passed before she regained enough control over her body for coherent thought or action.

• 253 •

"It was weeks before I could even make my toes twitch." Still more before she stood, then more before she walked.

She sighed, closing the fabric to stop herself staring at the scar. Next to her, Nicole sat rigid. A tear ran down her cheek. Val cringed as a surge of guilt twisted in her chest. "I'm sorry. Maybe I shouldn't have told you."

"No." Nicole slipped her fingers through the open buttons, running her fingers lightly over the scar, and Val trembled at the tumultuous wave of echoing pain and intense longing that surged through her. "I want to know."

"It's such a small thing, for the agony of uncertainty it represents. I spent months wondering whether I would ever get out of that bed, or if I'd survive without an army of machines holding my vitals together."

"But you did."

"Finally." She'd stared at her toes, willing them to move. Cried herself to sleep in frustration and rage at the impotence of her own will. Suffered excruciating days in which Kass had sat by her side cajoling, convincing, and sometimes downright pissing Val off just to get her to press on. Nicole knew none of this, could never know all that had filled the few minutes of her life between Val's departure and her return to the cabin, but her green eyes brimmed with tears nonetheless.

"Jesus." Nicole gripped her tighter, and despite it all, she relished the closeness. "To spend four months comatose in a hospital when a simple salve could make a gunshot wound disappear without a trace…"

"But I taught myself to walk again so that I could come back to you. So I could do this." She tipped Nicole's face up to her own and kissed her, tasting the salt of her tears and mustering every ounce of comfort she could pour into the touch. She held Nicole's gaze as she pulled away, one thumb gently wiping a tear from Nicole's cheek. "I'm here. I'm alive. We're together. Every day is better than the last. As long as I keep up my exercises, eventually I'll be good as new."

"I can't believe I almost lost you." Nicole whispered. "It's so much for just a few, short minutes." She sniffled. Sat up straighter, wiped her tears away, and shook herself. "But…what about the Sh'keth?"

"By the time I woke up, the peace talks on Luna were almost over. Apparently, throwing myself into the path of an armed human *and* a squadron of lethally pissed-off Protectors to protect the ambassador put truth to my story. They'd been skeptical that we'd saved the First Hive, but after seeing that, our story could finally be the true seed of peace. The ceasefire was in place two months before I woke. The end of the war was on its way, and I'd done everything I needed to do." She smiled and pushed a loose strand behind Nicole's ear, savoring her nearness. "It took a bit of convincing, but in the end I had enough clout to get myself a ticket home."

"Home," Nicole repeated with a watery smile. "I like the sound of that."

She sat silent a moment, her fingers tracing idly along the scar on Val's chest, and Val closed her eyes again to savor the touch she'd longed for, imagined, even clung to, in the endless months since she'd walked away down the riverbank. She sighed as the uncertainty and fear of those months washed out of her, relishing the simple feel of Nicole by her side and the comfort of their haven in the wilderness. She grinned as she felt another button come undone, Nicole's touch turning insistent. "Weren't we going flying today?"

Nicole looked over her shoulder at the perfect sky beyond the windows. Cerulean and emerald commingled in her eyes, reflecting a soul tied to the air and the land, and the heartache in them had given way to unadulterated joy. She smiled and Val's heart melted at the vision she'd kept locked in her memory for the agonizing months of her recuperation. Without Nicole, she would have failed. Nicole and her compassion, her love, were the keys that had unlocked a million better futures for humanity and Sh'keth alike. This woman, beautiful inside and out, was the true hero.

"I love you," the worlds tumbled from Val's lips as the truth of them swept through her again.

Nicole's gaze returned to hers. The smile remained, perfect, just for her. "I love you, too."

Nicole cast one last look at the blue expanse beyond the window. "The sky can wait," she said, and drew Val into her arms.

About the Author

Tessa is an engineer, pilot, and all-around nerd, born and raised in the woods of Alaska. She writes the stories she wants to read: women who love women, saving the world. She also drinks far too much coffee.

Books Available from Bold Strokes Books

An Extraordinary Passion by Kit Meredith. An autistic podcaster must decide whether to take a chance on her polyamorous guest and indulge their shared passion, despite her history. (978-1-63679-679-6)

That's Amore! by Georgia Beers. The romantic city of Rome should inspire Lily's passion for writing, if she can look away from Marina Troiani, her witty, smart, and unassumingly beautiful Italian tour guide. (978-1-63679-841-7)

The Unexpected Heiress by Cassidy Crane. When a cynical opportunist meets a shy but spirited heiress, the last thing she plans is for her heart to get involved. (978-1-63679-833-2)

Through Sky and Stars by Tessa Croft. Can Val and Nicole's love cross space and time to change the fate of humanity? (978-1-63679-862-2)

Uncomplicate It by Kel McCord. When an office attraction threatens her career, Hollis Reed's carefully laid plans demand revision. (978-1-63679-864-6)

Vanguard by Gun Brooke. Beth Kelly, Subterranean freedom fighter, is in the crosshairs when she fights for her people and risks her heart for loving the exacting Celestial dissident leader, LaSierra Delmonte. (978-1-63679-818-9)

Wild Night Rising by Barbara Ann Wright. Riding Harleys instead of horses, the Wild Hunt of myth is once again unleashed upon the world. Their ousted leader and a fey cop must join forces to rein in the ride of terror. (978-1-63679-749-6)

Heart's Appraisal by Jo Hemmingwood. Andy and Hazel can't deny their attraction, but they'll never agree on the place they call home. (978-1-63679-856-1)

Behold My Heart by Ronica Black. Alora Anders is a highly successful artist who's losing her vision. Devastated, she hires Bodie Banks, a young struggling sculptor as a live-in assistant. Can Alora open her mind and her heart to accept Bodie into her life? (978-1-63679-810-3)

Fearless Hearts by Radclyffe. One wounded woman, one determined to protect her—and a summertime of risk, danger, and desire. (978-1-63679-837-0)

Forever Family by L.M. Rose. Two friends come together after tragedy to raise a baby, finding love along the way. (978-1-63679-868-4)

Stranger in the Sand by Renee Roman. Grace Langley is haunted by guilt. Fagan Shaw wishes she could remember her past. Will finding each other bring the closure they're looking for in order to have a brighter future? (978-1-63679-802-8)

The Nursing Home Hoax by Shelley Thrasher and Ann Faulkner. In this fresh take for grown-ups on the classic Nancy Drew series, crime-solving duo Taylor and Marilee investigate suspicious activity at a small East Texas nursing home. (978-1-63679-806-6)

The Rise and Fall of Conner Cody by Chelsey Lynford. A successful yet lonely Hollywood starlet must decide if she can let go of old wounds and accept a chance at family, friendship, and the love of a lifetime. (978-1-63679-739-7)

A Conflict of Interest by Morgan Adams. Tensions rise when a one-night stand becomes a major conflict of interest between an up-and-coming senior associate and a dedicated cardiac surgeon. (978-1-63679-870-7)

A Magnificent Disturbance by Lee Lynch. These everyday dykes and their friends will stop at nothing to see the women's clinic thrive and, in the process, their ideals, their wounds, and a steadfast allegiance to one another make them heroes. (978-1-63679-031-2)

A Marvelous Murder by David S. Pederson. When a hated director is found dead in his locked study, movie star Victor Marvel, his boyfriend Griff, and friend Eve seek to uncover what really happened to Orland Orcott. (978-1-63679-798-4)

Big Corpse on Campus by Karis Walsh. When University Police Officer Cappy Flannery investigates what looks like a clear-cut suicide, she discovers that the case—and her feelings for librarian Jazz—are more complicated than she expected. (978-1-63679-852-3)

Charity Case by Jean Copeland. Bad girl Lindsay Chase came home to Connecticut for a fresh start, but an old, risky habit provides the chance to save the day for her new love, Ellie. (978-1-63679-593-5)

Moments to Treasure by Ali Vali. Levi Montbard and Yasmine Hassani have found a vast Templar treasure, but there is much more to the story—and what is left to be found. (978-1-63679-473-0)

The Stolen Girl by Cari Hunter. Detective Inspector Jo Shaw is determined to prove she's fit for work after an injury that almost killed her, but a new case brings her up against people who will do anything to preserve their own interests, putting Jo—and those closest to her—directly in the line of fire. (978-1-63679-822-6)

Discovering Gold by Sam Ledel. In 1920s Colorado, a single mother and a rowdy cowgirl must set aside their fears and initial reservations about one another if they want to find love in the mining town each of them calls home. (978-1-63679-786-1)

Dream a Little Dream by Melissa Brayden. Savanna can't believe it when Dr. Kyle Remington, the woman who left her feeling like a fool, shows up in Dreamer's Bay. Life is too complicated for second chances. Or is it? (978-1-63679-839-4)

Emma by the Sea by Sarah G. Levine. A delightful modern-day romance inspired by Emma, one of Jane Austen's most beloved novels. (978-1-63679-879-0)

Goodbye, Hello by Heather K O'Malley. With so much time apart and the challenges of a long-distance relationship, Kelly and Teresa's second chance at love may end just as awkwardly as the first. (978-1-63679-790-8)

One Measure of Love by Annie McDonald. Vancouver's hit competitive cooking show Recipe for Success has begun filming its second season and two talented young chefs are desperate for more than a winning dish. (978-1-63679-827-1)

The Smallest Day by J.M. Redmann. The first bullet missed—can Micky Knight stop the second bullet from finding its target? (978-1-63679-854-7)

To Please Her by Elena Abbott. A spilled coffee leads Sabrina into a world of erotic BDSM that may just land her the love of her life. (978-1-63679-849-3)

Two Weddings and a Funeral by Claudia Parr. Stella and Theo have spent the last thirteen years pretending they can be just friends, but surely "just friends" don't make out every chance they get. (978-1-63679-820-2)

BOLDSTROKESBOOKS.COM

Looking for your next great read?

Visit BOLDSTROKESBOOKS.COM
to browse our entire catalog of paperbacks, ebooks,
and audiobooks.

Want the first word on what's new?
Visit our website for event info,
author interviews, and blogs.

Subscribe to our free newsletter for sneak peeks,
new releases, plus first notice of promos
and daily bargains.

SIGN UP AT
BOLDSTROKESBOOKS.COM/signup

Bold Strokes Books is an award-winning publisher
committed to quality and diversity in LGBTQ fiction.